Lainey of the
DOOR
ISLANDS

"I just read *Lainey of the Door Islands* and found it to be an excellent read. As a licensed Master Captain and shipwreck diver I know the waters in this area as well as much of the local history and lore. This book brings to life the hardships endured by lighthouse keepers on the rugged islands, seas, and dangerous ice crossings in the winters. Combining their adventures with the Captains and crews of the sailing schooners that fought the winds and waters in these wild inland seas makes this book one you will want to keep on reading. Judy's accurate historical description of Lainey growing up in the Islands and Door Peninsula combines the rich history of this area with the adventures of the keepers, crews, and Captains and brings to life a bygone era of this beautiful Peninsula and islands."

—CAPTAIN JIM ROBINSON
U.S. Coast Guard Licensed Master, Shoreline Scenic Cruises & Charters, Gills Rock, Door County, WI

"*Lainey of The Door Islands* is a fantastic read. It hit all my emotions and transported me back in time. It's not only a story, but a glimpse into the lives of people who made up the Door Islands in the late 1800s. Wonderfully written and had me wanting it to not end!"

—SARAH R. GIBSON
Rasmus Hanson's Great Granddaughter, co-owner of Jackson Harbor Soup, Washington Island

"Calling all history buffs, lovers of Door County, lighthouse enthusiasts, and adventurers. In her splendid writing style, Judy DuCharme has created a story you'll read in one sitting because you won't be able to put it down. With the combination of real-life characters and the amazing history of Door County, Judy takes you on an exhilarating journey and lets you experience every moment through her dynamic writing, so much so, you'll almost be able to smell the lake air. This is the book you'll want to read again and give to your friends and family."

—MICHELLE MEDLOCK ADAMS,
Award-winning & bestselling author of more than 90 books including her latest children's book, *I Love You Bigger Than the Sky* (WorthyKids)

"Dear Readers: It is a joy to endorse Judy DuCharme's book *Lainey of the Door Islands*. Having lived on Washington Island and camped on Rock Island I can tell you it is a land of historic proportions filled with many romantic memories to those who have lived there and for those who have visited. The waters of Lake Michigan have their own personality, being feisty and also gentle depending on the season. Lainey is a true Islander and her escapades are heart-warming. You easily pour into the pages, turning one after another to escape into her world of Door County in the 19th century where living in northern Door and the remote islands brought huge challenges. The book is so delightful and can be compared to *Anne of Green Gables*. I love the research Judy did in the Washington Island archives to produce this book. My late wife Gay who lived much of her life on Washington Island would be reading this in one day! Surely this is a Good Read!"

—RICHARD JAMES HECKER
Author of the ebook devotional *Journey to the Promised Land*

"Infused with the rewarding, yet sometimes tragic, culture of 19th century lighthouse keepers, *Lainey of the Door Islands* is a vivid journey of hardship and loss, joy and purpose, and the balance between a tethered, predictable future and one rife with adventure and wanderlust. Author Judy DuCharme captures flawlessly the 19th-century setting of the islands surrounding the tip of the thumb of Wisconsin's mitten. DuCharme draws the reader into a time and place where storms were often unforgiving, but steadfast faith served as a beacon of light to guide the way."

—JULIE LAVENDER
Journalist, *Guideposts Magazine* contributor, and author of *365 Ways to Love Your Child: Turning Little Moments into Lasting Memories* (Revell, October 2020)

"Lainey is a gift to our world. This coming-of-age tale about a spunky young girl living in the Door Islands is a thoroughly delightful page-turner. Fans of *Anne of Green Gables* and *Little House on the Prairie* will rejoice as they discover this heroine who, though she faces great difficulty, embraces life with great love, joy, faith, and courage. Anyone looking for a wholesome, uplifting, and engaging read will be blessed by *Lainey of the Door Islands*."

—DENA DOUGLAS HOBBS
MDiv., Campus Minister to Episcopal and Lutheran students; Author of the upcoming book *When Anxiety Strikes*

"Judy DuCharme's latest offering, *Lainey of the Door Islands,* does not disappoint. The book follows the life of a young girl coming of age shortly before the turn of the century in the ruggedly beautiful landscape of the Door Islands of Wisconsin. Though Lainey experiences great loss and struggle, our young heroine reminds us again and again of the power of love, the love of those close to us and the love of our Lord and Savior, Jesus Christ. It's impossible not to be swept along with young Lainey on her journey toward adulthood.

—ALYNDA LONG
Founder and Editor of *Faith Beyond Fear*; Contributing writer to *Stories of Roaring Faith: Volume 3* and to *Dear Wife: 10 Minute Invitations to Practice Connection with Your Husband*

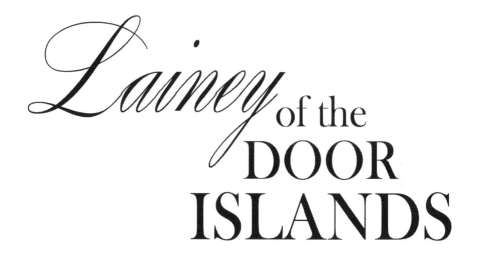

Lainey of the
DOOR
ISLANDS

Judy DuCharme

Ambassador International
GREENVILLE, SOUTH CAROLINA & BELFAST, NORTHERN IRELAND

www.ambassador-international.com

Lainey of the Door Islands

ISBN: 978-1-64960-002-8
eISBN: 978-1-64960-004-2

Cover Design and Page Layout by Hannah Nichols
eBook Conversion by Anna Riebe Raats

AMBASSADOR INTERNATIONAL
Emerald House
411 University Ridge, Suite B14
Greenville, SC 29601, USA
www.ambassador-international.com

AMBASSADOR BOOKS
The Mount
2 Woodstock Link
Belfast, BT6 8DD, Northern Ireland, UK
www.ambassadormedia.co.uk

The colophon is a trademark of Ambassador, a Christian publishing company.

DEDICATION

There was no question in my mind or heart that I would dedicate *Lainey of the Door Islands* to the memory of Gay Ellefson Hecker. Sadly, we lost this joyful woman in October 2019. She was everyone's best friend, loved the Lord with all that she was, and was an avid reader. She loved all my books and we planned for her to read the completed manuscript, but she was too ill. She had read close to half the book. It was special to her because her parents lived on Washington Island until they passed. Her mother, Barbara, was the Island Archivist and spent time with Gay writing historical notes for me to include in the book. Gay's extended family still lives on Washington Island. Her brother, Tully, is a Captain on the Ferry that transports thousands of tourists and residents to and from the Island each year. Gay met her husband Dick there when he was the Island Physician's Assistant, and they with their daughter Grace lived for a time on the Island as well. I had planned for the Rock Island light keepers to be named Ellefson but did not as another author used the name for the main character in her book set on Rock Island. Gay's gravestone is near Bethel Church, but she is not there, she resides in heaven now.

CHAPTER ONE

ONE MORE DAY. THAT'S ALL. Just one more day. The expanse of blue ripples before Lainey Louis sent a surge of excitement through her. A single gull called from its freedom land in the clear skies, and she looked up to trace its path. How she longed to join him in flight. The breeze carried the fragrance of deep waters. Lainey sighed. Soon, she would leave. The pounding in her heart to be free of this place was strong. Yet unseen strings tied her here. One more day and a whole new future would descend on her.

The door that never latched creaked open. One bounce, two bounces. She's not too mad. Three or four bounces indicated real trouble. Lainey braced for the shrill use of her name. Auntie Edith seemed to only yell her name lately. Just one more day. Why couldn't she call her Lainey? Here it came. With her back to the stone house, she heard the wheeze before the call sounded.

"Eeee-lain-ah, why are you out here staring at the water? That ship will arrive in its own good time. There is laundry for you to tend—it needs hanging. I'm not feeding you so you can just dilly-dally your hours away daydreaming about leaving."

Lainey turned and hugged herself. "Auntie Edith, I'm just so excited to see my parents again. I miss them."

"I know, child, but there's work to be done." Auntie Edith wiped her hands on the frayed apron that covered her striped dress, the one she always wore on Tuesdays. The apron still had Sunday's stains on it. After church, Pastor Gunnlerson's wife had sent five buckets of cherries. Auntie and Lainey spent the rest of the day pitting and putting up twenty pints of cherries and making four pies. Even though danger remained of staining the calico Sunday dress, she wouldn't change it. One day per dress, no matter what. Auntie Edith honored tradition, no matter how it came to her, and she wore one dress each day. That old apron covered it in work time—which was all the time—until it totally wore out. She owned one other apron that probably would soon take its place.

Lainey glanced down at her fingers. They still sported a red remnant of color, though she had scrubbed them as hard as she could after pitting the cherries. It was okay. She liked red. Mama said she'd bring her a red dress. Lainey hoped it had just a few ruffles on it. Not too much, just enough to make others notice. She didn't like being girly, but she liked being noticed. Except by Auntie Edith. Out here, it was no fun being noticed. It only meant work or trouble. Besides, there rarely dwelt but the three of them and a few chickens on small Pilot Island.

"Elaina, get in here. Are you deaf, girl? Why must I say it over and over?" She shook her head, and wisps of graying hair slipped out of the bun perched at the back of her head. Lainey often wished Auntie Edith would just let her hair hang down. It was probably quite pretty, and it would soften her appearance.

Once, she asked Auntie to let her hair down while Uncle Otis stood behind his wife. A sweet smile swept across his face, and he nodded. Auntie looked around and then rushed out the door. The door bounced five times!

Uncle Otis's eyes misted over, and he turned to gaze out the window.

Lainey ran to him and snuggled under his arms that were quick to wrap around her. "What did I say, Uncle Otis? She's really mad."

Uncle Otis stood mute for a few minutes. His voice sounded far away as he told Lainey, "One day, your aunt was combing her long, beautiful hair—down to her waist—truly lovely hair. I was out fishing. Our little girl managed to get outside without that door creaking. When Edith realized something was amiss, she heard a faint crying. Little Mandy, only two years old, had wandered to the island's edge and tumbled down the rocks into the water. The breeze was brisk, so it was hard to locate her cries. By the time Edith found our baby, she was gone. I came home to her cradling our dead little Mandy in her arms. After we buried her, Edith cut that hair right off. As it's grown, she refuses to brush it fully and keeps it in a bun day and night, only to take it down on occasion to wash and get some of the tangles out."

By the time Uncle Otis finished, he was convulsed with sobs and went up into the watch room of the lighthouse. When Auntie Edith returned to the house, she went to peeling potatoes and didn't say another word that day. Lainey never brought up her hair again, though she still wished her aunt would let it down once in a while.

Shaking off the memory, Lainey went inside and gathered up the wet laundry. She and her aunt each grabbed an end of a single garment or linen and twisted in opposite directions. The water that dripped from these would be used for washing the floor. Auntie Edith was a stickler on cleanliness, as was the lighthouse inspector, who only came occasionally but always unannounced. Auntie always kept one of the wet towels handy after the laundry. If Lainey did not cover every inch of floor on hands and knees, that wet towel was snapped at her behind. As much as she hated getting that swat, she knew she'd done an excellent job if she didn't get snapped. Lainey chose to make it a game—it was the only way to avoid the spank.

She knew her game accomplished Auntie Edith's plan of clean floors as well, so she chuckled to herself, despite the tiresomeness of her knees pounding the hard stone of the floor. Lainey loved to see the humor in things. Auntie Edith shook her head and called her a silly girl. Uncle Otis gave her hugs. Her father said her positive outlook would do her well and help her succeed in life. Mama, Auntie Edith's younger sister, was always quick with a laugh—full of life and kind words. Lainey wondered if Auntie Edith was like that until her baby died. She didn't ask—the hair question had obviously been too painful. She would see Mama in a day—one more day. Mama would answer her question.

As soon as the floor was scrubbed, Lainey took the piled damp laundry out to the line to hang dry. It was her favorite job. As lighthouse keepers, strict rules dictated no laundry was to be on the line after 11:00 a.m. They were so late today, but the inspection occurred just two days previous, so Auntie Edith assured Lainey no inspection would happen today. She'd chosen to pluck all the chickens this morning that the grocery boat had brought yesterday.

The breeze had kicked up while Lainey worked inside. The laundry would dry quickly. She loved the wind in her face and the choppy spray that spritzed across the water. Today, the wind blew from the east. She'd learned that was a bit unusual. Most wind in this part of Lake Michigan just off the Wisconsin mainland came from the west and north. Southerly winds she loved for the warmth they brought.

Lainey turned her face to the wind as she grasped the corners of each article. She deftly connected the corners of two pieces with one clothespin before grabbing the next. The rhythm soothed her spirit, and she gazed upward. "God, I appreciate this time, but I can't wait to return to the mainland with Mama and Papa. I know You love Auntie Edith and Uncle Otis—I do, too, mostly—but Auntie treats me like a slave. I don't mind 'cause there's not much to do here, but she's not a happy person. I like happy, God. Can You help her?"

The extent of Lainey's praying ended after a few moments as other things distracted her. A few more gulls called. It was a sound she loved, even though only a few found their way out to Pilot Island. She loved that they would come the two or three miles to say hello. Lainey never doubted they came to see her. The whiteness of their sleek bodies against the blue sky was a favorite sight. She glanced upward to see big clouds gathering about and snatching away the beautiful blue. The gulls cawed again and swept back toward shore. The white of the waves had moved from spotty ripples to frothy caps, and the wind whipped the remaining clothes into her face as she finished hanging them on the line.

Grabbing the empty basket before the wind carried it the short distance into the water, Lainey returned to the stone building that provided a home for her these months her parents traveled. Uncle Otis said the brick was Milwaukee Cream City brick. It was bright and soft in color at the same time. She always smiled at the hint of pink that she could find in the slightly golden hue. She loved colors. Mama said maybe she should be an artist. Maybe.

"Wind's picked up, Auntie."

"Keep an eye on the laundry. Did you secure it well? If it flies into the lake, I may send you in after it."

Lainey ran back outside to check each clothespin to make sure the laundry did not fly away. She knew how to swim, but the lake was getting rougher by the minute. A slight roar bawled from the north, and she walked down to the rocky side of the island. The teardrop-shaped spot of land in northern Lake Michigan held a length of only seven hundred feet and a width of four hundred feet, but Lainey found it fascinating to explore. The rocky shoals that the island sat upon were a danger to ships but so inviting to a young explorer. Occasional trips to Washington Island and to Newport Town on the mainland broke the boredom that rose up every few weeks.

The rocky north end enthralled Lainey. It seemed to change on a daily basis as the water swirled around in a constant churn. She had set herself to find every nook and cranny of the big rocks while heeding Uncle Otis' warnings of the dangers of slipping and getting caught between rocks. Obviously, that was where Mandy lost her life, and Lainey understood that was why Auntie Edith never came here and never wanted to hear her discoveries of tiny caves and roots, artifacts that washed up from shipwrecks, and lost items that floated in from the mainland and surrounding islands.

She stood with her arms wrapped around herself as if it kept her from being blown away. Her long hair curled around her face, and no amount of shaking her head kept it out of her mouth. Her uncle's voice faintly sounded in her ears. "Lain . . . stor . . . your . . . with . . ."

Lainey turned a full circle straining to hear, then looked up. Her uncle stood on the gallery, the balcony walk that surrounded the lighthouse watch room, waving and pointing. His mouth moved, but the wind snatched the words away. He pointed to the east. The clouds darkened the horizon. Finally, she made out the words, "Storm coming." Then he pointed toward the west. Lainey gasped. Auntie was removing the laundry. Her face heated, despite the chill the wind gave. The door must have bounced four times. Lainey ran to help.

"Hurry, hurry, a powerful storm is forming. They're almost dry anyway." If Lainey thought she could stand with mouth agape, she would have; but the wind continued to pick up speed, and Lainey sensed the urgency to get the laundry inside. Auntie Edith didn't seem angry, just focused. Auntie stuffed a large load of garments into Lainey's arms, then put her foot into the basket to hold it in place while she crammed more laundry in and slid the basket along the ground below the clothesline. Lainey struggled to get the door opened. Once inside, she carefully laid the clothing on the table, knowing not to let them wrinkle too much.

Hurrying out to get the next load, she almost collided with Auntie trying to balance the basket while opening the door. "Hurry, Elaina. Get the last few and then get in here."

Lainey fought again with the door on her return, spilling the laundry as she managed to get through the entryway. Auntie Edith was busy shuttering the windows tight. "She's a gale, all right. They often come up sudden. This was a quick one, and the seas are running high already. Hope there're no ships out there." She stopped and turned toward Lainey. "I'm sure they're okay, Elaina. The ships see this coming. Your folks' ship would've gotten out of the storm. Don't worry. They'll be here." Auntie Edith turned back to the shutters.

Lainey couldn't move. What if . . . Her parents had to return.

"E—lain—a, I need help with this shutter." Lainey could see her aunt struggling and willed herself to move. Her feet stayed put, though. Auntie Edith peered over her shoulder, both hands trying to pull the determined shutter from flapping against the outer wall. The anger fled her aunt's face. She gave the window cover one final yank and latched the window closed.

Lainey saw Auntie coming toward her. She flinched, knowing she had earned a slap. Instead, Auntie Edith stood in front of her and grasped her shoulders. "Elaina, now . . . look at me." She gave the girl a little shake, and Lainey woke from her daze. "Elaina, listen to me. Ships are designed to take the waves and the wind. Your folks might be delayed, but I'm sure they'll be here."

Lainey nodded, but the sickening feeling in the pit of her stomach only grew. She picked up the clothing and began to fold the laundry. A few pieces were not completely dry, and she hung them over the drying rack they kept in one corner. It slowly dawned on her that Auntie Edith had shown her kindness, not anger. It helped her to almost stop thinking about the storm and her parents out in the lake somewhere returning on a ship, a ship that could sink.

A southerly gale had blown up just the previous December, shortly before she came to stay with her aunt and uncle while her parents traveled the world. The *H.M. Scove* was carried by that gale all the way from Milwaukee, two hundred miles down the coast of Wisconsin. The ship, skippered by Sam Thorson, was stranded on a shoal between Plum Island and Detroit Island, the two smaller islands between tiny Pilot Island and the larger Washington Island. His crew of six made it, but the ship could not be salvaged. The storm, the winter ice, time, and the weathering of the lake prevented its rescue. *The people all survived, though.*

The wind howled. "Is Uncle Otis up in the lighthouse?"

"He is, Elaina. If you promise not to disturb him in any way, I'll let you take his supper up to him."

"Oh, yes, Auntie! I'll be careful and not disturb him. That light might be for my parents."

Auntie Edith smiled, a rare occurrence, even though it was a sad smile. "Yes, Elaina, it just might. First, help me get it on the table. I know he's getting everything ready and so intent on watching for ships that he won't be thinking about food for a while."

Auntie Edith got out the beautiful china that she used every day for dinner, not the lighthouse board-issued china all lighthouse keepers received. Her set displayed an ivory background with lovely pink roses all around the fluted edges. The center held one large rose, slightly redder than the others. Lainey always thought it beautiful. As amazing as her mother was, she used her best china only on special occasions. With all of Auntie Edith's flaws, Lainey loved that she used her beautiful china every day.

There remained only one occasion where Auntie Edith wouldn't use the china. That was when the fog horn blew. The other main building on the island housed the fog horn, which ran by steam power. When its loud and mournful sound went out for a period of time, dishes actually broke; milk curdled; and the chickens stopped laying their eggs. Auntie Edith said some of her china dishes shattered the first time that fog horn blew, and ever after, she wrapped them in towels and tucked them in cushions at the first hint of fog. Uncle Otis told Lainey that the fog horn on their very own Pilot Island was the loudest on the Great Lakes. Lainey put great energy into attempts to never break a plate.

The pot on the stove held chicken, dumplings, carrots, and cabbage. Lainey's mouth set to watering as that sickening feeling of worry in her stomach turned to a gnawing rumble of hunger. She laughed, as she was sure the rumble could be heard above the howl of the gale outside.

Auntie Edith set a platter on the table. "I heard that growl in your stomach. We forgot our afternoon tea with all the commotion of getting our chores done late." Auntie had been raised in an English home, where tea was deeply ingrained in her daily routine. "I thought, at first, that today would be too warm for chicken and dumplings, but since Rasmus Hanson brought so many fresh chickens to sell from his schooner store yesterday, I knew I needed to cook it today. Plus, he always has such great vegetables—my carrots and cabbage are almost gone from the garden."

"I saw a couple cabbages out there, Auntie."

"And they'll last several more weeks—at least, till the first frost—if this wind doesn't blow them away."

Lainey paused setting the table. "Aren't there carrots stored in the cellar room?"

"Of course, but we want to use them in winter, not now."

"Will you stay in the lighthouse this winter?"

Auntie Edith loaded two plates and set them on the table. "We will if the lighthouse board tells us to stay. It will depend on whether the Ann Arbor Railroad Car Ferries need to get through the channel. Otherwise, we'll be back at Irvin Goodlet's place on Washington Island."

Lainey pulled up her chair and smiled at her aunt. "Dinner smells so good."

"Let's thank the Lord and ask protection for all those in this storm, whether on land or sea."

After her aunt's prayer, Lainey sat just a moment and inhaled the fragrance of the meal. It always seemed like the right thing to do. *Thank You, Lord. And if it's quite all right, thank you, chickens, for giving your life, so I could have this absolutely delicious meal on the last day before my parents finally arrive. Thank You that I have survived being a slave.* Lainey quickly looked over at her aunt, hoping she had not thought aloud. Auntie was cutting her food with great attention. Her diligence in always cutting every bit of her meal tickled Lainey.

Lainey ate every morsel on her plate. "Auntie Edith, it was a wonderful meal. Thank you for all the good food you've provided for me while I've been here."

Auntie Edith laughed. It was such a nice sound that Lainey didn't even wonder if her words sounded funny. "Elaina, are you starting your goodbyes already?" She gazed toward the ever-darkening window. "I do suppose it's a good choice—a wise pattern." She stood. "Let me get you your uncle's plate. Now, mind you, be careful."

Bossy Auntie is back. Lainey didn't mind. She'd really had a good time. And she'd made a forever friend while here—Rasmus Hanson's daughter Rose. Rose had arrived with her father yesterday, knowing Lainey would be leaving soon. They squealed upon seeing each other, hugged, and ran off. It was right after tea time, so Auntie Edith and Uncle Otis invited Rasmus in for cherry tarts and gave the girls a bit of time to say their goodbyes. They rushed to the rocks and the little cave area they declared their own.

The Hansons lived in Jackson Harbor on the northeast corner of Washington Island. Rose could see Rock Island from her bedroom window. Her father and Uncle Hans built the schooner that they used as a grocery store boat. Twice in the summer, Auntie Edith and Uncle Otis allowed Lainey to travel with them back to Jackson Harbor and spend a few days. It was the highlight of her time in the Door Islands.

She would miss Rose the most. They promised to write each other. As Lainey climbed the narrow circular steps to the lighthouse watch room, she practiced remembering Rose's face so she would never forget her. To remember people and places, she worked to see a picture in her mind. Then she would stare at the picture and memorize every detail. Sometimes, she closed her eyes, and occasionally, she simply stared at the actual image. That worked when it was a place. It was a little harder if the person looked back at her.

Now, she kept her eyes open as she pictured Rose's face, so she didn't miss a single step or lose her balance. Each narrow, wooden step challenged balance and demanded attention from the climber. To climb without holding the smooth rail teased Lainey every time and mocked her when she stumbled, but her determination to conquer the climb urged her to continue. Not only narrow, the climb was steep. Uncle Otis would often say, "It's not for the faint of heart." She squinted her eyes as she attempted her memorization of Rose's face and that of her family. She stopped a moment, so she could close her eyes and get the picture set.

"Eee—lainnn—ah! Are you watching your steps? If I have to come up there to take your uncle's dinner . . ."

Lainey's whole body shivered, and the plate wobbled in her hand. She felt her face go white as she looked down at her aunt, who stood, hands on her hips, at the bottom step. "I've got it. Just taking my time, so I don't miss a step."

Auntie Edith shook her head. "Girl, get up there. And be careful. Your uncle can't be worrying about you right now."

"Yes, ma'am." Setting pictures in her mind would have to wait. She carefully wound her way up the narrow stairs to Uncle Otis.

Lainey breathed in the wood smell with what she called the fishy, watery fragrance of the lake. She'd come to love that smell. It stirred in her peaceful memories of pleasant days gazing at the water and feeling satisfied. Overall, it had been good here with her aunt and uncle and all the occasional visitors. A slight pang sounded in her heart. That was the loneliness for her parents that pinged in the background, just like the haunting call of the fog horn on those dense, gray days. At least, that loneliness wasn't every day. Still, if she wiggled around inside just right, she knew it never really left. But tomorrow they would return, and she would leave the Door Islands.

A shutter banged below, and Lainey almost stumbled on the steps again. Auntie Edith would not forgive that. Lainey's pride in mastering the narrow curve of the lighthouse stairs returned, and she refocused on her speedy ascension without hanging on to the rail. She would always remember this game she played with herself, counting the steps faster and faster. However, since she carried Uncle Otis' dinner, she'd best go slowly. And pay attention—why did she feel so distracted?

"There you are, my girl. Just set the food over there. We have quite a blow tonight, so I can't sit and visit."

"Do you see any ships out there, Uncle?"

"I'm looking, but even if I don't see them, we want them to see us."
He chuckled. "We like visitors, but not because they run aground on
our shoals. This is a strong gale, and sudden. You go back downstairs
now, young lady."

Lainey turned to the stairs and then turned again. "Can I go out
on the gallery one more time?"

"Not tonight, honey. Those winds'll blow you away. Maybe tomorrow, before your folks get here." He paused from his intense observation out the windows and placed a hand on her shoulder. "They'll be
here; don't worry."

Lainey could hold it no longer. She threw her arms around her
uncle and sobbed. "What if . . . What if . . . "

"Oh, sweetie, I'm sure it'll be just fine." He kissed the top of
her head. "You go downstairs now and get your things together.
Tomorrow will be a big day." She inhaled his scent—fishy air and
sweet aftershave, although he maintained a short beard that tickled
her cheeks when he kissed her. His big arms were strong as trees, and
yet his gentleness steadied her. His uniform was always on when he
worked in the lighthouse, and the hint of mothballs still clung to it.

Lainey hung to the rail as she backed down the stairs to the main
floor. The steps were too steep to go forward. She'd tried it once and
almost fell. Going down never invited her to hurry and never became
the game as going up did. The wind outside now rattled the house.
Or maybe it was just her insides that rattled. Her excitement earlier
in the day fled like the sunshine when clouds arrived. Now, it felt
like hunger deep within her and even worse. Each step down added a
weight of fear to her mind. *Sinking, like a shipwreck.*

Auntie Edith folded clothes in the small sitting room at the foot of the stairs. "Elaina, you need to get these in your trunk, so you're ready when . . . Why, Elaina, you're white as a sheet. Are you feeling ill?" She set down the shirt she held in her hands and walked over and placed the back of her hand on Lainey's forehead. "You don't feel warm. Let me look at you." She stuck a finger under Lainey's chin and lifted her face. "Oh, heavens, girl, is this your drama again? Your folks will be here tomorrow, and there is still work to be done. It's not like we haven't had a gale or a blow before. Get to your room and get your packing done. Fear and tears won't change anything."

Lainey nodded, picked up a pile of her things, and went to her room. The small space was just that—small—but she actually loved it. The bed was just her size, and even though Auntie Edith seemed harsh at times, she had a good sense of decorating. The quilt was creamy white with little roses all over it, just like the china dishes. Lainey paused. *I wish I could give this to Rose. It would be such a wonderful parting gift.* Lainey shook her head. Auntie would never approve. Her trunk stood over to the side and doubled as a nightstand. She carefully set the lantern and her books on the small chair by the window and opened her trunk. She would leave the next day with her parents. Her parents would arrive tomorrow. Lainey dropped to her knees. "What if . . . " The terrible thought wouldn't leave, but she couldn't let it finish either. Perhaps their ship had already landed in Ellison Bay, and they would take a skiff out for her tomorrow. They were surely already on solid ground, and everything would be all right.

A sound came through the window, like rocks scraping—grating sounds. The wind stole much of the sound away but delivered snatches. She could hear men shouting, or was that Uncle Otis?

"Elaina, get out here. I need to get upstairs to help your uncle see. There's a ship running hard aground on the shoal just off the island. He needs to go out. I'll go upstairs and direct the light. You stay by the door and open it if anyone comes. Put some water on to heat in case we have injuries or they just need to have something warm. Put the leftovers back in the fire to stay warm. Do you hear me, Elaina?"

"I do, Auntie. I'm here."

Auntie Edith climbed the steps, and immediately, Uncle Otis descended. He donned his slicker and boots as rain pelted the sides of the lighthouse.

"Now, Lainey, push the door closed tight, but don't latch it. We may have people that need to get in, so pay attention." He went out the widened door designed for carrying injured people through to safety, a feature common in lighthouses.

Lainey nodded and pushed the door tight as her uncle disappeared into the driving rain. At the same time, she pushed the dread concerning her parents down into deep recesses within her. *No time for that now. People need me to be ready to assist.* She grabbed her sweater as the wet and chill seeped into the house. She stoked the fire and retrieved the pot with chicken and dumplings from the ice box and placed the cast iron kettle onto the hook in the fireplace.

She went to the chest in the next room and removed the extra quilts. *What if . . .* She stuffed it down. All her senses were on alert. This was the life of the lighthouse keeper, and she would put her needs aside.

Auntie Edith's voice drifted down the stairs, but Lainey knew the words were not for her. Her aunt had opened a window and hollered what she saw to Uncle Otis. More than likely, the wind would steal the words away, but Auntie Edith always had more words to replace any that were lost. Lainey could see the light focused to the north-west corner of the island through the window that had lost its shutter. She couldn't see Uncle Otis, though. *Oh, what if . . .*

The thought of losing her uncle had never occurred to her before. It shook her, like the wind shook the lighthouse. "Stop it," she scolded herself. Now was the time to be like Auntie Edith. Tough, unwavering, focused. Maybe that's why she was like that. She had to be to live this life.

Lainey saw something go by the window. She ran to the door and eased it open. It flung back, almost slamming her to the floor, but she recovered and grabbed it. It was a man, soaked with rain. His beard dripped, and his eyes held gratitude and fear both at once. Lainey had never seen that before. He stomped his feet and wiped his face with the back of his hand, sending water spray everywhere like a dog shaking himself after a swim. Lainey struggled to get the door back in place.

"Oh, my, thank you, little lady. Forgot my manners—just so glad to be outta that gale. Name's John. Let me hold that door. The rest of the crew should be along soon. Glad your pappy is the lightkeeper. It sure enough saved us, though the *Gilmore* may be lost."

Lainey grabbed a quilt to hand to John, just as they heard shouting outside. Uncle Otis and another man burst through the door, half-carrying a third man. "Think we got a broken leg here. Lainey, find a crate, so we can prop up his leg. Don't want it getting worse than it already is." He pointed to John. "See what you can do for him. I have to go back out. Lainey will help you get whatever you need, and my wife will be down as soon as we get everyone in. She's tending the light."

John held the leg out from the settee, where the injured man was placed, and Lainey ran to the storeroom by the kitchen and pulled out an empty crate. She ran in, sliding on the water on the stone floor, barely stopping before colliding with John. She slipped the crate under the injured man's leg. His face held no color; his sunken eyes darted about the room; and his skin-plastered clothes soaked the chair.

"Let's see if we can get Ben's coat off. Stay with us, Ben." John looked at Lainey. "I think he's passing out from the pain." Sure enough, his eyes rolled back, and his head nodded forward. "Young lady, do you have any coffee? We need to keep him awake."

Lainey let go of his coat she had gotten part-way off and ran to get the pot of coffee still on the stove. She poured a cup that she knew would be very strong, but maybe that was good. Auntie left it on when the storm blew up, knowing Uncle Otis may be up late. She tiptoed back to the sitting room with a cup half-full, not wanting to slip and spill any of it.

John took it from her and then handed it back. "Hold on a minute." He turned to Ben and slapped his face. "Ben, wake up. I know it hurts, but we need you awake."

Ben's eyes worked open, but he seemed unable to focus. John took the coffee and held it near his lips. Ben seemed to notice the fragrance and looked at John, then at the coffee. He reached up to take the cup. Instead, John held it to his lips.

"Drink it, Ben. I'll hold it."

The door flew open again, and in stomped four more men with Uncle Otis. With them came wet and wind and debris.

"Shuck your wet stuff here. Keep some of it on till we can gather dry clothes for you; we have womenfolk present."

The men dropped coats and pulled off boots. Lainey ran for towels to wipe up the floor. Auntie Edith came down the stairs and went to the storeroom to bring out shirts and pants that they kept for just such a situation. Lainey had seen those and often wondered why Uncle Otis had so many clothes but didn't keep them in the bedroom.

Auntie herded them into the assistant's quarters with orders to change and leave wet things on the floor, not the bed. Lainey shuddered at what might happen if the wet stuff got left on the bed. Although designated for assistant lighthouse keepers, Uncle Otis and Auntie Edith used the quarters as needed for visitors, shipwreck survivors, and storage. Occasionally, they let Lainey and Rose play there. It took up one-third of the brick building and had its own kitchen. Auntie Edith was just as insistent about keeping it clean as the main quarters.

Her aunt ordered her to get the plates—yes, her good china plates—and she quickly loaded them with the chicken stew. Lainey set each plate at the table, except the one for Ben, who seemed to be awake but in great pain. She tentatively offered it to him, and he smiled. "Thank you, young lady. Are you about eleven? My daughter is eleven. Thanks to your pappy here, she'll get to see me again—well, once I heal."

Lainey smiled and stuffed the what-if back down. If anything had happened, then surely someone was helping her parents right now. Fear and hope swished around her, and she hurried back to get cups and coffee for everyone.

The men ate silently; and then, as they settled in, conversation took over.

Ben nodded at Uncle Otis. "Sir, thank you; you saved us. That gale caught us by surprise, and the winds kept changing; but we've been in gales before. Seeing your light helped us maneuver, but no amount of compensating kept us off that reef."

"Cap'n, you think we can salvage her? We rammed that reef pretty hard starboard side."

"Once the winds settle and we have daylight, we'll be able to see." The captain turned to Uncle Otis. "Sir, you surely saved our hides tonight. Thank you for your hospitality."

"Name's Otis—Otis Severson. You know the *Scove* ran aground near here just last December."

The conversation and stories of this and previous wrecks continued late into the night until the men bedded down in the assistant lighthouse keeper's rooms.

Long before that, Auntie Edith scooted Lainey off to bed. As she climbed into her night clothes, she looked at her trunk, still standing open, waiting for her to pack her belongings. Lainey felt her heart was still open for hope that indeed her parents would arrive in the morning or the afternoon the next day. She drifted off to sleep as men's voices still filled the sitting room.

CHAPTER TWO

"AHOY, AHOY, THE LIGHTHOUSE."

Lainey opened her eyes. It must be late, as sun filled the room. The sun! That meant the storm had ended. She peeked out the window and saw the men from the night before examining the ship that had slammed into their island last night.

Then she heard the call again. "Ahoy, the lighthouse." Someone was here, perhaps her parents! This was the day! Lainey scrambled into her clothes and ran for the door. As she pulled it open, she saw Auntie Edith doubled over with hands to her face. She must be sick. Lainey forgot her excitement and ran to help her aunt.

By now, her aunt sobbed loudly; but when she saw Lainey, she straightened and grasped her, hugging her to herself. Confusion rose, and then realization dawned on Lainey. This was not sickness; this was grief. Who could have . . . ? No, it couldn't be . . . No, it will never be . . . She would not let this be.

She tried to pull herself away, but Auntie Edith wouldn't let her go. Lainey turned her head, and the skiff was leaving. No—that should be her parents. Maybe they were delayed. She could stay a few more days.

Auntie Edith gripped Lainey's shoulders and stepped back. Her eyes were filled with moisture, and tears dripped off her chin. "That was Glen Jansen from Newport Town. He—he brought news of another—shipwreck. Oh, Lainey, I'm so sorry . . . your parents . . . my sister . . . " Auntie Edith looked up to the sky and then squeezed her eyes shut. "They were lost . . . They are no more."

Lainey's knees buckled, and Auntie Edith dropped to the ground with her, rocking her and giving way to sobs. Lainey couldn't move. Only the rocking of her aunt gave her any motion. When her aunt paused, Lainey fell to the ground and buried her face in her arms.

Lainey had no idea how long she remained there. She vaguely remembered hearing the voices of the men, perhaps the voice of her aunt. When she felt she could open her eyes, she sat up. Uncle Otis sat beside her and held her hand. He didn't say a word. Tears began to form, and she couldn't see. Soon, a great groan enveloped her mid-section and began to rise. She felt she was choking and drowning at the same time. Uncle Otis put his arms around her and pulled her to himself.

Lainey awoke to quiet voices in the kitchen. Her room stood to the left of the kitchen door. She saw daylight through the muslin curtains and wondered why Auntie Edith had let her sleep so long. The shipwreck of the *Gilmore* rose in her thinking, and she realized the voices were the crew. They must be consuming Auntie Edith's amazing breakfast. The few chickens they had on the little island laid delicious eggs, except when the fog horn sounded, and Mr. Hanson brought on his grocery boat the best bacon she'd ever had. She was glad to have learned to cook and bake bread with Auntie Edith. She knew she could cook better now than her own moth—Lainey fell back against the pillow. Her parents. Her mother . . . her father . . . surely, it was a bad dream. She had just dreamed that because she was so excited about their return, and then the *Gilmore* had run aground.

"Poor little thing . . . almost inclined to take her home with me . . . got two little ones already. She'd fit right in but have to talk to the missus first."

Other voices chimed in with "yes, me, too." And "That's right admirable, Simon."

Uncle Otis's voice came across loud and clear. "We'll have none of that. Lainey is family. She'll remain with us."

Lainey sat upright and stared at her hands. It was real then. Her parents . . . No, it couldn't be. Her stomach growled, and a sharp pain penetrated her head. She laid on her side and pulled the blanket over her head. Surely, life was no longer possible.

Life did continue, though in a daze. Auntie Edith didn't yell at her anymore. In fact, she didn't say much. Auntie did the chores, fed the chickens, cooked the food, made pies, and did laundry. She reminded Lainey to help her but left her to herself to work out her grief. She still called her Elaina, but it didn't bear the screaming quality it usually held.

The fall colors began to appear on the islands. Pilot Island had a handful of trees, and one sported a fine, orangey color. On that one, Lainey found a branch she could climb onto and just think. Going down by the rocks held no privacy now, as the *Gilmore* crew remained two months on the island and spent considerable time getting the ship emptied of its important equipment. They hoped she could be salvaged before winter arrived.

Rather than a church funeral, Pastor Gunnlerson came to Pilot Island to hold a small memorial service. Mr. Hanson brought him on his grocery boat along with Rose. The only other attendees were the men from the *Gilmore*, Uncle Otis, Auntie Edith, and Lainey. Lainey could only sob against Uncle Otis. She couldn't remember anything the pastor said but managed to thank him for coming. Uncle Otis offered to make a small cross and place it somewhere on the island, but Lainey thought it would be too hard to see each day.

School started, and Lainey went as often as she could. Rose's dad would pick her up and let her spend a few days with Rose while attending school. If the weather held, Uncle Otis or one of the *Gilmore* crew ferried her to Washington Island and brought her back. The teacher always gave her work to continue, in case she couldn't return for a time.

When she spent days with Rose, they also attended church. At first, she wasn't sure God would want her there. She was angry with Him and wondered if He was angry with her. Perhaps God spoke with the pastor and told him she wasn't welcome. Rose said she didn't think it worked like that; and since she wanted Lainey to go with her, Lainey did.

She'd always loved to go to church. Auntie and Uncle insisted on going when the seas were not too rough and there was no fog. Lainey found she craved hearing about a God Who loved her. Understanding why Jesus died escaped her a bit. Auntie certainly made it clear that Lainey was a sinner. She grasped that concept well. It was the forgiveness she wondered about. And now, did God forgive her for being mad? Did she need to forgive God? What about her parents? How come God didn't love them enough to save them? The pastor said Jesus died to save everybody because He loved them. It didn't make sense.

To Lainey's thinking, if Jesus forgave her, she was free. And before her parents died, she felt free—until she got in trouble or had a bad thought. She had lots of bad thoughts now. Why wasn't that freedom of forgiveness forever? It just seemed it should last longer. She talked to Rose about it.

Rose shrugged her shoulders. "Maybe we should ask God ourselves."

Lainey frowned. "I like to ask Him questions but always wonder if I'm being too forward. So, you think we can ask Him big questions by ourselves?"

Rose stopped. She looked Lainey in the eye. "I think so."

"But if we do, won't the devil hear us, too?"

Rose's eyes got big. "Oh, my, that wouldn't be good."

"Shoot, let's try it anyway. Maybe the devil needs the answer, too."

"Do we have to get on our knees?" Rose looked around.

"Let's do it." The two girls knelt and grasped the other's hands. "I'll start, since I guess it was my question. Dear God—er, Jesus—this is Lainey and Rose, and we have a question. Well, I do, anyway." She paused. "Rose," she whispered, "can I keep my eyes open?"

"Better close them, Lainey."

"Okay, God, now my eyes are closed. I'm wondering about forgiveness. I know You died and rose again so we could have it, but I don't know if I have it. I mean, sometimes I feel free, and that's when I think I'm forgiven—even though I doubt Auntie Edith thinks that. Anyway, it just seems it should be forever. Could you tell us if it's forever or have someone tell us? That would be helpful. Thank You."

Rose opened one eye. "Amen."

The next Sunday, Rose and Lainey giggled together in the back row of Bethel Church. Auntie Edith was not there, and Uncle Otis had let Lainey sit where she wanted. Rose's parents gave them a stern nod, and the girls put their hands in their laps and lowered their heads. Soon, their little shoulders shook, and their hands covered their mouths.

Lainey's head popped up. The pastor had said her name. The color drained from her face as she looked at Rose, eyes big. Rose frowned and looked down, hands again in her lap. Lainey bit her lip.

"Lainey?" Pastor Gunnlerson called her again.

She gulped and looked up, ready to apologize for her rude, unmannerly ways. Auntie Edith would be so disappointed. A whipping? Well, a long list of chores, for sure. She should tell Auntie Edith before Uncle Otis did. But wait, maybe he wouldn't say anything.

"Would you come up here, Lainey?"

She stood. Her shaky steps betrayed her shame. Remorse shadowed her, and her head hung. Her shoes echoed loudly on the worn, wooden floor as she made her way down the aisle. She felt the eyes of the islanders, who sat primly in the smooth, wooden pews, follow her all the way to the pastor.

"It's okay, Lainey. You're not in trouble. I think you'll be blessed by this."

The words could not penetrate. Blessed? Whatever did he mean? She managed to climb the two steps to the podium, where the pulpit stood. It must have taken her two weeks to get there. Every eye remained on her, and she could not meet their eyes. The pastor must be teasing. She struggled to look up. He smiled down on her. It confused every cell in her body.

"Please stand right here by me—face the congregation, Lainey." He chuckled and placed his hand on her shoulder. "You all know this delightful young lady."

The congregation murmured yes and nodded their heads. Lainey began to shake again. Pastor Gunnlerson gripped her shoulder a little stronger as if to steady her.

"And we all grieved with her over the loss of her parents in the recent shipwreck near Egg Harbor as they were returning to Ellison Bay to reunite with her."

A big gulp developed in Lainey's chest, and uncertainty filled her. Could she hold back tears? Why must he do this in front of everyone?

"Well, let me tell you a little history." He looked down at Lainey. "It's okay," he whispered. He returned his gaze to the congregation. "Lainey's grandfather, Lieutenant George Collins, her mother's father, was a hero in the Civil War. He fought for the Union and risked his life to rescue eight men at the battle of Chattanooga."

Lainey heard twitters of approval waft through the congregation. She remembered her parents telling her this a few times. Auntie Edith had mentioned it, too.

"For his heroic act, he was awarded the Congressional Medal of Honor. Lainey's parents took the medal with them on their trip, and it went down with them in the shipwreck."

The collective moan brought tears to Lainey's eyes. Why must she stand here while he told the story?

"This last Tuesday, the salvage company—you all know Jim Sanderson. Well, his crew was finally able to raise the *Hackley*. Partway up, the hull cracked, and one section was lost forever, possibly with some of the bodies still not recovered."

Lainey put her hand over her mouth and saw people in the congregation wiping their eyes. The pastor wrapped his arm around both her shoulders. She could feel herself shaking against his arm.

"Amazingly, they found a few belongings. Most were damaged beyond redemption, but one item was in incredible shape. I have it here." He lifted up a thick, short ribbon, and on the end gleamed what looked like a gold coin.

Lainey found herself staring at it.

"This, Lainey, is your grandfather's medal of honor. We grieve with you over the loss of your parents. But we hope this will be an honored keepsake for you to remember your proud heritage."

He turned to face her and very gently laid the medal in her hands. *This may have been the last thing my mama and papa held.* Lainey didn't even realize that she was sobbing—she just couldn't understand why she couldn't see the medal anymore. Before she knew it, Rose had wrapped her arms around her, and Uncle Otis stood beside her awkwardly trying to wipe her eyes with his handkerchief. When Lainey could finally see, she whispered, "Thank you" to the pastor and then gazed out at the congregation. Everyone stood and clapped their hands.

At that, the pianist played the first hymn, and everyone joined in the singing as Rose and Uncle Otis helped her back to her seat on the last pew. Uncle Otis allowed her to remain in the back row but sat next to her and held her hand. What would she have done in all this without Uncle Otis?

At the end of the service, Pastor Gunnlerson asked a young couple to stand. "I'd like to introduce you to the newest lighthouse keepers on Rock Island. They recently arrived, and we want to welcome Anna and Reinhardt Engelson. They started out at the lighthouse on Cana Island and then returned to Kenosha for a time. They have now taken this new assignment. Please welcome them as you go out."

Lainey saw many parishioners go to the new couple and chat and shake their hands. Just as many came to her and gave her a hug, shook her hand, or patted her on the shoulder. Several asked to look at the medal. She noticed they held it with such respect and told her they were praying for her as they handed it back. Usually full of words, she could say nothing. But she felt an uncanny peace that somehow this deep sadness would not derail her forever.

She and Uncle Otis walked outside the church. Rose had already left with her parents, with a promise to see her soon. The blue sky caught her attention. It must be brighter today. She couldn't remember a blue sky for some time. Could it be because she'd been so sad? Was this how Auntie Edith felt every day after the loss of her little girl?

"Lainey? Mr. Severson?" Lainey looked up into a very sweet face. It was the new lighthouse keepers the pastor introduced. "Could we speak with you for a few minutes?"

Lainey turned to her uncle, who nodded.

Uncle Otis extended his hand to shake theirs. "Certainly, and welcome. Always happy to chat with fellow lighthouse keepers. It can be a lonely job at times, but we are honored to do it."

"We've heard amazing stories of how many lives you've saved, Mr. Severson."

"Well, it's part of the job. Did you have a question?"

Anna and Reinhardt exchanged glances, then looked at Lainey. "Could you sit here on the steps with us a few minutes, young lady?" Anna sat down on the brick church steps and patted a space beside her. She reminded Lainey of the sweet way her mother would talk to her. Lainey sat down, and Uncle Otis leaned against the huge maple tree that stood just a few feet away. Reinhardt sat down next to his wife.

"While we were at Cana Island, we had two children, Carter and Rena. He was two, and she just eight months when we returned to Kenosha. My father was ill, and my mother needed us to help her. About the time that he passed, a terrible influenza swept through the city. So many were deathly ill. Our little Rena got the sickness and was unable to get over it."

Lainey's head shot up. "You mean she di . . . I mean she didn't . . . "

"That's right, Lainey. She passed away, and our hearts were broken."

Lainey looked up at Uncle Otis. "Like you and Auntie Edith." Uncle Otis wiped his face with the back of his hand and nodded.

"Yes, we heard about your little girl, Mr. Severson, and we are so sorry."

"Thank you." Uncle's voice sounded hoarse.

"Lainey, we were on the ship with your parents."

Lainey couldn't move. She gulped. "Did you meet them?"

"We did; we rode the train from Chicago to Marinette with them as well. We ate together and became friends. They told us all about you. She told me how you loved red and that she had purchased you a beautiful red dress in New York City."

Lainey's stomach tightened, and she felt the sobs begin to rise again.

Uncle Otis walked over and placed his hand on Lainey's shoulder. "You okay, girl? We can go if you want." He looked apologetically at the Engelsons. "This has been a lot for the girl."

Anna reached and took Lainey's hand. "Please, let us finish."

Lainey nodded and swallowed the sob that lodged in her throat.

"We told your parents about losing our little girl, and they were so kind to our little boy, Carter—he's inside now with the Gunnlersons." She looked at her husband.

Reinhardt stood, then sat down again and leaned out around his wife so he could talk to Lainey. "When the blow hit the *Hackley*, the captain just couldn't bring it around to face into the waves that came up so quickly. It was a small ship bound from Marinette to Ellison Bay. The blow hit us in sight of Egg Harbor just after we turned north. So, the ship got battered portside, and then the waves went right over the ship. She started to sink almost immediately."

Lainey hugged herself and looked at her lap. The blue skies had dimmed again.

"Our little boy, Carter, was immediately swept into the water, and we feared we'd lost two children. Both your parents, Lainey, jumped in to save him. They got him back to us; and then a huge wave crashed over them, and they both went down. We all tried to find them, but the whole boat was sinking and creating a suction that pulled all of us. We ended up on the other side of the boat, where a piece of the cabin roof was floating. We managed to get Carter up there and just hung on. Everyone tried to find your parents and the others who were dragged down, but it wasn't possible."

Reinhardt put his face in his hands and wept. Anna placed her arms around Lainey. "Lainey, your parents saved our son. They gave their lives for him. He is alive because of your parents. If you ever need anything, anytime, we will gladly give it. We are so sorry, but so grateful."

Lainey buried her face in Anna's chest and sobbed. The tears flowed for several minutes. When Lainey opened her eyes and pulled herself from Anna's embrace, the pastor sat on the steps with handkerchiefs for everyone.

When they all had composed themselves, Anna took Lainey's hand again. "So, Lainey, your parents deserve that medal of honor as much as your grandad. You come from strong stock, young lady. We are forever grateful for their sacrifice and are so sad that it took their lives to keep our son alive. We concluded that they chose to not let us lose two children. And, as we said, we will do anything that you ever need. To start, please come visit us some time on Rock Island."

Lainey nodded and blew her nose. Just then, Carter came running out of the building.

"Are you Lainey? Mama said you were really special. I fell off the ship, and your mama and papa grabbed me. The waves were really big, Lainey. I'm five. How old are you? Will you come and visit us sometime? Mama, I'm hungry." The little boy threw his arms around Lainey. "Could you be my big sister?" His blue eyes matched the sky.

Lainey looked up. She couldn't understand it. The sky was bright blue again. She smiled. "Carter, I'd like to be your sister. Maybe we can play together some time."

CHAPTER THREE

EARLY OCTOBER WAS THE MOST beautiful Lainey had ever seen. The fresh scent of water wafted across little Pilot Island. The pain in her heart stung deeply, but the beauty of the skies and the colors of the trees on the mainland and Washington Island tickled her senses. The constant amazement of the brilliant colors across the waters helped her focus outside herself. If she looked within, the pain and grief from the absence of her parents pulled her down, making her gasp, unable to breathe, drowning with them. The colors brought her back.

Uncle Otis let her spend as much time with him in the watch room of the lighthouse as she wanted. He taught her how to fill the light casing with the heated lard that kept the light burning. He also showed her the intricacies of focusing the light and keeping it clean. She began to notice the many ways to determine the speed and direction of the wind and found her observation skills noting weather conditions and water situations improved daily. She loved to see ships pass through the channel and began to understand their route—how they must line up with the day markers on Plum Island in order to stay off the shoals around Pilot Island. Uncle Otis pointed out Nine Foot Shoal that lay between Pilot and the mainland, a treacherous spot for any ship.

Each day, Lainey anticipated observing and identifying the ships that passed the southwest corner of the island. Her favorite part of the day was to go out onto the gallery to wave. She even enjoyed writing the reports to keep track of wind direction and speed, water conditions, and ships sighted. It helped her take her mind off the pain. School work occupied her quiet time around Auntie Edith. She knew her aunt shared her grief and that it all stirred up her hurt over the loss of Mandy. She wondered if Auntie Edith could love her like she loved Mandy, like her own mom had loved her. She pretended sometimes that her aunt was her mom and tried to hug and snuggle with her as they sat reading before bed. Auntie Edith tolerated the closeness for about twenty minutes and even smiled at Lainey with an almost-motherly smile. After the twenty minutes, though, Auntie got up for some reason and busied herself in the kitchen until Lainey went to bed.

Rose remained the best of anybody. When they were in school together, they were inseparable. Lainey always stayed a night or two with Rose's family. It was the most like home, and secretly, she prayed she could stay there forever. She wanted to ask Rose and hoped Rose or her parents would ask her, but they never mentioned it.

Church lifted her every time she went. Pastor Gunnlerson always seemed to preach something that helped her refocus her thoughts from a negative view to a positive one. Plus, occasionally, Carter and his parents were there. She'd fallen in love with Carter at that first hug. She'd always wanted a little brother, and her mother had indicated that they might think about having another child after they returned from the trip. Lainey hoped they'd have a boy. Carter clung to her, and she never wanted to say goodbye to him after church.

Lainey pondered all this as she sat in her little cave-like spot on the north rocks. Auntie Edith didn't act like she even noticed Lainey spent time there. Lainey figured she knew but just had no energy to tell her to be careful. She found she missed her aunt's bossy remarks. Somehow, those remarks meant they were family. That's what parents do, and Auntie Edith and Uncle Otis had to be her parents now. Would they do that?

"Lainey, do you mind staying up here a few minutes while I go down and eat my dinner? It's been a long day, and you're very observant. The wind is not letting up today, and so I'll be here most of the night. Just keep your eye on the water, mainly to the south . . ."

"Because it's a southern blow, right? The winds were fifteen miles per hour, south-southwest earlier, but they look like they are now up to thirty to thirty-five miles per hour, due south."

Uncle Otis beamed. He planted a kiss on the top of her head. "Well, looks like you may be our next assistant lighthouse keeper, young lady. You're learning well."

"I like it, Uncle Otis. It's a little lonely, but I love the light and the water. I don't know if I could rescue anybody from a wrecked ship, though." The pain rose up, and she dropped her head.

"Lainey, we do what we must. We're not prepared for so many things, but the good Lord helps us get through." He pulled her into his arms and hugged her.

She stepped back in the small space. "I know. You go enjoy your supper with Auntie Edith. I will be your assistant until you return."

"Now, mind you, Lainey, don't go out on the gallery. Too danger-ous tonight with the gale."

Lainey gave her uncle a salute and took up a position gazing south. The near waters whipped up by the gusts brought crashing, frothy waves on the rocky southern edge of the island. That end of the island was a small pebble beach. Uncle Otis always told her not to let that trick her as submerged rocks made up a shoal that created havoc for the unprepared ship captain. One day, when a southeast wind attacked the waters and shoals, he pointed out how the waves rose and tumbled into the island. Then those mounds of waters bounced off the rocky shoals and returned, bumping into the oncoming waves to create thunderous claps that sent shivers down her spine.

Now as she watched, a gray curtain rolled across the lake from the mainland. Fog. She didn't like fog. It was chilly and damp and always made her sad. She knew Uncle Otis would need to fire up the fog horn. Perhaps she should go help Auntie Edith cushion her china. *So glad we got the eggs already, and the hens have been laying well this week. If this fog continues, there'll be no eggs for a few days.*

She turned to go partway down the stairs and call her aunt and uncle to report the fog when something caught her eye. What was that? A light? Out in the channel? A reflection of the lighthouse light off the fog? She studied the southern end of the island, even though the fog already hid most of it. Just then, the fog horn started. Lainey jumped; then she saw it again. A light off the southern end. Who would be out there now? Then a sound. It sounded eerily like the scraping sound she'd heard when the *Gilmore* ran aground. But not as loud. Maybe it was the door scraping closed when Uncle Otis returned from starting the fog horn. Or Auntie Edith moving the trunk where she put her good china. She pressed her face against the glass. The image came into view. The bow of a ship. Too close! Way too close! The screeching sound reached her ears over the fog horn.

"Uncle Otis! Uncle Otis! A ship is running hard aground! Southern end. Uncle Otis, do you hear me?" Lainey didn't know how she got halfway down the stairs, but she found herself there.

"Good girl. I'm on my way. Keep the light on it. Can you do that, Lainey? I need you to do that. Your aunt will get things ready here."

Lainey drew on the training that Uncle Otis gave her over the last month. She knew how to focus the light by shifting the prism angles of the Fresnel lens. *Should have already done that as soon as I heard the sound.* She remembered when the *Gilmore* rammed the rocks and Auntie Edith took that job. *God, please help me do this. Help the people on the ship. Help Uncle Otis.*

Lainey spotted the small telescope on the window ledge. She grabbed it and put it to her eye. The rain that now fell in earnest and the fog made her vision of the scene difficult to discern. She soon realized that the ship must have struck on a shoal maybe a hundred yards in distance from the southern edge. Vaguely, she saw Uncle Otis guide the small rescue boat in the direction of the ship. Lights flashed from the ship. They must be trying to signal him. *Please, God, help me guide the light.*

Lainey set down the telescope. She wiggled the light a little to the right. In a pause of the driving rain and a slight lifting of the fog, the light fell on the bouncing boat Uncle Otis bravely rowed to pull alongside the ship. She could barely see men climbing into the boat. She tried to provide a span of light back to the island, but she wasn't sure where the boat should arrive. Would he want to come to the southern tip or come around to the west side, where the dock stood? *God, please help me again.* The thought of those in the storm with her parents rose up. What if the little boat capsized? Most likely, they could all swim, but the wind could blow them away from the island. She felt herself begin to sink, imagining her parents in the water. *No, Lainey, help them! Just like you wish someone could have saved Mama and Papa.*

Again, she turned the focus of the light. She found them. Uncle Otis located the dock, and the men clamored out and up toward the house. Relief enveloped her. A deep breath. She started down the steps as the men came through the door, and Auntie Edith greeted them with strict instructions of where to change into dry clothing.

"Ma'am." One of the men interrupted her. "Keeper Severson is going back to the ship. There are others. He asked that the light continue to be directed."

"Ee—lain—ah!" Lainey halted on the steps. "Stay up there. Your uncle is still rescuing." Lainey willed herself back up the steps. She had not heard fear in her aunt's words before, and it unnerved her. Before she took another breath, she was redirecting the light and finding the ship. Her hands shook, and sweat beaded on her forehead. Why was she so nervous now? What caused Auntie Edith to sound so scared?

Peering through the telescope, she barely caught sight of the small boat. She again turned the light the slightest bit to provide extra vision to her uncle. As he came up beside the ship, she saw that it now floated at a different angle. The high seas battered the ship against the submerged rocks of the shoal. *No wonder they have the range lights to guide the ships away from these shoals. These strong winds sure cause danger.*

Lainey thought the ship looked much lower in the water. *It's sinking!* She silently willed Uncle Otis to rescue the remaining men from the ship. The fog fled with the wind, and Lainey saw one of the men slip and tumble into the water. The other men grabbed his arm and pulled him awkwardly into the boat. The boat rocked and turned broadside the waves and nearly capsized. Lainey had no idea how Uncle Otis kept the boat upright and commandeered it back to the dock. This time, she remained with the light until she was sure all the ship's crew arrived safely inside.

Relief and exhaustion swept over her as Uncle Otis' voice rose over the others as they all thanked him. "Edith, was Lainey on the light all that time? She did an amazing job! I have to go up there."

"Get your wet things off first." Auntie Edith was always a stickler. Lainey smiled.

"I'll change in a few minutes."

Lainey looked down the steps as Uncle Otis started the steep climb.

His eyes lit up when they met Lainey's eyes. "You are a great keeper of the light, Lainey. I'm so proud of you. I couldn't have done it without you." Uncle Otis glanced down before taking his next step. As he lifted one foot, the other foot slipped backwards on the water dripping from him. As the back foot went down, the other foot caught on the upward step. His back and head slammed against the railing. Unable to grab anything, he lurched down the steps with one leg folding under him and the other dragging awkwardly behind. He landed with a thud.

Lainey and her aunt both screamed and called his name. The men ran to him.

"Sir, can you hear me. Are you okay?"

Uncle Otis moaned. Auntie Edith knelt beside him and grabbed his hand. "Otis, Otis, talk to me."

Lainey heard his moans as she carefully backed down the slippery stairs. As she turned, she screamed again. "Your leg! Auntie, look at his leg!" Her aunt turned, and Lainey saw the color drain from her face.

"No, no. You can't break your leg. We need you to be the keeper." She buried her face in her husband's chest and wept.

Two of the men lifted Auntie Edith off Uncle Otis and took her to a chair. "Cookie, check the kitchen for tea. We need to get her calmed down."

Another man knelt beside Lainey's uncle. He glanced up at Lainey, who remained on the bottom step. "I'm the ship's medic. I'll need you to find the supplies." He ran his hands lightly over Uncle Otis's leg. He shook his head. "This is a bad break. Young lady, is there a stretcher? We'll need to move him to a bed and see if we can set this. Also, we'll need the strongest scissors to cut these wet clothes off him. He's a hero, but . . . " The man didn't finish.

Lainey showed the men where the stretcher was and ran to find the scissors. She heard her uncle scream as they lifted him. Guilt washed over her. If she had just come downstairs before he started up so quickly to tell her what a good job she'd done . . .

The medic and a few men from the ship's crew managed to get Uncle Otis on the bed. His wet clothes and theirs soaked into the quilts and dripped all over the rug. Auntie Edith said not a word about the wet. She took several sips of tea, thanking the ship's cookie for making it. She took a deep breath and stood. She looked around but did not appear to see anything, then turned toward the bedroom. Pausing, she reached out toward Lainey.

"Come with me, child."

Lainey caught her breath and then took her aunt's hand. Chills went up and down her spine. Had Uncle Otis died? It would be too much. Whatever would they do?

The men parted when they came through the door. The medic had two poles lined up on each side of Uncle Otis' leg. "Ma'am, young lady. I must set his leg, and it will be painful. It's a bad break. It's best you stay out. The men will help me. I do apologize for getting everything wet. Your husband here saved us all, and we will do our best to give him the best chance to walk again."

Auntie Edith walked over to Uncle Otis, took his hand, and then she kissed it. Uncle Otis opened his eyes, and he smiled at his wife. Lainey saw strain all over his face and wondered how much pain he felt. Her aunt put her arm around Lainey and led her out of the bedroom.

"Elaina, go back up to the light and make sure it's reset for the night. There may be other ships out there. Can you do that? Your uncle is real proud of the way you handled the light."

"Thank you, Auntie. Will he be—"

"You go tend the light." Her aunt smiled, but the way she held herself so stiffly unnerved Lainey.

Halfway up the stairs, she heard her uncle yell. The groans that followed felt like the blows of a sledgehammer against her spine. *Dear God, make him okay. He must be okay. Help me focus on the light. Help Auntie Edith—she's had too much heartbreak.*

It eventually quieted downstairs, and Lainey hoped it meant Uncle Otis was sleeping and not dead. She stood gazing out at the rough waters that continued to hammer the island. Occasionally, she passed the light over the ship, and each time it sat lower in the water. Her confidence sank along with the ship.

Lainey shook herself and began to calculate its angle so she could write a report. Uncle Otis always wrote a report each day. He recorded when he saw ships; the ship's name, if he could see it; whether it was a schooner, passenger steamer, freight steamer, lumber hooker, fishing boat, or whaleback. She could see this ship was a freight schooner. The difficulty of determining length bothered Lainey, but she could ask the men. She discerned easily the angle at which the schooner sat—it was already at forty-five degrees, and the lower hull was gone from sight. The rocks of the shoal hovered close to the surface, but the depth of the water was seventy feet not far from the shoal. Lainey was sure the schooner was going that way and estimated that by morning it would be totally submerged.

"Little lady, may I interrupt you? You appear very focused."

Lainey jumped. She looked over her shoulder at a huge man. He filled the space behind her, and she wondered how he'd maneuvered the steps. *His feet must be as big as two steps.* Lainey kept herself from gazing down at his shoes. The man's beard was trimmed near his jaw, and his spectacles slid down his nose. *At least, he's in dry clothes.*

He smiled and held out his hand. "I'm Captain Benjamin Clow of the *A.P. Nichols*, the schooner. Your uncle deserves a medal for saving us. I'm the one who landed in the water, and at great risk, he pulled me back in the rescue boat. And, amazingly, your aunt had extra clothes that would fit me. I'm impressed at your ability to keep the light on the rescue."

Lainey smiled, but no words came out of her mouth. She simply marveled at his size.

"Your uncle's leg is badly broken. You may have to fill in for him for some time."

Lainey coughed. "Well, Auntie Edith will probably be doing that, sir."

The man smiled a sad smile. "Young lady, your aunt seems very undone by this accident. You are going to have to do a lot to help her and your uncle. I can see from your light that our schooner is sinking and will most likely be a total loss. Because of that, my crew and I will not remain here long. We'll help all we can for the next few days. I was raised by a lighthouse keeper, so I can help with the reports." He paused, glancing at Lainey's notes. "Why, young lady, you have calculated the length and angle of descent quite well. You possess an uncanny knack at the skills required of lightkeepers for one of such a young age. My appreciation."

Lainey felt the blush run up her face. She smiled. "The length of the ship is difficult for me. The angles seem easy."

Captain Clow picked up her notes. "You have 150 feet, and it's actually 145—that's a good estimation when the weather is clear, but you accomplished it with the fog and rain."

"Thank you. When do you think Uncle Otis will be able to continue?"

The captain looked past Lainey. "I don't know. I'm not sure he will be able to continue as lighthouse keeper."

Lainey gulped. *This couldn't be. Would it be too much for Auntie Edith?* She felt a tear escape her eye. She brushed it away with the back of her hand. "What did Auntie Edith say?"

The captain laid his huge hand gently on her shoulder. "Young lady, we haven't told your aunt yet. You need to be strong for her. She's struggling with this and is just busying herself with food, cleaning, dry clothes, and where we are to sleep right now."

That was Auntie Edith. Lainey nodded her head.

"When the blow settles down, we'll go to the mainland or Washington Island in your skiff and bring back the doctor. Hopefully, we've set the leg so it will heal fully, but we're not sure. Tell you what—I'll stay up here and tend the light. You go down and get something to eat. Your aunt has a meal ready for you."

Lainey squeezed around the big man and found her way carefully down the steps.

Auntie Edith bustled to the stove and dished up a plate for Lainey as soon as the girl entered the kitchen. Lainey examined her aunt's countenance, but it revealed nothing of her feelings. "Eat up, Elaina; you have a long night in front of you. You tend the light. I must tend your uncle." The scent of tarts wafted from the warming drawer.

Lainey picked up her fork and stared at the little roses around the edge of the plate. Auntie Edith must not have had anytime to cushion the china. Lainey hoped none had broken due to the fog horn.

She was so hungry, but first, she needed to know how Auntie Edith perceived things. "Is he . . ."

"He's sleeping now. They had a little whiskey with them to cut the pain, and it knocked him right out. That's a good thing. He needs to rest now."

"Will he be all right, Auntie?" The words scraped Lainey's throat one by one as they came out.

Auntie Edith turned to the sink and washed a pot before answering. "Of course, he will. What a silly question, girl. What else could he be? Nothing has ever kept him down." She set the pot on the sideboard and placed both hands on the edge of the sink. Her head hung down. Then she turned to Lainey but stared at the floor. "We'll take turns with the light until he's well enough to keep the light. He says you're a natural up there, and that's good. It will be a lot of work till he's well enough to work again. I don't know how much schooling you'll get—you'll just have to make it up later."

For the first time, she met Lainey's eyes, then looked at her plate. "Why, Elaina, you need to eat your food before it gets cold. I didn't hold that for you so you could just sit there and stare off into the distance and ask questions. Finish your dinner and then get back up to tend the light."

Bossy Auntie Edith returns. I guess that's a good sign. Lainey ate her meal with such diligence, it seemed she inhaled it. She knew it was good, but she knew she needed to return to the light and possibly be there all night. Uncle Otis needed her to do that. So did Auntie Edith. She would do it.

"Thank you, Auntie. I'm going back upstairs now." She waited till she was almost outside the kitchen, hoping to prevent upsetting her aunt in any way.

"Elaina, get a sweater. It will be chilly up there tonight. Here, take some cookies and a little jug of milk. You might get hungry." Auntie Edith placed the items into her hands without looking at her.

"Yes, ma'am."

After retrieving her pink sweater from her room and a little bag in which to carry the cookies and milk, Lainey tiptoed past the kitchen door and went into her uncle's room. Indeed, he slept. She looked at his leg and cringed. The vision of the fall and the sound of the break played in her mind and threatened to overwhelm her. She gazed at his face. Pale and sweaty. He must be in pain. She took his hand. He squeezed her hand, and she thought she detected a slight smile. Perhaps it was a grimace. Either way, it gladdened her that he responded. She bent and kissed his forehead and hurried to the light.

"Thank you for watching the light for me, Captain Clow."

"My pleasure, young lady. It's been a rough evening for all of us. I'm going to get a few hours' sleep and then return here so you can get some sleep. It's already 9:00 p.m. I'll come back at midnight and stay till first light." He glanced at Lainey. "Don't you worry about your aunt. I'll clear it all with her first." Captain Clow chuckled. "She reminds me of my grandmother when I was growing up. Don't worry. It'll be okay." He patted Lainey's shoulder and proceeded down the stairs.

True to his word, he returned a few minutes after midnight. Lainey wasn't sure she'd ever been up this late, and it had been difficult to think through anything, but she forced herself to pay close attention to the light and the lake. The blow had settled a bit, and she hoped morning would be clear with little wind. That would make it possible for the crew to deliver a doctor to see Uncle Otis.

Captain Clow's eyes held a bit of grogginess, but he acted quite chipper for the middle of the night. "I helped myself to some cookies in the kitchen on my way up. Hope your aunt doesn't mind."

"I'm sure it's fine. Thank you for relieving me, Captain."

"You get some sleep. You've had a long day. And you've done a great job as a lightkeeper."

Lainey smiled and carefully picked her way down the stairs. She fell into bed with her clothes on and went to sleep instantly.

CHAPTER FOUR

THE MORNING AFTER THE ACCIDENT, the last of the exposed ship slipped off the shoal and sunk into the waters of Lake Michigan. When Lainey went up the stairs to reclaim her post, Captain Clow was standing at attention with his hand in a salute. She followed his gaze to see the last of the mast disappear from sight.

"Oh, my, sir. I'm so sorry."

The captain smiled. "It's a big loss; but all the crew is alive, and that's most important. We'll be okay."

After a big breakfast, Captain Clow and three of his crew left for Newport Town in Uncle Otis' skiff. They purchased supplies, reported the loss of the *Nichols*, and returned early afternoon with Dr. Corbin, a kindly gentleman with bushy hair. Lainey came partway downstairs when she saw he'd arrived.

"Otis, Otis, whatever have you done to yourself?" He stood in the doorway to the bedroom and laughed with his belly shaking. His white beard and hair reflected the light. Lainey chuckled to herself.

Uncle Otis laughed as well. "I just wanted to have an early visit from Santa Claus. Sorry you had to come all the way out here."

"It's a nice day on the water. So sorry to hear of the shipwreck, but I hear you're quite the hero. Brought you a newspaper, so you can catch up on all the news."

Uncle Otis shook his head. "Just doing my job. That's all."

"Can I get you some tea and a cherry tart, Doctor?" Auntie Edith came into the bedroom behind Dr. Corbin.

"Edith, Edith, it's good to see you. You both are so healthy, I never get a visit. Sorry to have to be here now. Let me examine this leg, and then we'll talk a bit over the tea and tarts. Lainey . . . " he looked out the door as she descended the steps. "I hear you have become a great lightkeeper. You sure are a help to these two." He laughed again, and his belly actually shook. Almost instantly, his face became sober, and he gently closed the door, effectively shutting out both Auntie Edith and Lainey.

"Well, I never." Auntie Edith stalked into the kitchen to make the tea and warm up the tarts. Lainey could hear her mumbling the whole time. She wondered why the doctor didn't allow them in while he examined Uncle Otis. Then she heard the moan. Dr. Corbin said something, and Uncle Otis responded; but Lainey couldn't make out what they said.

Twenty minutes passed. Dr. Corbin opened the door. He smiled at Lainey, but it wasn't near as jovial as it first had been. He walked into the kitchen. Edith poured tea and set the tarts on the table. She motioned Lainey to join them. "She needs to hear your assessment."

Lainey sat down, but her longing for cherry tarts had waned. Dr. Corbin took a sip of tea and a bite of tart. Then he looked at Auntie Edith with somber eyes. He laid his hand on hers. "Edith, I hate to tell you this, but you know it was a bad break. He's going to be fine . . . " Lainey pulled in a deep breath of relief, but it was short-lived. "However, I doubt he'll ever tend light again."

Auntie Edith sat stoic. She nodded slowly. "That's what I feared. I'm officially the assistant lighthouse keeper, but I can become the main keeper and Otis the assistant. That way, we can remain here and get all the stipends and supplies as before. Otis can help me with the reports. Elaina can do a lot of the work as well." She looked down and wrung her hands and then rubbed the back of her neck. "But if there was another shipwreck . . . And how would Elaina ever get to school? I just don't know if we can do this."

"You know I'll help, Auntie Edith. I'm happy to." Lainey took a bite of cherry tart.

"I know that, but it isn't a life, a full-time life, for a young girl. Not much of a life for Otis and me either if all he can do is sit down here while I do his work as well as mine."

Lainey sat straighter. "But Uncle Otis will walk again, right? He can do everything, just not climb the steps. That's what you mean, don't you, Doctor? I'm strong. I can carry up the lard fuel. I can wash the windows and clean the light. Uncle Otis even taught me to direct the light and calculate wind speed."

Her aunt laid a hand on Lainey's arm. She knew it meant to stop talking. She looked down. "Elaina is a big help, Doctor. Do you think Otis will walk again?"

Lainey's head shot up. "What! He'll walk—won't he?" *He has to. This is Uncle Otis. I need him to walk.* Lainey felt her hands shake as she waited for Dr. Corbin to answer.

Dr. Corbin ran his hand over his mouth and then frowned. "By 'bad break,' I not only mean it's a severe and ragged break; but also, through no one's fault, it was set awkwardly. It's not going to heal correctly. If it had happened near my office, maybe. But this is remote. The medic saved his leg—maybe his life—but he didn't have what was needed to set it correctly. No infection set in, which is wonderful. He'll be okay. He may walk, but at best, with a cane. I doubt he'll be able to climb steps again." Dr. Corbin reached across the table to place his hand on Auntie Edith's. "It's probably time to get an assistant lightkeeper out here. I can send a message to the U.S. Lighthouse Board if you like."

Lainey set her elbows on the table and rested her chin on her hands and stared into space. Assistants? That might be nice. It might be a family with a girl or a boy her age. But would they think Auntie Edith was the assistant? Would they take over? She glanced at her aunt. Auntie Edith is wondering the same thing.

Auntie Edith stood up. "Dr. Corbin, thank you. Otis and I need to talk this through. Thank you for your offer, but please wait—don't contact the lighthouse board yet. And I will pay your bill on your next visit."

Dr. Corbin shook his head. "Edith, you and Otis are like family. There is no bill—let's just say it was a visit long overdue, and why don't you put a few of those tarts in a bag for me. The kids and Agatha love your tarts."

Auntie Edith nodded. She pulled a small flour sack out of a drawer and placed a dozen tarts in it for Dr. Corbin. "Thank you. Your kindness is appreciated."

"I'll say goodbye to Otis and show myself out. I'll come back next week."

As Dr. Corbin went out the door, Auntie Edith turned to her niece. "Elaina, you need to go upstairs and clean the light and wipe down the windows. Be careful on the gallery. I'll heat the lard and bring it up later, and you can help me pour it in. We'll need to get a schedule set. I don't want you up there all night long. The crew from the *Nichols* will leave soon, so it will be up to us to take care of your uncle's needs and determine our ability to be up at night."

Lainey started to go into the bedroom to see Uncle Otis before going to the light.

"Elaina, go now." Auntie Edith's voice left not a bit of wiggle room.

She longed to have Uncle Otis hug her and tell her everything would be all right, but she'd have to see him later. She gave herself a little hug after determining Auntie Edith wasn't looking and said in as deep a voice as she could muster, "It'll be all right, girl. It'll be all right, girl."

She continued her mantra all the way up to the light. Taking a deep breath, she set to cleaning the light. The thick glass had tinges of oil smoke darkening the interior. She loved the Fresnel lens. Uncle Otis told her a French scientist invented the lens, and installation took place about twenty years previous. She found fascination in its capability to focus in a wide spray of light or a more pinpointed beam.

After cleaning all the glass, she polished the brass of the back side of the lens. The brass sides prevented the light from shining where it wasn't needed. Uncle Otis impressed upon her the need for proper lighting whenever she spent time with him. Unnecessary light could confuse a ship that depended on the range lights between Plum Island and the light of Pilot Island. Adding extra light could throw a ship too close to a shoal. Most of the waters of Death's Door ran deep and rough, sporting danger in many places. Even her lighthouse was named Porte des Morts—Door of Death. Lainey shivered when she thought of it. She preferred to call it Pilot Island Lighthouse.

She next opened the narrow door and went out onto the gallery to wash the windows. She enjoyed this as much as hanging the clothes on the line. As the breeze blew her hair in her face and the sun lowered itself in the sky, a peace settled upon her. "It will be all right. I don't know how, but it will be all right. I can do this job. I love it. I've lost my parents, but at least I have Uncle Otis—and Auntie Edith." Lainey chuckled. "Yes, Auntie Edith is okay."

Lainey wondered if her aunt needed help with the fuel. She could smell the heating of the lard on the stove. Carrying the heavy bucket up the steps was tricky, but it wasn't a choice. It was daily life. Lainey had managed to carry it up twice. The handle of the bucket cut into her hands, leaving red marks, and the weight made her back and shoulders hurt. But she could do it. *It'll be all right, girl.*

Auntie Edith probably had her hands full if she was trying to cook dinner for everyone on the *Nichols* crew, keep an eye on Uncle Otis, and heat the fuel. She backed down the steps. About to call to her aunt and offer to take the lard oil up to the light, she heard voices. It was Uncle Otis. He sounded upset.

Lainey tiptoed toward the kitchen. She debated calling out, so it wouldn't appear she was trying to eavesdrop, which she most definitely was doing. Uncle Otis' voice rose.

"Edith, we are not going to let her go. We can manage this. I'll be better, and I've trained her well."

Lainey froze.

"You know we can't do this forever—not now that you're injured. This is no life for a girl. She'll never get off the island. It's a demanding job. You know that, Otis.

Uncle Otis sighed. "I know. Maybe we should request an assistant."

"But then we'll have to split the rations and stipends provided by the lighthouse board. Right now, we get both. Plus, I'm sure they would demote us to assistant. We'd be in the smaller quarters with less provision. There wouldn't be enough for three of us."

Uncle Otis groaned.

"Otis, you have to try to sit still till there's more healing. Getting agitated over this isn't helping your leg."

"Nor my disposition, my dear wife."

Lainey heard the swoosh of Auntie Edith's skirt. She scooted into the kitchen and waited. Auntie Edith probably was checking if she was nearby.

Her aunt continued, but her voice lowered. Lainey moved closer to the door. "I got a letter from your cousin Alma after the shipwreck claimed my sister. She said the orphan train would be traveling from Chicago to Nebraska and stopping in Milwaukee shortly before Christmas."

Lainey gasped. Fortunately, Uncle Otis slammed the newspaper down at the same time.

"What are you thinking, Edith?"

"That we can't support Elaina. If she can get on that train, a family that is looking for an extra girl would take her. She's a good worker, and she's a happy girl. Lots of families would love to have her."

Lainey couldn't breathe.

"Edith, some of those families are only looking for servants, for slaves. We are her family. We can't turn her out."

"Otis, we are in danger of being turned out. Then, what would we do? We'd have no home, no work. Better that we give her an opportunity to find a good family that has provision."

"I can't listen to this. I can't consider this. I don't know yet what we'll do, but we will not turn out that girl. She has the most resilient spirit of anyone I've ever met. We can't destroy that."

"But we can't provide for her. How can we handle winter if the lighthouse board orders us to remain for the railroad car ferries? It would be too much work for her; she'd never be able to leave, be a child, be a young lady. And even if we winter on Washington, you can't lumberjack anymore. It would be charity for the Goodlets to have us stay there. It won't work, Otis. Something has to change."

A tear trickled down Lainey's face. This was far more serious than she realized. What could she do? Auntie Edith's chair scraped, and Lainey realized the conversation was over—or, at least, on hold. She ran to the stairs and climbed up a few steps, then stopped. As Auntie Edith came out of the bedroom, red-faced, Lainey pretended she'd just descended from the light. Forcing her voice to sound cheery, she offered to take up the lard.

"No, I'll take it up and stay a while. Uncle Otis has eaten. Why don't you eat? But don't bother your uncle. He needs to rest. You can do schoolwork for the evening."

Lainey dished up stew from the pot on the stove. It was one of her favorites. But tonight, it had no taste. Time passed. Lainey jerked herself awake. Where had she been? She'd eaten, but somehow, she must have shut down. The darkness blocked the windows like darkness now blocked any sensation of life. The orphan train. She'd heard that children abandoned or honestly orphaned—well, that was her, wasn't it—were put on the train with a few nurses who took care of them. The train then made stops in various towns; and farmers, store owners, and childless couples took the children. Some became servants to earn their keep. She'd heard some were made slaves. Others were given a home and a family. But she had a family—Uncle Otis and Auntie Edith. They weren't Mama and Papa, but they loved her. Well, Uncle Otis did.

A fog descended on her, and a gale blew in her heart. Her life had run aground just like the *Nichols*. Would she sink, or would she survive? Uncle Otis coughed. Lainey gathered her dishes and quickly cleaned and put them away.

Peeking up the stairs and seeing no sign of her aunt, Lainey scurried to Uncle Otis' bedroom and tiptoed in. His face lit up. "Climb up here with me, girl. How are you? I've missed you."

Lainey kicked off her shoes and hopped up on the bed. She crawled over and squeezed under his arm. He kissed the top of her head.

"Tell me what you did upstairs today, girl."

"Well, I cleaned all the glass, lens, and windows. I even polished the brass."

"And what conditions did you record?"

"The windspeed was ten to fifteen, temperature in the fifties. It was mostly sunny. There were the puffy clouds—what are they again—not cirrus, but cummel, culus . . ."

"Cumulus."

Lainey clapped her hands. "Yes, cumulus. It was a pretty day. I saw two vessels. One a fishing boat, the other a schooner heading south." She held her hand up, stopping him from asking. "I would say it was an empty freight schooner, as it sat high in the water. And I would say it was a hundred feet long."

"Good girl, Lainey. What a great lightkeeper you are. All the young men will have their eyes on you. A beautiful young woman who can be a lighthouse keeper will be in great demand. I hear that the keeper at Eagle Bluff Lighthouse has seven sons—one of them might be right for you."

Lainey laughed, a deep laugh. The fog lifted, and the gale lessened. She was safe with Uncle Otis. She playfully punched his arm. "Uncle! I'm not interested in any boys."

Her uncle chuckled. "Oh, but they'll be interested in you. Your aunt Edith was the catch when I was young."

"The catch?"

"Oh, the most beautiful young woman. Like you, she loved the lighthouse and was capable. There were a few of us who wanted to be keepers, but the U.S. Lighthouse Board said we had to be married. I think five of us were wooing your aunt. Now, your mama was a beauty, too, but she was much younger. At that time, all we saw was your aunt."

"But were Mama and Auntie raised in a lighthouse? I don't remember Mama telling me that."

"No, but Edith's best friend grew up in a lighthouse. Mildred was already spoken for. Her parents had arranged it long before most young people start thinking about courting and marriage."

"Elaina." The voice at the doorway made her jump. Auntie Edith had told her not to bother Uncle Otis. Lainey looked at her and hung her head. Her aunt's words were strained. "I'd like you to spell me a couple hours. It's been a long day." Glancing up, Lainey observed a smile, but it was sad and tired. "I'll take a nap and then come up for the rest of the night. Can you handle that, Elaina?"

Lainey nodded. She swiveled and kissed Uncle Otis on his cheek, then scrambled off the bed and hurried to the stairs.

"Elaina, remember to be careful." How tired Auntie Edith's voice sounded.

When her aunt relieved her, Lainey fell into bed fully dressed again and never stirred till daylight peeked through her curtains.

CHAPTER FIVE

LAINEY CHANGED HER CLOTHES AND washed her face with the chilly water that sat in the bowl on her nightstand. October stood strong and colorful, but the whisper of winter was in the air. She shivered and longed for summer again—before her parents died, before Uncle Otis broke his leg.

Still, autumn's colors and fresh nippy breezes drew her in. The crackle and rustle of the leaves, the crispness of the air made it her favorite season. Autumn's only downfall was that winter followed; and even when life was wonderful, winter had a forlornness about it. The gray sky, gray waters, white snow, and lack of leaves always brought sadness to Lainey. But now, she dealt with true sadness, real loss—her parents and possibly her aunt and uncle—orphan train! Really, could it be? What could she do? In more ways than one, winter was on its way into her life. *I must be strong. I want sunlight, not winter. I don't know how, but I don't want to be sad forever like Auntie Edith. Dear God, help me live. Help her live.*

Lainey walked into the kitchen. The wooden table was cleared. Only the vase with the wilted leaves she had brought in a few days previous sat on the wooden table. The sink was empty of dishes. The pump sat alone on the counter with the promise of bringing water from the cistern below the floor, if only someone would work the handle. No pots of leftovers or preparation of future meals lingered on the stove. Auntie Edith must still be upstairs with the light.

Her twelfth birthday would soon arrive with no red dress, no party with her parents, and perhaps only a trip to the orphan train. She wouldn't remind anyone of her upcoming birthday. Too much occupied everyone's mind.

Lainey determined to make breakfast for everyone, unless she'd slept too late. If that was the case, she'd best eat a piece of bread and cheese and get upstairs to clean the light and then get the lard oil ready to fuel the light tonight. She exited the kitchen to check upstairs when she heard lowered voices from the bedroom.

"Edith, you can't really be thinking this. I was sure you were in shock yesterday. The orphan train is not the place for Lainey. And you need her help here . . . Edith, she loves the lighthouse, and she's learning the weather, the kinds of ships."

Auntie's voice rose a bit. "She loves it now, but soon, she'll hate it. It's too isolated here. She has the wanderlust like her mother. Don't you remember? Emma only wanted to travel, to 'explore the world,' as she put it. She would have withered had she been tied down in any way. Look, she left Elaina with us, so she could take the big trip . . . "

A tenseness crept up Lainey's back and spread to her shoulders. Did Mama love travel more than her? A tear formed in her eye. *But Mama wanted me. Do you, Auntie Edith? Where else could I go?*

Uncle Otis's voice sounded thick, gravelly. "I don't think I can let her go, Edith. She's too precious. She's a part of us now. She needs us." There was a pause. "And I think we need her. I know no one could ever take Mandy's place, but she sure fills a lot of that empty space."

Lainey heard a muffled sob. "Otis, it's not that. We can't support her. I can't do the job of keeper and take care of you."

"But—"

"You must listen, Otis. Please, listen. At best, we can be assistant keepers, which brings less provision from the lighthouse board. If we remained as main keeper, what would we do if there was another shipwreck? We couldn't help—at least, I can't. Do you want her trying to help save a crew? Also, you are going to need some help concerning your injury. We really should be on the mainland. We don't know if we can find work. I could take in laundry or cook, but you can't lumberjack or stone-chip. I don't even know of any assistant keepers needed on the mainland."

"I can do accounting and records, Edith. I don't need my legs to do that."

"Yes, but at an entry level, we would barely be able to support ourselves. I know we have some funds saved from our winter work, but we can't live on that very long. Lainey deserves to be well taken care of—good schooling, grand clothes, and many friends. We can't give her that. I don't want to turn her out, Otis, but everyone I'm connected to has been injured or died. I can't do it anymore."

Lainey found herself back in the kitchen, staring out the window. Her limbs were limp, and it seemed a cloud had entered the room. Movement fled her being, and breathing came in short gasps. To wrap her mind around the conversation challenged all her strength. She forced herself to pump some water into a pan and some into a glass. She drank it but spilled a good portion down her shirt. Opening the door, she walked into the sunshine. It was too bright. She turned slowly, realizing she had left the door open. She looked at her hand and mentally pushed it back to the handle to close the door.

Stumbling, she entered the henhouse. The occupants looked at her, and their clucking ceased. *They must know I can't stay here.* Lainey fell to her knees in the straw. *God, help me to handle this.*

A hen poked her. Lainey lifted her head. Three hens stood facing her. "Oh, Tilly and Muffin and Henny." Lainey felt the giggles rising as she considered what the hens must be thinking. "It's okay, girls. I'll just get some eggs from you." She wiped her eyes with her sleeve and rose. Seven eggs awaited in the nests. "I can make breakfast for all of us." Lainey nodded to the hens. "If you can live here and be productive, well, so can I. That is, if they let me stay." With that, she turned back to the house, her back straight. No matter what, life must be lived, and she would live it as best she could.

When she had made breakfast of scrambled eggs and bread, she carried it to Uncle Otis and Auntie Edith, who still sat in the bedroom. "I slept a little late, but here's a good breakfast for you. I'll get right upstairs and get the windows and light cleaned as soon as I finish my meal. We may be too late for laundry today, but I can work on it tomorrow if that's acceptable to you."

Auntie Edith nodded. "Thank you, Elaina."

Lainey quickly left the room and went through the motions of eating, cleaning, and washing windows.

Sunday dawned pleasant with calm winds. The autumn air held a chill but an invitation to explore. Lainey stepped outside and longed to run, to hide, to play, to explore. The cravings for activity coursed through her and confused her. Perhaps it was the weather. Perhaps it was the wanderlust Auntie Edith said her mama possessed. Perhaps it was the inability to face the concerns she overheard her aunt express to Uncle Otis. But the restlessness threatened to overtake her.

The door opened. Lainey held her breath and waited to count the bounces. There were no bounces. Instead, she felt a hand on her shoulder. "Elaina, it's a nice day. Let's go to Washington Island and go to church. It's been a long time since we've been able to go."

Excitement rose within her, but she pushed it away. "What about Uncle Otis? Should I stay and sit with him?"

Auntie Edith smiled. "No, child. He'll be fine for a few hours. I've made him plenty of food. It's by the bed. You go in, get something to eat, and dress. We should leave in thirty minutes."

Lainey want to skip, but instead politely walked back to the house to get ready.

As they shoved off and rocked in the lapping waves, Auntie Edith's eyes held Lainey's. "Elaina, you know we have some difficult decisions ahead of us due to your uncle's accident."

Lainey gulped and nodded.

"You're a good worker, Elaina. Otis is so proud of your learning. But being a keeper isn't easy. If they send assistants to help us . . . I mean, you and I would be little help if another shipwreck occurred. If they sent assistants, they probably would dismiss us. I don't know what work your uncle can do, but I don't think we'll be able to stay here."

Auntie Edith stared off toward the mainland. The blueness of the sky and the blueness of the water brought a thrill to Lainey's very being. Gulls cawed in the distance. Perhaps they were welcoming her.

She loved this place. She dragged her fingers in the water as the sun glinted off the surface of the slight chop of waves. The strength of Auntie Edith's arms as she rowed the boat impressed Lainey. *She's so strong in so many ways. Why can't she be strong for me?*

"Elaina, I don't know if we can keep you." Her aunt bit her lips. "You need to be with a family that can give you more. I don't know if I can give you what you need. We think we know about some families that might be able to care for you."

The orphan train! Lainey wanted to scream, to jump in the water and swim away; but she sat still, looked down, and wrung her hands in her lap.

"We'll discuss this more, Elaina." Auntie Edith continued to row and not say anymore. She didn't look directly at Lainey for the rest of the journey, which suited the girl just fine.

After tying the boat at the familiar wooden pier, the two gathered shawls and hats and a small basket of food and began the three-mile walk to the church. Lainey was happy for the exercise, but it was short-lived.

"Miss Edith, Lainey, are you here for church on this fine day?" Lainey observed a wagon with an elderly couple coming toward them. The Wickmans were retired lighthouse keepers from Plum Island. They now lived with their daughter's family, helping with the lavender farm and the grandchildren. "Let us give you a ride." Mr. Wickman stepped off the wagon and offered his hand for Lainey and her aunt to climb aboard.

Auntie Edith tried to lead the conversation by asking about their family and well-being. Soon enough, the conversation came to concern for the Seversons.

"Edith, how's Otis? We heard he broke his leg quite badly. How long till he can return to the light?"

"It may be quite a while." Auntie Edith pursed her lips and then smiled. "But we'll be fine. Tell me again how many grandchildren you have now."

Lainey saw the questioning look that crossed the faces of both Mr. and Mrs. Wickman, but they asked no more after Otis.

Upon entering the church, old friends descended upon both Lainey and her aunt. Questions about their activities and Otis dominated the conversations. Lainey took her lead from her aunt and simply said that her uncle was healing, the break was bad, but they hoped he'd be on his feet soon. She looked around for Rose but didn't see her. She noticed Anna and Reinhardt Engelson. They, too, must have decided to take advantage of the calm waters and beautiful day and travel the waters to church. Carter ran to her with a squeal. Lainey dropped to her knees and embraced the young boy. "How are you, little brother?"

Carter beamed. "I miss you, but Papa and I are exploring Rock Island. Can you come visit?"

"I hope so, Carter."

"Elaina, we need to take our seats."

"Auntie Edith, did you see any of the Hansons? I don't see Rose."

"Her brother just told me she has a cold, and they decided she should remain home today. She'll be sorry she missed you."

Lainey hung her head. *Oh, Rose, I needed to talk to you.* She followed her aunt to a pew near the side aisle. After three hymns, everyone greeted each other and sat down. Lainey gazed around at the families present. She saw smiles, nudges, and parents putting their arms around their children. Some provided looks that said "behave," but she perceived the love behind those looks. She heard Pastor Gunnlerson's voice, but it didn't register. Instead, her mind filled with the conversations she'd overheard between her aunt and uncle. Wanderlust . . . orphan train . . . can't provide . . . can't walk . . . find another family for her. A fog horn of words and fears blew around her. Again, the urge to run, to flee, rose up within her, and she couldn't resist. She got up; and though inside she raced, she made herself walk to the back. She hoped Auntie Edith assumed she left to use the outhouse. Instead, she ran down the road and into the woods.

Finally, she slowed to a walk. The soft sound of the breeze whispered across the path. Lainey looked up. The leaves, tinged with fading color, gently waved at her. She smiled. The rustle of the leaves already fallen crunched beneath her feet. Soon, all the leaves would fall and leave the trees bare. A wave of loneliness swept over Lainey, and she wanted to cry. Why must the leaves fall? Why must the leaves leave? They go with magnificent color and glory. She paused. Why must they die after such a glorious display? That was what her parents did, wasn't it? They gloriously saved Carter so his parents wouldn't be without two children. But now she was without two parents—and probably without an aunt and an uncle as well. Not only that but her twelfth birthday most likely would come and go with no celebration, no red dress, no parents, and maybe no family at all.

She continued walking. The leaves return—they grow again in the spring—but her parents wouldn't return. *But I am with you forever.* She remembered Pastor saying Jesus said those words. She'd been told her parents remained with her in memories. But they were not present to take care of her. *But I am here with you.*

"Who is saying that? Is that God? But who will take care of me, God? Uncle Otis can't work, and Auntie Edith only wants to help him. She doesn't want me." The tears flowed freely. Lainey sat on a low limb of a huge tree and leaned back. "Carter now has his two parents; and I'm glad, but I'm alone. If Auntie Edith has her way, I'll be totally alone." She closed her eyes and tried to stop the heaving sadness that filled her chest. She felt a niggle inside. What was it Carter's parents said that day on the church steps? *If you ever need anything . . .*

A strong gust of wind rose up and almost tipped her off the limb. She thought she heard voices and wondered if God was speaking to her again. He did say He was with her forever. She listened and heard her name. And then, there was Carter—he threw himself into her lap. She wrapped her arms around him and smelled the sweet fragrance of soap in his hair. His little hands squeezed her, and she felt she could hug him forever. Peeking over his head, she saw his parents and Auntie Edith. Oh no, this meant trouble. She quickly stood up, gently letting Carter down to the ground.

"I'm sorry, Auntie Edith. I just had to get some air, just walk . . . I won't do it again, I promise."

"Elaina, it's all right." Auntie Edith actually smiled.

Anna, Carter's mother, took Lainey's hands in hers. "Lainey, we heard about your uncle and heard about the troubles this creates for your family. We want you to be ours, Lainey. Your aunt and uncle have agreed, and the pastor thought it would be a good idea."

Lainey gulped and shook her head. She looked at Anna and Reinhardt, then at Auntie Edith. "But—but Uncle Otis . . . "

"Your uncle and I discussed this last night, Elaina." She looked down at her hands. "We've been discussing it for some time." She walked over to her niece. "I'm sorry, Elaina, if you overheard some of our talks and arguing. I truly care for you, and you have been such a help—not to mention what joy you bring to your uncle." She smiled. "But I've been so worried and so tired and so afraid of what's to come since your uncle's accident—not only for your uncle and me, but also for your future. How could we provide?" Auntie Edith looked away, and her voice softened. "But last night, Otis remembered the conversation with Anna and Reinhardt and asked me to talk to them about our dilemma. We didn't know if they would be open to the idea, but we knew we had to check. Otherwise, his cousin in Milwaukee . . . "

"Uncle Otis agrees?"

She placed her hand on Lainey's shoulder. "He does, Elaina. It was his idea. And if Anna and Reinhardt were agreeable, then he wanted to make sure Pastor Gunnlerson felt it was a wise plan. The pastor thought it was excellent and prayed for all of us."

Anna stepped closer. "But, Lainey, are you agreeable? We are lightkeepers on another island."

"A lot bigger than Pilot Island." Auntie Edith rolled her eyes and chuckled. "A lot more room for you to explore."

Lainey wondered if she actually saw a twinkle in her aunt's eye. "I . . . I . . . " She stepped back and looked at everyone. They all looked hopeful.

"Please, Lainey!" Carter again wrapped himself around her. "Please be my real, real sister."

Anna gently pulled Carter back. "Lainey needs time to think about this. It's a bit sudden." She and Reinhardt turned as if to walk back to the church.

"No, no, wait. Auntie Edith, are you sure?"

"Yes, Elaina, I think it is the right and best solution for all of us. Your uncle and I may have to leave Pilot or be assistants—and we don't know how we'll manage—but we want the best for you."

"Uncle Otis is truly agreeable with this?"

"Yes, Elaina." Lainey noticed Auntie Edith didn't raise her voice. "As I said, it was his idea."

Lainey looked at Anna and Reinhardt. "And you want me? You're sure? Not just to be a slave?" Lainey coughed and looked with big eyes at Auntie Edith, who just laughed. "I mean, not just to be household help. I mean, I'm a good worker, and I'm happy to help, and I've learned a lot." Lainey looked down and back up. Auntie Edith had her hand over her mouth, and her shoulders shook a little. "Auntie Edith, I'm strong, right? And I can do a lot of good work, right?" Auntie Edith nodded but kept her hand over her mouth, and Lainey was sure she heard a laugh leaking out of her. Lainey looked back at Anna. "But, I mean, you want me as part of your family—a sister for Carter?"

"And a daughter for us. Yes, Lainey, we want you more than we can express, and we are so honored that your aunt and uncle would trust us with your care and upbringing." Anna reached out and grabbed Auntie Edith's hand. Lainey's aunt turned and put her head into Anna's shoulder and wept. Anna patted her back. "It's good; it's okay. It's God. It's right."

Auntie Edith stepped back and wiped her eyes. "Thank you, Anna. Elaina, do you want to be with them?"

"I do. I do with all my heart. I . . . I'm amazed. I prayed, and . . . and . . . and here you are."

Anna enveloped her, and Lainey cried and then laughed. She saw her aunt stand by with tears on her cheeks but a smile on her face.

"So, when do you want me to come?" Lainey looked from Anna to Auntie Edith.

Reinhardt spoke up. "We can get you a week from Thursday. That will give you time to pack and say your goodbyes. And it will give us a few days to prepare your room as well and get things set up. Does that work?" He looked to Auntie Edith and back to Lainey.

Auntie Edith put her arm around Lainey. "That will be fine. It will give us a little time together as a family before she joins her new family. And time for Elaina to help me until the lighthouse board can provide the additional help we'll need. Thank you for that." She reached out and grasped Reinhardt's hand. "Thank you. You will let her come visit?"

Reinhardt's hearty laugh filled the air. "Absolutely. You are now our family as well, and we hope to see you as often as we can."

Lainey smiled all the way back to Pilot Island. The longing for a birthday celebration and a red dress began to fade. She now had the adventure of a whole new family to grow with and enjoy.

CHAPTER SIX

Two and a Half Years Later

July, 1890

LAINEY HUGGED ROSE HANSON. "I'M so excited. It's a perfect day." She turned to Rose's dad as she squeezed her hands together and rocked up and down on her toes. "Mr. Hanson, thank you so much."

"My pleasure, young lady. Rose has been excited for days." Rasmus Hanson waited for the girls to gather their skirts about them and take a seat in the stern.

Rose's brother Sam pushed the boat off from the dock and jumped on. "It'll be so nice not to hear all the giggling and girl plans for a few days." He dodged Rose's playful swipe, then coiled the lines near the cleats, making them ready to throw at the next stop of his dad's grocery boat.

"Lainey! Lainey!"

Lainey stood to wave to Carter.

"Bring me some candy, please!"

"I will, Carter. You be good to Mama. Papa, thank you for letting me go."

Papa paused as he loaded his wagon with supplies delivered by the Hansons. He stood next to Carter and blew a kiss to Lainey.

Rose grinned. "I love that you call them Mama and Papa. It's so wonderful that you're here on Rock, Lainey."

Grabbing Rose's hand, Lainey sat down again. "I know. I mean, I still miss my parents. It's been almost three years now that their ship went down; but I love the Engelsons, and they've made me part of their family. Carter is so much fun, and guess what? Mama's pregnant."

Rose squealed. Sam paused and shook his head. "Girls."

"She told us a few days ago and said I could tell everyone."

The two girls sat huddled against the wind as the small ship chugged toward Pilot Island. "I love the water, Rose. I love living in the Door Islands. Do you think your dad will let us get out at Pilot?"

"He already suggested it. He knew you'd enjoy visiting with the keepers."

"It'll be odd to not have Uncle Otis and Aunt Edith there, but I'm happy he found a job on the mainland." Lainey had returned to Pilot three times after going to live with the Engelsons on Rock Island. As they thought, assistant keepers had moved in as Aunt Edith was designated the main keeper. Due to Otis's inability to climb the stairs, they would not allow him to be named the assistant keeper. Thinking about all that had transpired sent Lainey down memory lane.

> The new keeper was one of the seven sons of the Eagle Bluff lightkeeper and had recently married. Even as Uncle Otis introduced the keeper and his wife to Lainey on her first visit, he got a twinkle in his eye. "Lainey, he has six brothers. You might want to meet them all some time. Maybe we could plan it."
>
> Lainey laughed and shook her head. "Uncle, you are funny. You told me about them once before, and I'm still way too young to think about that."

On her second visit, she was informed that the assistants would become the main keepers and Auntie Edith the assistant.

"Oh, Auntie, I'm so sorry. Can I help you move into the assistant keeper quarters?"

Auntie Edith chuckled. She seemed so much more relaxed. "The new keepers will help, Elaina, but thank you. And . . . " She glanced at her husband.

"Go ahead. Tell her, Edith." Uncle Otis beamed.

Auntie Edith walked over to Uncle Otis and stood behind him, placing her hands on his shoulders. "We thought this day would come. We need the new keepers, but they don't really need us." Uncle Otis reached up and squeezed her hand. A small tear escaped her eye, and she quickly swiped it away. "We've been able to obtain a position in Newport Town."

Lainey gasped. "Oh, Auntie!"

Uncle Otis continued. "The lumber company has grown so much. The need for lumber in Chicago after the great fire has waned, but they've expanded into supplying furniture companies and places other than Chicago. They need an extra person to help keep the books. Plus, they know me and have a place for us to live that's owned by the company."

"So instead of keeper of the light, you'll be keeper of the books."

Uncle Otis chuckled. "I guess so. I guess so."

"Auntie Edith, are you happy about this move?"

She smiled, but Lainey could see that she might never really be happy—too much loss and hard work. "Yes, it's a good move for us. And I'll be able to take in laundry, which will help."

"But she only has to do as much as she wants," Uncle Otis interjected. "She has worked very hard and deserves to be a part of a quilting bee or just have tea and tarts with the ladies of the town. We'll be fine."

"Can I come to visit you in Newport Town, Auntie?"

Auntie Edith walked to Lainey and hugged her. "Elaina, you will always be a part of us. You're always welcome to visit. Are you happy with the Engelsons?"

Lainey coughed. The hug touched her deeply. As time went by, she realized that Auntie Edith knew she needed a growing family and more space. The appreciation for all her aunt had given her in so many ways surged in her chest.

Her aunt frowned. "Elaina, are you not happy?"

"Oh, Auntie Edith, I am so happy. I'm finding I want to call them Mama and Papa." She raised her eyebrows and looked to her aunt and uncle. "Do you think that is all right? Do you think Mama and Papa would mind if I did that? Do you mind?" Lainey wrung her hands.

Auntie Edith took her by the shoulders. "Elaina, you are healing, and we couldn't be more pleased. I believe your parents would wholeheartedly agree."

"Come here, girl."

Lainey ran over to Uncle Otis and sat on his lap like a little girl and let him hug her. "Uncle, am I hurting your broken leg?"

"Oh, no, I'm done with pain—just can't walk wonderfully." He laughed. "I sit very well now. I've missed you. We are so happy for you and the Engelsons. I know they will continue to be good to you. But if you don't come and visit, I'll have to have a talk with them."

The next time Lainey visited her aunt and uncle, she helped them load their stuff in the skiff and say goodbye to the island. That day, she took time to walk the perimeter.

Memories flooded her mind, and her thoughts floated back in time. As she stood on the north shore and the rocks called her to explore, she noticed the remnants of the shipwreck off to one side. *My life was almost a shipwreck, but now it's full.* She wandered down to some of the lower rocks and slid into one of the crannies, half-expecting to hear her aunt's warnings to be careful. Nothing thrilled her more than sitting on those rocks and letting the fragrant water scents fill her heart with peace. She ran her hand over the damp rocks and felt the smooth roughness, weathered over the years.

After what seemed hours, but she knew was only minutes, Lainey walked the shoreline past the house, the chicken coop, and the fog horn house and went to the pebble beach at the southern end. She could see the shoal just below the surface that extended well into the channel. It had been the demise of the *AP Nichols*.

Shipwrecks. So much loss. Parents gone. Where would she be now if they lived? Probably in Chicago on a pretty little street. Maybe with little brothers and sisters. Maybe right back here with Uncle Otis and Auntie Edith, as her parents loved to travel. Maybe she would have traveled with them to New York or Europe. Well, she could only imagine. But here she dwelt. Water, trees, beauty, friends, a new mama and papa, and a little brother. She didn't end up on the orphan train—that could have been wonderful or awful.

Lainey observed the outline of the *AP Nichols* under the surface of the water. That night of the shipwreck played in front of her eyes. The ship was lost, but lives were not. Lives were changed, however. Uncle Otis broke his leg, ending his ability to be the lightkeeper. He loved his job and taught her well; and now she lived in another lighthouse, and life sang around her. The comprehension of it all escaped her while it filled her with a deep-seated peace. The pastor said God works to make all things flow together for good. Some of it just baffled her.

Her aunt's voice pulled her back. "Elaina, it's time to go. This is our last trip. The boat is loaded, and Mr. Hanson is arriving to take you back to Rock." Lainey could feel the sad smile she knew filled the face of her aunt. Never before had she felt such love for this woman, who had taken her in and helped her survive. Auntie trained her and took care of her. She'd lost a daughter and her younger sister and now their means of support. Her husband was injured. Still, she kept going, and Lainey knew that spirit of survival dwelt also in her. She ran to Auntie Edith and threw her arms around her.

Auntie Edith hugged her tightly, and an unspoken bond passed between them. Her aunt stepped back and put her hands on Lainey's shoulders. They pierced each other's eyes with a hundred thoughts of thanks and approval. "You're a good girl, Elaina. You're strong. I'm glad." She pulled her once more to herself and then turned and climbed into the boat.

Uncle Otis stood with his cane on the tiny, wooden dock that had withstood many a gale. Once more, he called with the words she loved to hear. "Come here, girl."

Lainey ducked into his arms. "You know we love you, Lainey, and the Engelsons are the right fit for you. We want you to come and visit. I've already told Rasmus that you're to bring Rose when you come. You be a good girl now, you hear."

So many words ran into Lainey's mouth, but none would come out. Instead, the tears that burst out of her eyes some-how held the words of her heart. She was sure her aunt and uncle understood every one of them.

Rasmus Hanson called to her uncle, "As soon as you pull off from the dock, I'll pull in and get Lainey. Let us know if you need anything. You're not that far, and I can get over there right quick."

"Thanks, Rasmus. You're a good friend. Make sure you and Hannah come to see us when you visit Newport Town."

The memories of that moving day faded as Lainey heard Rose's voice bringing her back to the present. "Lainey, we're almost to Pilot. Did you fall asleep?"

"Oh, Rose, I was just remembering my last few visits to Pilot. I miss Uncle Otis." She giggled. "I even miss Aunt Edith. I hope they enjoy having us for a few days."

Rose nodded. "They invited you, so I think they'll be happy to have us."

Sam shook his head. "No, once they see what the two of you are like together, they'll send you home as quick as they can."

Exchanging glances, the girls laughed. "They might, Sam; they just might. Rose, we'll have to try not to be too silly."

"Here, we are. Ahoy, Pilot Island. Grocery boat docking."

Julius Claflin scurried out the door. It bounced twice. Lainey felt a quiver in her spine. "I still cringe when I hear that door, Rose. I always expect to hear Aunt Edith's anger."

Rose grabbed her hand. "Not anymore, Lainey. Not anymore."

"You're right. Thank you."

Julius Claflin caught the line that Sam tossed to him and helped secure the boat to the dock. "Good to see you, Rasmus and Sam. Girls, my wife Marla has tea and tarts waiting for you. I'll get the supplies."

Rose and Lainey squealed. They put out their hands, allowing Julius to assist their exit from the ship. They skipped up the path to the house and greeted Marla, who held the door open.

Marla ushered the girls in and hugged them both. "Oh, it's so good to have company." She brushed her long, dark hair behind her shoulders and let them into the kitchen.

Lainey took a deep breath and turned full circle, using her memory method of staring to take it all in. So much was just as she remembered, though she saw the touch of Marla's decorating. The lighthouse board china dominated the dishes that sat on the table waiting for them. A sprig of flowers graced a small bowl on the table. "You have flowers!"

Marla grinned, and her large brown eyes sparkled. "I had to have flowers in this isolated little place. I miss people and flowers the most, but I am happy here. I took part of the vegetable garden and planted flowers."

Rose clapped her hands. "Marla, they are beautiful, and the arrangement is so nice. So is the tablecloth." The yellow gingham brightened the kitchen. She had kitchen curtains in the same material.

Marla, Lainey, and Rose chatted about life on the islands—the beauty; the isolation; the fog horn and its terrible effects on the chickens, milk, and dishes; and the shipwrecks.

Rose took one more tart. "Marla, can you give me this recipe? My mom would love it. She's thinking about opening a little café."

"Certainly. I have so many wonderful recipes from Julius' mother." Marla got up to get some paper and laughed. "She raised seven sons. She must have cooked and baked from dawn to dusk."

"I know." Rose smiled. "I think we've met all seven. Lainey's uncle brought several to one of the school functions. I think he wants each of us to marry one."

Lainey chuckled. "They are a fun bunch. Marla, how did you and Julius meet? Did you grow up in a lighthouse?"

"No, my father is a fisherman out of Fish Creek. I went to Blossomburg School with Julius and his brothers."

Lainey stood. "While you finish writing the recipe, may I go up to the light and gallery?"

Marla reached out and took Lainey's hand. "Absolutely. You are always welcome to any part of this place. Your uncle told us how you managed the light so wonderfully the night of the Nichols wreck."

Lainey shook her head. The memories of her uncle's fall washed over her. "My uncle was the hero that night. I'll not be long." She turned and went to the stairs and then carefully made her way up, silently timing her climb as she did when she was younger. Everything was the same, and that comforted her. *Why would it be different?* She stepped out onto the gallery as memories of shipwrecks and storms rose up. Soon, reflections on the beauty of Lake Michigan and pleasant thoughts of her parents refreshed her thinking.

Her eyes drifted northeast to Rock Island, her new home with her new parents. A strange feeling swirled within her. Somehow, Pilot Island was her pivot place. Here, she waited for her parents, learned to love and listen to Aunt Edith and Uncle Otis, grieved her great loss, learned to keep the light, and traveled to Washington Island, where she met Rose and found her new family. She sighed. So much. She loved the lighthouse, loved the water, loved the lake breeze in her face.

Her mind drifted back to her new life on Rock Island, reminiscing about the last two-and-a-half years.

Reinhardt and Anna filled the hole of her loss like she never thought possible. And Carter was the joy of her life. Though six years her younger, she enjoyed nothing more than taking hikes with him throughout the island. The five-mile perimeter had so much variation that they often spent the whole day exploring. Anna encouraged them to go at least once or twice a week.

Chores had to be completed most days before they had adventures, so they rose at dawn. First, they conquered the steps to obtain water for the day. Even though they had a cistern that collected rainwater for their kitchen needs, it had a small leak. What they collected from the lake provided their cleaning purposes. As she did with all chores, Lainey made it a game and helped Carter to join her positive attitude. Fifty steps down were strenuous enough, but returning with the weight of water in the buckets without spilling challenged all her strength. She persuaded Carter to sing with her on the way down.

After collecting water from the lake, they prayed. "Oh, Lord, give us strength. Send your angels to guard us, so we don't spill or slip. Amen."

After ten steps, the two stopped. Lainey would start a story. Sometimes, it was one they knew well, and sometimes, she started a new one. When the stop at step twenty came, it was Carter's turn to continue the story. Another ten, and Lainey picked up the story again. Usually by the time they returned to the top, the laughing overtook the weariness, and breakfast was ready. One more trip was required after breakfast. On the second trip, they practiced their math functions, trying to stump each other.

Lainey and Mama worked together on the laundry, while Carter helped his father with the cleaning of the glass around the light. Lessons followed the chores, but on beautiful days, Mama would smile and say, "This is a day meant for exploration. What better lessons are there? Make yourselves a lunch and be back for dinner."

The kitchen on the first floor of Pottawatomi Lighthouse on Rock Island held a cheeriness that Lainey loved. The amazing stove had arrived Lainey's first summer. The white metal beauty trimmed in black boasted a huge oven, a place for wood fire, and a warming spot on top. It was Mama's joy. Mr. Hanson's grocery boat delivered it from Washington to Rock, and Rose and her brother Sam came along. Papa, Mr. Hanson, and Sam found Mama's pride and joy a heavy gift. Carefully, and with difficulty, they loaded it onto the wagon. Sam and his father rode in the back to steady the stove, while Papa urged the horse to pull the extra load along the rough path that traveled uphill a mile. Carter rode with his dad, and the two girls laughed and skipped behind the wagon.

The stove pipe for exhaust was secured by the two men with much discussion and exertion. By afternoon, the stove sat in its privileged place, and a load of wood burned in its core. While the adults finished the stove preparation, Lainey and Carter gave lessons to Sam and Rose on milking the cow. The Hansons traded vegetables and eggs for milk from their neighbors on Washington Island, who owned several cows, so Rose and Sam never learned to milk a cow.

Soon, Mama walked into the little building, where Mattie the cow resided. "I'm hearing so much laughter and giggles, I came to see what's happening." Mattie let out a long moo. "Oh, you poor girl. What are these young hooligans doing to you?"

She doubled over in laughter and then patted Mattie's head. "They have more milk on them, Mattie, than in the bucket."

"I think I've got it now." Sam nudged Rose off the stool and sat down, trying to use the rhythmic pull Lainey showed him. Mattie stamped her foot and shook her head.

Mama placed her hand on Sam's shoulder. "Slow down, Sam. There, that's better." Mattie calmed down, and milk flowed easily in the bucket.

Lainey grinned. "I tried to tell him. He just wanted to get more and be faster than the rest of us."

Sam turned a sheepish face to Lainey's mama. "That's true. Do you do this every day?"

"If we want milk, we do. I think we've troubled Miss Mattie long enough. This should be sufficient. Lainey, the men have the stove pipe in now, and we're going to prepare a meal. Why don't the four of you get some water to replenish the cistern with what we'll use for cooking. One trip will do with four of you. I'll start dinner. The wind is picking up, so don't be long. The men are returning to the boat dock to more firmly secure the boat in case you have to spend the night."

"Spend the night!" Rose and Lainey embraced each other and jumped up and down.

Carter grabbed Sam's hand. "You can sleep in my room, Sam, and be my big brother."

Sam dropped down on his knees. "I'll be happy to be a big brother to you. But we'd better go get that water. I hear you have a lot of steps."

"Yes, we have fifty, and we tell stories on the way back."

"Speaking of stories, the library box came last week, Rose." Lainey led the others to the side door of the lighthouse to gather buckets. "There are a whole bunch of new books for us to read."

"What's the library box?" Sam picked up two buckets.

"Every two months, the U.S. Lighthouse Board delivers a box with several books in it. It's so exciting. I love to read." Lainey handed buckets to Rose and Carter.

"I do, too." Rose started down the steps.

Sam rolled his eyes. "I think reading is work, but it's okay."

Lainey stopped. "Sam Hanson, Carter is learning to read and tell stories—don't you mess that up."

"Yes, ma'am!" Sam laughed, and Carter giggled.

Lainey loved the Hansons' visit that summer, and today, she and Rose would soon be on the mainland visiting Aunt Edith and Uncle Otis. She was glad Marla and Julius were happy here on Pilot Island. He had grown up on the mainland in a huge family. Lainey wondered if they were lonely at times but hoped it was a good fit for them. Time would tell.

Carefully backing down the steps as she'd done hundreds of times, she rejoined Rose and Marla just as Mr. Hanson called to them to return to the boat.

"Now, don't be strangers, you two." Marla hugged each one. "You are always welcome here."

"Maybe you can come visit on Rock Island sometime, Marla. I know Mama would love it."

Marla sighed. "I would love that. Thank you."

CHAPTER SEVEN

LAINEY SPOTTED AUNT EDITH AND Uncle Otis waiting on the long, wooden dock of Newport Town. Ships were docked and loading cords of wood, railroad ties of hemlock and cedar, and bundles of bark. The buzz of activity sent shivers of excitement through Lainey. Horses pulling wagons laden with lumber and furniture strained on the dock, while wranglers guided them to the proper ships. Calls and orders filled the air and sounded contradictory.

"Forward! Back! Now! Wait! Come! Go!" Horses whinnied and stomped. The thud and scraping of loading and unloading punctuated the yells.

Lainey took it all in and determined to avoid getting in anyone's way. The men loading the ships nodded to Lainey and Rose as they disembarked the grocery boat. Some men stopped, stepped aside, and tipped their hats as the girls hurried past them.

Lainey ran to her aunt and uncle. "Here we are. We're so happy to see you. Thank you for having us. We're so excited."

Aunt Edith laughed, and Lainey stopped. How rarely had she heard such a relaxed and easy laugh from her aunt. She recovered, hoping her aunt had not noticed her surprise.

Uncle Otis embraced her and kissed the top of her head. "We are thrilled to have you. We've missed you, girl. Or should I say 'young lady'? You're fourteen already and what a beauty."

Lainey felt the familiar creep of heat on her face. "Uncle!"

He laughed and turned to Rose. "Hope you're hungry. Edith has fixed a big pot of stew."

Rose rubbed her hands together. "Oh, we are. It's really busy here."

Aunt Edith took one of Rose's bags. "We're constantly amazed at how much business they do. It's good—keeps your uncle busy."

The little town with its dirt path roads was filled with clapboard buildings painted white. Some were businesses and some houses. Laughing children ran by the girls and the Seversons. Soon, they came to a small path lined with flowers. Lainey looked at Aunt Edith. "Did you plant these? They're beautiful."

Aunt Edith smiled. "I did. I've always loved flowers, but never had time on Pilot. Now I have time. It's been nice."

Lainey grabbed her hand. "You look happy."

"Oh, Elaina, I am. I loved being a lightkeeper, but I was duty-bound. Now, I've learned to enjoy life a bit more. We're so glad you've come to visit."

The table was set with the rose-patterned china that Aunt Edith used every day on Pilot. Lainey ran her finger over the pattern and smiled. Rose took their bags into the bedroom and called Lainey in. "Look, the rosebud quilt you had in your bedroom on the island."

A rush of joy ran through Lainey as she looked around. Everything was just like the island, yet all in a different setting. A nostalgic peace settled over her.

They visited late into the evening, and then Lainey and Rose giggled for another hour before falling asleep in the four-poster bed just off the sitting room of the spacious home. Breakfast was made when they arose, and Auntie Edith displayed no anger or concern that the girls slept in a bit.

The second day, the girls awoke at dawn. Aunt Edith busied herself in the kitchen with laundry as the girls emerged sleepy-eyed. "Aunt Edith, you're doing laundry already? Would you like us to hang it on the line for you?"

Aunt Edith smiled. "That would be nice. I still feel like I must have it done and dry by 11:00 a.m., even though they don't have that rule here."

The girls dressed and carried the laundry to the lines. Just beyond the house was a huge pine forest. Much of it was being lumbered, but the lumberjacks chose places a distance from Newport Town to cut trees. The forest was abundant, despite a huge fire a year previous, and promised many years of good harvest.

"Smell that, Rose? The sweet pine smell of the trees and the fresh water smell from the lake. I love it." Lainey turned her face to feel the breeze coming from the shoreline.

"I love it, too, but it's rather damp out with the mist. Do you think they'll dry well?" Rose deftly pinned the clothing on one line, while Lainey claimed the other.

"I think the fog will burn off soon. Did you hear the fog horn on Pilot last night?"

Rose rolled her eyes. "How could anyone miss it? Papa says it's the loudest thing he's ever heard."

"It is. I almost got up in the night to pack towels around Aunt Edith's dishes."

A horse and buggy pulled up to the Severson home. The lady waved to the girls and hurried into the house.

The girls finished up and went inside. Auntie Edith sat at the table with the lady from the buggy. "Girls, this is Alice Landin, my good friend from Ellison Bay. Her husband, Albert, is a fisherman and a cherry farmer. After breakfast, you're to take the wagon and follow her to their home and pick us a batch of cherries."

The girls ate, gathered buckets for the cherries, and put on their bonnets to protect their faces from the sun, knowing the mist would lift. Uncle Otis had the horse and wagon ready for them. He held their hand as they climbed into the seat of the wooden wagon. "Fresnel will take good care of you. He's a good horse."

"Uncle, you named him Fresnel?"

Uncle Otis laughed. "I miss the lighthouse lens a bit, so I still have a Fresnel to take care of."

The girls giggled as they took the well-worn and rutted road through the woods and fields. They traversed seven miles on their journey to the Landins' home, which stood in the woods high on the bluff above the waters of Green Bay. Mrs. Landin encouraged the girls to get right out to the orchard and start picking before the sun came out strong and provided a scorching. She put on her apron. "I'll have some food ready for you when you return."

The fog still clung to the trees, but as the sun's warmth penetrated, the mist reluctantly moved out of reach, leaving only a bit of dew in the grass as evidence of its existence. Rose and Lainey whispered, though no one was around, while quickly picking the savory cherries and filling their buckets.

"Mrs. Landin said we could pick as many as we wanted."

"Oh, I love picking them, but pitting is so much work." Lainey moved to the other side of the tree.

"Well, there will be three of us with your Aunt Edith, so it won't take so long." Rose stopped and looked to the east. "Oh, I love seeing the sun come through the foggy air."

Lainey paused to view the scene when a movement in the distance caught her eye. As the young man emerged from the hazy mist, her heart emerged from a heaviness that she didn't realize still dwelt within her.

Rose turned back to her friend and followed her gaze. "Lainey, you're staring." Rose nudged her. "Who is that?"

The young man strolled down the grassy lane like a king in one of her favorite books. His gait was easy and confident. His casual demeanor brought no warning to Lainey, and yet all her senses stood alert. The breeze blew fresh, and the sky cleared as late morning sauntered into the orchard and the young man sauntered into her consciousness. Never had she seen such strength, such kindness, such wonder combined in one person in one moment.

However, the fog now shrouded her voice. She wasn't sure whose voice she heard then. "I . . . I don't . . . know, but . . . "

"Lainey," Rose whispered. "Put your arm down. Put the cherries in the basket. It's just a boy. A really nice-looking boy." She grinned.

The young man approached down the grassy path. The sun glanced off his shoulder. His presence was so casual and his stroll so easy that Lainey stood staring again. "Good morning, ladies. You must be the Seversons' niece and her friend. I'm Clifford. My uncle Albert Landin owns this orchard."

Lainey pulled herself up and shook the haze off. "Mrs. Landin gave us permission to be here." The fog within her was totally dissipated now. How dare he assume she and Rose were stealing!

He laughed. It resonated full and long and warm. It melted all her short-lived resolve. She glanced at Rose, who watched her with eyes sparkling with humor. Lainey could hear the giggle Rose attempted to hold within herself.

"Aunt Alice suggested I help you carry the cherries." He paused and stepped back. He met Lainey's eyes. "That is, I'm sure you're strong enough to do it all by yourself, but I can carry any extra you want to pick."

Lainey studied her feet. Her boots had a film of moisture on them. Rose stepped up beside her and kicked Lainey's foot while extending her own hand. "I'm Rose, and this is Lainey. We're happy for the help. It's so beautiful out here. We can't wait to make cherry tarts and sauce. Do you help with the orchard?"

"I do. I help with whatever my uncle needs with the orchards or fishing. I hope to be a sailor or captain someday, but I don't mind learning on a fishing boat." He laughed again. "A bit smelly, but I thoroughly enjoy it." He glanced at Lainey again and gave his head the slightest tilt. "Here, let me help you pick. I brought a couple extra pails. I'll start on this row."

Rose pulled Lainey's arm. "We'll finish these two rows we've started."

Lainey gulped and followed Rose.

Rose leaned in close. "Lainey Louis, you are smitten."

"What? No. I mean . . . Is it really warm out?"

Rose laughed.

Lainey wondered why Rose kept mumbling at her and not speaking clearly. Rose giggled every time she looked at Lainey. Before she knew it, her pail was full, and Rose took it from her and handed her another. Then she saw Clifford standing to the side with two full buckets of cherries. Were his lips moving? Was he talking, laughing?

He moved closer. "Lainey, I think we have enough. We'll be pitting all day. Are you okay carrying both buckets? They are a bit heavy."

Lainey just stared at him. His blue eyes were quite beautiful. The shock of blond hair that cascaded across his forehead caught her attention. He set down a bucket and brushed his hair aside. "Lainey, you okay?" He looked to Rose. "Do you think she's gotten too much sun?"

Rose bent over and laughed. "Too much something!" She set her buckets down. "Let's get you back, Lainey, and get some water—maybe you are sun-struck." She leaned into Lainey's ear. "Or love-struck."

Lainey shook her head. "What—oh, are we done? Yes, let's go. Water would be nice." She picked up her buckets and turned to follow Rose and Clifford. Soon, Rose shifted behind Lainey and Clifford.

"I think I dropped my bracelet while we were picking." Rose rubbed her wrist. "You two go ahead. I know my way back." Rose turned to walk back to the cherry trees.

"Rose, we can help you look for it." Lainey glanced at Clifford and raised her eyebrows.

"Certainly." He set his buckets down.

Rose set her buckets down as well and waved her hand. "No, no, I think I can find it. It shouldn't take long. You go ahead."

"Well, okay, if you're sure. Lainey and I'll get started on the pitting." He bent to retrieve his cherry buckets, brushing Lainey's hand as he did so.

The tingle startled Lainey. It traveled up her arm and down her back. She couldn't describe it. Nothing in her understanding could compute it. She put one foot in front of the other and listened to

Clifford. His conversation was easy. She fought to focus. His voice was so pleasant.

"My parents own the little store in Ellison Bay, and I grew up stocking shelves and sweeping the floor. We live upstairs. But I would always hurry to get done, so I could go explore by the water. Sometimes, I would sneak onto the fishing boats just to look at them. If I could get out of the house early, I went to watch the fishing boats leave each morning. I wasn't thrilled about fishing, just about boats, and I decided I wanted to captain a ship."

"What kind of ship—a schooner, passenger ship, a freight ship?"

Clifford stopped. "You know ships." He smiled.

"My uncle Otis taught me when I lived with them on Pilot Island. He was the lightkeeper. And we had shipwrecks while I was there."

"I've heard about those. My parents worry that if I pursue shipping, that will happen. But Uncle Albert is an amazing shipman. He's taught me how to read the water and the weather, know the day markers and the range lights, and check water depths. Most shipwrecks around here don't end in loss of life. There was one two or three years ago . . ."

"My parents died in that one." Lainey met Clifford's eyes, then hung her head.

Clifford stopped again and set his buckets down. "Lainey, I'm sorry. I didn't know that. I thought the lightkeepers on Rock Island were your parents."

"No, they've taken me in, and I absolutely love them. They were on the ship with my parents and knew them and tried to save them. My parents saved their little boy before they drowned."

Clifford touched her arm, and the tingles flew again through her body. "Wow, I don't know what to say."

Lainey smiled. "Clifford, you don't need to say anything or feel sorry for me. I'm okay and have a new family. I mean, I miss them, but I'm happy. Aunt Edith is my mom's older sister, and I stayed with them; but it was too much for them when Uncle Otis broke his leg." Lainey started forward again. "Tell me more about your life. You like to explore?"

Clifford picked up his buckets, and they turned down the rutted path that served as a road and led to his uncle's home nestled in the tall woods. "My parents say my love of exploring is a wanderlust. Uncle Albert says it's the love of life."

"Aunt Edith said I had the wanderlust, too. I just love the adventure of discovering the beauty and treasures of different places. I'd like to travel. I love helping with the lighthouse. Mama—my new mother, Anna Engelson—would agree with your uncle. She just tells Carter, my new brother, and me to go explore and wander when our chores are done and then asks us all about it when we get back. I think my first mama would have done the same."

"I plan to start training to be a sea captain this winter. I'm not afraid of the water. I feel drawn to it. It speaks to me. I heard a Bible verse once that said the voice of the Lord is upon many waters. I think it was in Psalms, but there's a calmness, a strength I feel by the water."

Lainey nodded. "It's refreshing."

"Exactly." Clifford smiled. "Here we are. You think Rose found her bracelet and will find us?"

Lainey turned. "There she is, just coming around the corner from the orchard to this path."

After a light lunch of sandwiches and apple slices, the three teens and Clifford's aunt spent the next hour pitting the cherries, telling stories of their families, and laughing. The Landins' home stood tucked back in wooded acres of maple, oak, and birch. The simple log house, pitched on the outside with black tar, sported several windows filling the indoors with light.

Mrs. Landin started pitting another bucket of cherries. "Albert loves light. I think that's why he loves the water so. There are so few shadows out on the boat—only when he's inside pulling the nets in, which is a good part of the time. But the out-of-doors and daylight are just a few feet away. The wind and the breeze, even when cold, are his favorite things. He keeps these windows open well into November if he can." The house held one big room, which included the kitchen. Two bedrooms stood next to the large room.

"Do you have a summer kitchen, Mrs. Landin? At the lighthouses, the kitchen is always at one end in case there's a fire and because it gets so warm. Rose's mom has a kitchen away from the main house to use in the summer when it's too hot to heat up the whole house."

"Albert didn't want that. Because we have so much shade around, it doesn't get as hot as it might, and like I said, he keeps the windows open all the time." Mrs. Landin picked up the bowl she'd held in her apron between her knees as she pitted, set it on the table, and went to a cupboard. "I think it's time for a break." She retrieved a plate of cookies and a pitcher of milk.

"Oohh. This is the best." Rose stood to help pour the milk. "Lainey, we should probably go soon. We don't want your aunt and uncle to worry."

Lainey took a bite of the oatmeal cookie and closed her eyes. No sound broke the silence of chewing for a full minute. "You're right, Rose. I'm glad Uncle Otis let us take his wagon and horse; it would be a long walk back to Newport Town."

"Let me help you load the cherries on your wagon. You'll be busy baking for a few days, I think." Clifford scooted his chair back and picked up a bucket of pitted cherries.

"Thank you so much for letting us take some of the cherries and helping us to pit them." Lainey carried the plates and glasses back to the counter.

"Some?" Mrs. Landin placed her hands on her hips. "All of these are yours. You picked them. Did you not see how many cherry trees we have?" She shook her head before Lainey could respond. "You tell your aunt Edith that she is welcome to come visit and get more cherries or whatever else we have anytime."

Rose climbed up on the wagon and slid over. Lainey joined her, and Clifford placed the cherries securely under the seat. "Thank you, Clifford. Thank you, Mrs. Landin."

Mrs. Landin turned to go back in the house, but Clifford lingered by the wagon. He and Lainey held each other's eyes, but no words came. Finally, Rose cleared her throat. "Time to go." Lainey startled as if shaken.

This time, Rose did not hold in her laughter. "Thank you, Clifford." She took the reins and guided the horse back out to the road. When out of earshot, Rose burst out laughing again. "Lainey, you are so funny."

"What is this?" Lainey shook her head. "Am I sick? I feel so unusual."

"I would say love-sick. And you have it bad."

"How can that be? I barely know him." Lainey shook herself. "Oh, my, did we get the cherries? Aunt Edith will have my head if we forgot them."

Rose laid her hand on Lainey's arm. "We have the cherries. What concerns me is if you are here."

Lainey looked at Rose and rolled her eyes. "I think I'm okay now. Do you think he likes me?"

"I would say there's a good chance."

"Just a chance?"

"Lainey, I'm sure he's as smitten as you are. Do you think you'll get to see him again soon?"

The horse cantered along the road and gently moved the wagon down the hill into the little village of Ellison Bay. The sun remained high overhead, and the blue of the July sky spread like a canopy. The view of the water as they proceeded down the hill mesmerized Lainey. "Isn't it a grand view, Rose? I think I love the water as much as Clifford does."

Rose nodded. "Maybe he'll take you out on the fishing boat sometime."

Lainey wrinkled her nose. "Well, no, I don't think so." She leaned into Rose. "Was I awful back there?"

Laughter rang out from Rose. "You were pretty bad, but it was kind of sweet. Oh, is that his parents' store?"

"It must be. I wonder if that's his mother sweeping the porch."

"Want to stop? We have a few minutes." Rose guided the horse to the front of the building and tied the reins to the railing.

The sign said Ruckert's Supply. The woman sweeping smiled at the two young women as they walked by her. The man sitting on the bench next to the door tipped his hat. Behind him, the windows were lined inside with lamps. Rose opened the door and entered. A potbelly stove stood to the side, giving promise of warm visits come winter. An array of smells from baked goods, meats, and cleaning supplies greeted them.

Lainey could not remember seeing such abundance since she was a little girl with her mother shopping. Boots and shoes filled shelves, while brooms stood against the wall. Tables held bags of flour and coffee, and candy filled the jars. Barrels of pickles stood against another wall. Lainey looked up at hams hanging from the ceiling. On the wall hung a chart with the temperature of every day for the whole year to the present date.

The man at the counter was purchasing eggs and cherries from a local farmer. "I'll see you in two days, Frank. These will go fast. Everyone wants cherries right now."

Rose grabbed Lainey's arm. "I forgot about the cherries. We should get going. Your aunt will want to do some baking with us as soon as we get back."

"Let's buy a piece of the cheddar cheese. I'm a little hungry."

Rose giggled. "You don't even remember eating with Clifford and his aunt, do you?"

"I promised Carter some candy, too. I'll get some here."

Lainey handed the clerk two dimes to pay for the candy and a hunk of cheese. After they pulled away from the store, she broke the chunk in half and gave it to Rose. "This is such a fun day. I'm so glad you came with me to visit Aunt Edith and Uncle Otis. Do you think your parents will let you stay a few days on the island when we get back?"

"Maybe . . . that would be wonderful."

The girls continued on in silence, munching their cheese as the horse carried the wagon along.

Lainey hummed as the trees went by and the sun lowered itself a bit in the sky behind them. "Clifford said he loves the sunsets over the bay. I always loved them, too, from the lighthouse galleries."

"Does his uncle fish out by Rock Island? I've seen fishing boats out that way. Maybe he'll come to visit you." Rose slapped the reins gently on Fresnel's rump. "I hope we're not getting back too late. It must be about 3:00 p.m. I love summer when the days are so long."

Lainey sat up straighter. "I'm being a little silly, aren't I? I'm way too young to be thinking about boys." She sighed. "But he is rather splendid, don't you think?"

Rose grinned at her friend. "Yes, yes, and yes. You're silly; you're young; and he's very nice-looking. And he is just nice."

As they arrived at the house, Aunt Edith came out to greet them. "Oh, look at all the cherries, and you pitted them already. I made some dough, so we can roll it out, add sugar and flavor, and have fresh cherry pie with supper. Your uncle will be home soon, so it will be perfect timing. Lainey, take Fresnel into the stable and rub him down. Rose, I'll help you get the cherries in the house. Did you have a good time?"

"We did. I think Lainey had a wonderful time."

Lainey threw her a look. "Rose."

Aunt Edith paused. She looked from Rose to Lainey and back. Without another word, she picked up two buckets and carried them into the house. As Rose followed her with two more buckets, Lainey unhooked Fresnel and shook her head at Rose. Rose laughed and then pursed her lips and nodded at Lainey.

As she rubbed down Fresnel, Lainey found her mind wandering back to her time with Clifford. Soon, Fresnel nudged her shoulder. Lainey laughed. "I am so silly. Sorry, Fresnel. Did I stop rubbing you down? It's just that I met a boy today, and I can't stop thinking about him."

"A boy?"

Lainey whirled around. There stood Uncle Otis at the entrance of the stable. "Uncle Otis, how long have you been there?"

"Long enough." He chuckled. "Does this boy have a name?"

Lainey placed her head against Fresnel's flank and mumbled.

Uncle Otis walked over to Lainey. "I can finish the rub-down. I see that Fresnel really likes you—and you did just meet him—but who is this other boy?"

Lainey stepped back and handed the brush to her uncle. "His name is Clifford. He's the Landins' nephew, and his parents own Ruckert's Supply in Ellison Bay."

"They're a nice family. Is my little girl growing up?"

"Oh, Uncle Otis, I don't know. I feel so strange. I can't think. I feel happy. I feel silly. What is this?"

"You know, I was a little older than you are now when I first met your aunt. And I felt the same way. But you are young, Lainey, so realize you'll feel this way about other boys, too. Relationships take time to grow and become lasting love. What you feel is very normal. Just enjoy it and don't try to figure it out. But don't think it's permanent."

"I hope it's not permanent—I can't get anything done like this. I can't think." Lainey laughed. "Thank you, Uncle Otis. I should help Aunt Edith with dinner and the pies." Lainey skipped out of the stable and hurried into the house to wash her hands. "Uncle Otis is home and finishing up with Fresnel. I can help with the pies now."

"Here, roll this pie dough out, Lainey. Let's make some extra pies. You girls did an amazing job, getting so many and pitting them all. Rose said you had a little help . . . Alice's nephew, Clifford?"

Lainey looked up as Aunt Edith winked at Rose. She felt her face heat up. Aunt Edith reached over and patted her hand, sending flour across the table. "You're growing up, young lady."

Rose grinned and poured cherries into the pie dough-lined pan. Aunt Edith deftly lifted the top crust across the pan, fluted the edges, and cut the extra. They worked in silence for a few minutes, finishing five pies before placing them all in the wood-fired stove.

"You each can take a pie home when you go, and we'll eat one tonight after dinner."

After a dinner of chicken and biscuits, the Seversons sat on the porch with Lainey and Rose and ate pie.

Rose set her empty plate down. "This pie was so delicious. Thanks for having us. It's so much fun. Do you miss Pilot Island?"

"Oh, on occasion, but we are content here." Aunt Edith stood up. "Girls, come with me. I want to show you something."

The girls followed her around the house to the edge of the pine forest. Its fragrance wafted over them with the evening breeze. Shadows gathered on the forest floor, mixed with ferns and fallen logs. She led them down a well-worn path that brought them near the water just north of town. The rock shoals greeted them, covered with a bit of wet moss, just past a narrow sandy beach.

Aunt Edith abruptly stopped. The shadows had overtaken the beach, but the sunlight still glistened on the lake hundreds of feet out in the water. She pointed. "Look over there." The girls looked in the direction of her fingers.

"Ohhh, Aunt Edith! Pilot is lit up like, like . . . a lighthouse." All around them, shade stood prominent. The sun had dropped behind the trees at their back sufficiently to cause darkening, yet out on the water, and specifically on Pilot Island, the sun shone like a beam. "It's stunning."

Aunt Edith took Lainey's hand in hers. "I noticed this not long after we moved here, and every time I see it late in the day like this, I think of you."

"Me? But why?" Lainey shook her head.

"This is what you did to the island and to our lives, Lainey. You lit up our lives with your sweetness and your grace and your spunk. When there was darkness and sadness all around, you displayed life and hope. We are so glad you were with us for a while, and we certainly want you to always keep us in your life."

CHAPTER EIGHT

December, 1890

LAINEY CLIMBED THE STEPS WITH only one hand on the rail. In the other, she balanced the cup of hot chocolate. Inside herself, she heard the echo of Aunt Edith's voice: "Ee-lain-ahh! Be careful." Lainey chuckled and brought her arms in and shoulders up as if a hug wrapped her. Mama never yelled; she just laughed, even when reminding Lainey. Rarely did Mama go about with anything but a smile on her face. Lainey recalled Auntie Edith's way with peace and joy now and was glad she could visit her and Uncle Otis on occasion. They were her blood relatives, and that held great import with Lainey. But the love and happiness she felt in this place, Pottawatomie Lighthouse on Rock Island was—dare she say it—as wonderful as she experienced with her very own mother and father.

"Here, let me take that from you, Lainey. Those steps feel more slippery when it's cold out." Papa reached down from the small space around the Fresnel lens and retrieved the cup of hot chocolate.

Lainey squeezed into the close quarters. "Do you want a sip before you go down, Papa?"

He winked. "No, I'll get a full cup as soon as I get down. Then I'll take my time heating up the lard for the light. Thanks for coming up to spell me."

"Oh, Papa, you know I love it. Take as long as you like." She lowered her voice. "I think Carter is hoping you'll read one of the Christmas stories to him. I started *The Christmas Carol* by Dickens. He may want to hear a little more with you. Take your time. I'm happy up here."

Papa placed a light kiss on Lainey's cheek. "You are a precious blessing to us. How's Anna doing with all the preparations?"

"She has her feet up right now, but she's been busy getting everything ready for our guests. I'm so excited to see everybody. She is, too. Carter and I will continue decorating the tree when I come back down. And the food preparation we have all planned out."

"All right, I'll be back up soon." Papa backed down the steps, humming "Joy to the World."

Lainey took up the refrain and stood gazing out the windows at the snow-covered terrain in front of her. The glow of the sun created a dazzling sparkle on the white blanket that lay gently on trees and buildings. A slight sweep of her eyes across the ice toward Washington Island revealed a southerly wind that brushed wisps of snow to the north. But her view to the east unveiled a bright blue sky and an equally clear blue Lake Michigan. Though the lake rarely froze beyond Rock Island, ice had claimed most of the waterway to Plum and Pilot Islands. As she peered out the window, she discerned a few whitecaps traveling toward the north.

However, the trees held her attention now. The whisper of peace arose within her. Perhaps it came from the trees. Perhaps from God. Her breath almost fled at the beauty she beheld. The richness of the greenery in the summer, the filigree pattern created by the shadows of the branches on the paths of the island, and the colors in the fall thrilled her. Her insides were engulfed with wonder as she wandered in her explorations. But this, the snow on the evergreens, the majestic oaks, and the maples was like a reflection of God. Lainey couldn't explain it. She was captured by the thought of how everything imperfect was now made perfect because of the layer of soft and sparkling snow. *It's like God's love. Everything that's imperfect is covered and made right by God's love.* Lainey sighed. She could hardly believe she lived here in such beauty, with such kindness from a family who totally loved her.

She sipped her hot chocolate and debated whether to go out on the gallery but knew her folks disapproved of it this time of year. Instead, she gazed at the gorgeous vista below her and imagined the exciting days ahead. In only two days, Julius and Marla Claflin from Pilot Island and the Hanson family would arrive from Washington Island. They planned to arrive early in the day and would spend the night, returning to their homes late on Christmas Eve. Few families could be gone for long visits due to work with the lighthouses, farms, and stores, so to have whole families spend one night was a delight.

Two of Julius' six brothers, Phineas and Walter, would keep the light on Pilot Island while he and Marla came to visit the Engelsons. Marla and Julius would then return, and the young men would spend Christmas Day with them. They would remain to assist in shutting down the lighthouse for the winter, unless a late order came from the U.S. Lighthouse Board to remain open.

Lainey and Rose had not seen each other for several weeks, not since Rose had visited in early November for Lainey's fifteenth birthday. Lainey could hardly contain herself thinking of seeing her best friend. She knew Mama couldn't wait to see both Marla and Hannah. Marla's company just satisfied Mama's need for a friend, and Hannah—Rose's mother—created a safe place for Mama to learn motherhood, cooking, surviving in isolation, and trusting God. Mama was a wise woman, but Hannah held the status of a mother to her, though only ten years older. Mrs. Hanson never got flustered, even with four children and all the work of the grocery boat, the boatbuilding, the gardening, and perhaps a café. The garden took up so much space, Lainey thought of it as a farm. Plus, they had chickens and a pig. Their neighbors would check in on the animals while the family spent the night on Rock Island.

Lainey found herself mentally calculating everyone's plan. Uncle Otis and Aunt Edith had considered coming, but he found the cold created more pain in his leg and so declined to travel. Besides, his cousin from Milwaukee had chosen to visit them. Lainey cringed. She was the one who told them about the orphan train. Lainey made a point to often pray for all the children that traveled that train, that life would become wonderful for them in every way—like life had become wonderful for her.

The Claflin brothers would take a skiff and maneuver between ice chunks to get from Newport Town to Pilot. Julius and Marla could probably walk to Detroit Island on the ice but bring the skiff in case the ice broke. Uncle Otis had recounted several stories of walking the ice and the ice breaking. There always needed to be a clear plan as winter was fickle and demanding. Mr. Hanson could bring his sleigh from Washington to Detroit Island to fetch Julius and Marla.

Lainey heard Papa on the steps and set down her now-empty cup. His smiling face appeared at the top of the steps as he lifted the heated lard container.

"Let me help you pour it in, Papa. I've been daydreaming up here and didn't even wash the windows or the lens."

"Oh, the windows are clean, and I cleaned the lens shortly before you came up. All is well."

Lainey opened the portal, and Papa hoisted the bucket. With great dexterity, he poured the liquid into the place where the flame would create the light magnified by the Fresnel lens.

"Anna seems a bit tired today, Lainey. Could you gather the eggs and see if the cow needs milking? She's going to make lunch and then take a nap. You and Carter can make the popcorn to string the tree and make extra decorations."

Lainey frowned. "Is she okay? She's not due for almost a month."

"She's fine, and she was a week late with both children. I think she's been putting pressure on herself to have everything ready for our company."

"Papa, I am so excited to have everyone come. Carter and I can also do cookies and make some pies, so she doesn't have to think about it tomorrow."

"That would be great, as long as the two of you don't eat it all before our friends arrive." He chucked her lightly under the chin.

"I'll make extra dough and bake the cinnamon and butter rolls. Aunt Edith taught me to make those." She threw her arms around him. "Papa, we'll be good, and we will make sure she rests so we can all enjoy our company."

Lainey turned to go backward down the stairs. "Papa, maybe Carter and I could do all our baking on the second floor in the assistant keeper's residence. That way, we won't be in Mama's way if she wants to do food preparation or make too much noise if she wants to rest. Plus, she can't do the stairs very well, so she won't be able to try to help us."

Papa nodded. "Good idea, and you two can also make sure all the rooms are ready for our guests. That would help Anna a lot."

Lainey tiptoed into the room where Carter sat near his mom. Carter had a book in front of him, and his lips were moving. Lainey tapped him on the shoulder, and he jumped, making them both laugh. Lainey put her finger to her lips. "Don't wake Mama. Come with me. We need to get the eggs and check the cow."

Carter hopped off the chair and quickly donned his coat, boots, and hat. He and Lainey went out and walked to the chicken coop. The cackle of the hens greeted them. Lainey and Carter both had lost all fear of reluctant chickens that would peck at them removing their eggs. Carter ran his hands over the fluff of feathers on two of the hens and then reached in and removed the eggs underneath. Lainey did the same.

After collecting eight eggs, they headed to the small shed where Mattie, the cow, looked lazily at them while chewing her cud. Carter walked up to the huge animal and rested his forehead against hers. A low moo emitted from the animal, and Carter stepped back and patted her head.

Lainey grabbed the pail from the hook of the shed, pulled up the short stool, and slid her hands in a rhythmic motion, pulling the sweet milk into the pail. After a few minutes, she rubbed the cow's side. "Good girl, look at all this milk." She retrieved a cloth and wiped the udder dry. Then she and Carter each carried a pail back to the house—one of eggs and one with milk.

The two hung their coats and hats on a hook and set the pails in the cooler part of the entryway. They hurried in to warm their hands by the wood stove. Mama still slept, so after whispering to each other, they carried all their ingredients to the second floor. If they had assistant keepers, this would be their home. As it was, it beckoned them daily as a wonderful place to read, sew, and play games. Soon, it would be the guest quarters for the Claflins and the Hansons.

"Carter, I'll need you to practice your reading and read the recipe to me and help make sure I have all the ingredients."

"Okay, if you forgot anything, I'll go down. I'll be careful not to wake Mama."

Lainey set Carter to sifting the flour while she created a fire in the stove. She then quickly mixed the flour, lard, and milk and spread it out with the rolling pin. She deftly lifted the crust into the pie pan and fluted the edges. She opened one of the jars of cherry sauce she and Aunt Edith canned in the summer. The whole jar filled the pie tin. She rolled out the upper crust and found herself lost in thought of that time picking cherries. Meeting Clifford. Even now, her cheeks heated up. She glanced over at Carter, who was poking the fire in the stove making sure it was firing well.

While the pies baked, the two made cookies. After cleaning up the area and making sure the whole second floor was ready for their guests, they headed downstairs to join Mama, who was about to make dinner. Instead, Lainey made sandwiches for everyone and insisted Mama sit with her feet up. "We'll be eating so much in the next few days, we don't need a big dinner." After eating, Lainey popped popcorn so they could string it and adorn the tree. Papa continued reading *The Christmas Carol* aloud, while Lainey and Carter drew and cut out extra decorations until it was time for bed.

Anticipation woke Lainey. Her heart pounded. Christmas Eve eve had arrived, and guests were on their way. She hurried out to the smell of eggs cooking. "Oh, Mama, you're up."

"I am, Lainey. I'm so excited. You're just in time. Carter, are the dishes out?" She turned while rubbing her stomach that stood out under her apron.

"Yes, Mama, I have them all ready." He threw his arms out to display the table set with four place settings.

Mama laughed. "It's beautiful. Go call your father, and we'll get breakfast done."

Carter hurried out of the kitchen, sliding along on the wooden floors in his stocking feet.

Mama turned to Lainey. "You and Carter did an amazing job yesterday while I rested."

"Are you feeling okay?"

She ran her fingers through her hair. "I'm much better. I was so very tired." She stopped suddenly. "Oh, this little one is excited, too. Come, Lainey, feel him—or her."

Lainey walked over by the stove. Anna placed Lainey's hand on her stomach. Lainey gasped. "Oh, he kicked me. Or she. Oh, Mama, that's amazing."

Mama bent and kissed Lainey's forehead. "I'm so glad you came to our home."

"We are, too!" Papa and Carter exclaimed together as they entered the kitchen.

Soon after breakfast, Papa climbed the steps to the light. Upon descending, he announced he had viewed a sleigh leaving Washington Island.

Mama clapped her hands. "Oh, they're on their way. Carter, go help your father hitch the horse to the wagon and grab blankets to keep them warm. Oh, and put the snowshoes in the wagon in case there is not enough room for everyone."

"May I go, Mama? I'm jumping up and down inside. And I can snowshoe all the way back. I don't mind." Lainey bit her lips and looked from Mama to Papa.

Mama's face softened as she tipped her head, but Papa interrupted. "They'll all be here soon. I'd feel better if you stayed with your mama and help with any last-minute preparations."

Lainey's face fell, but she quickly recovered. "You're right, Papa. It's okay." She kissed him on the cheek. "Hurry back. I can't wait." He chucked her under the chin again. "We'll be back sooner than you can say 'jack rabbit.'"

Papa and Carter hurried out the door.

Mama pumped some water into the sink and began to wash the dishes. She stopped, placed both hands on the edge of the sink, and leaned with her eyes closed.

"Mama, you're still tired. Go put your feet up. I'll clean up. We don't have that much to do. We'll be perfectly ready when they arrive. And I'll make you a cup of tea." Mama did not argue and sat down on the settee in the parlor room next to the kitchen. She smiled sweetly when Lainey brought the tea. Lainey hesitated. "I'm going to just go up to the light for a moment to see if I can see them."

"Oh, yes, let me know if you see them. I am so excited, too. When you get down, will you get the tarts out and make more tea?"

Lainey nodded and then scurried as fast as she could up the stairs. The arriving sleigh greeted her eyes and quickly disappeared from sight, meaning her friends were very close to shore. She returned to the parlor. "Mama, they are probably loading into the wagon now."

When Mama didn't answer, she went closer. She was asleep. Lainey smiled and went to the kitchen to put out the tarts and make more tea. She finished the dishes and doublechecked the fire in the stove, knowing that the ham dinner would be put in once everyone greeted and visited a while.

Singing. Lainey heard singing. She called to Mama, then ran to the door and saw their friends tumbling out of the wagon. Her heart filled with joy. A wonderful visit was ahead. Rose ran in and embraced her. "We're here, Lainey, we're here. Merry Christmas. Wait till you see—"

"Hello, Lainey. Merry Christmas!" Lainey looked up from Rose's hug and went limp. There stood Clifford. How could this be? Had they invited him? But what did that matter? He came along. He was here.

"Mer—ry, Christ—mas, er, uh, Clifford. How did you . . . I mean . . . welcome to our—home."

"May I come in?"

Rose took Lainey's arm and shook her head. "Come in, Clifford." She pulled Lainey aside. "Oh, Lainey."

Confusion and joy churned in Lainey's mind. Clifford stood before her. Carter yanked his arm. "Clifford, let me take your bag. You can share my room. I want to show you the light. C'mon, Clifford."

Clifford smiled and followed Carter. Papa winked at Lainey. "Merry Christmas, darling daughter. We thought you'd enjoy this."

Sam rolled his eyes. "Oh, man, bad enough with Rose and Lainey together, but now this—Lainey over the moon."

Rose swatted her brother and grabbed Lainey's arm, pulling her to Lainey's room. "Wake up, girl. You can do this."

"You're right, Rose. I'm glad you're here. I've missed you. I'm just so surprised. Tell me what you've been doing." She gazed up the stairs where Carter took Clifford.

Rose shut the door, bumping Lainey's nose in the process. Lainey looked at Rose, and both burst out laughing and fell on the bed. "Pull yourself together, girl. I know he came to see you, so enjoy it."

Lainey's face heated. "What about his parents? Didn't they want to have him spend Christmas there?"

"Well, they went on a trip with the Landins, and your aunt and uncle suggested he come here."

Lainey's face lit up. "Really, but . . . "

Rose bounced on the bed and pulled her legs up under her. She grabbed a pillow and hugged it to herself. "Okay, your aunt and uncle made a point to talk with Clifford's parents. As you know, they were already friends with the Landins and knew his folks from the store. They like Clifford. And, of course, they know the Claflins from the Eagle Harbor Lighthouse, so Clifford traveled with them to Pilot, then with Marla and Julius the rest of the way."

Lainey giggled. "Yes, Uncle always mentions the Claflin boys. I like Trygve the best, but he's just a good friend, more like a brother."

Rose tilted her head and raised her eyebrows.

Lainey clapped her hands. "What, Rose? What are you telling me? You like one of the brothers?"

"I do, Lainey. I do!"

The two girls squealed and hugged each other.

"Tell me; tell me."

"Well, remember Niles? He's two years older than us and came to see my parents with your uncle one time. He escorted me to church and then had dinner with my family."

"Oh, my, Rose. You're sweet on him . . . I mean, do you think it's for real?"

"I don't know. I mean, I like him, but I'm not ridiculous like you." She jabbed Lainey with her elbow. "You're the funniest when you're around Clifford."

"He makes me . . . I mean, I can't think. What is that, Rose? I mean, that isn't love, is it? My parents were in love, and my new parents love each other, but I don't see them acting so silly." She spread her hands.

"My dad said he was like that when he first met my mom. He stumbled over his words and couldn't think. He tripped one time and fell right on his face in front of her." Rose laughed. "Mama likes to say he really fell for her."

Lainey shook her head. "Well, we're too young to think of anything forever."

"I know; I know."

A knock sounded at the door. "Lainey, Rose, can you help with dinner now?"

The girls popped up and scurried out the door into the kitchen. All the women worked together putting the ham with potatoes and carrots in the oven, making the biscuits, and setting the dining room table with the best dishes they had—their everyday, government-issued china.

The tablecloth was special, though. Rose's mom brought it as a gift to Mama for hosting the dinner. She had Rose put it on the table, while she occupied Mama in the kitchen talking about the baby. When the table was set, Rose and Lainey called her in to the dining area.

"Look, Mama." Lainey ran her hand over the lace cloth.

Mama's hand covered her mouth. "Oh, my, what a beautiful covering. Where did you get that?"

Rose's mom grabbed her hand. "It's our gift to our gracious hostess."

Mama turned and threw her arms around Hannah. "Thank you. I love it. I've been wanting a new one. Ohhh!" Her eyes got big, and her hands went to her swollen belly.

"Mama, are you okay?" Lainey ran to her side.

"I think it was just a big kick. This little one is ready to meet us all, but we have a few weeks to go yet."

"Anna, do you think you should leave a little earlier, so you're sure to have the baby on Washington Island?"

"Well, Reinhardt felt we should stay till about January tenth. The baby isn't due until January twenty-fifth, and both Carter and our little girl were late. We should be okay. He's probably making plans with Rasmus right now to help us with the move."

Hannah nodded, then crossed her arms. "Hmmm. I do wonder if it might be wise for you to come back with us and have Christmas at our home—or at least come before New Year's, especially if you have these pains again."

"Oh, I think it's just kicking." Mama rubbed her belly and then leaned forward and rubbed her back with one hand.

"This baby may be getting in position to be born, not just kicking. Has he or she dropped?"

Lainey looked at Mrs. Hanson and back to Mama. "The baby is lower. I noticed that."

"If nothing else, maybe Rose should stay. She's been around a lot of births and could help if the baby comes early."

Marla set down a water pitcher on the table. "Julius' mom has told me so many times that each baby came earlier than the previous one. I would think leaving early is a good idea."

Carter, Sam, six-year-old David, and Clifford entered the dining area after returning from the upstairs. Four-year-old Catherine tagged along behind them. Sam picked her up and gave her a kiss.

Clifford glanced at Lainey but turned toward her mother. "I could actually stay as well if you need help with firewood and water, even the light. My folks and aunt and uncle aren't returning until early January. It wouldn't be a problem."

Lainey tried to swallow and couldn't. A cough burst out, and she doubled over.

Mama reached out to her. "Lainey, are you okay? Your face is red."

Rose laughed, and Clifford smiled. Sam shook his head.

Lainey barely squeaked out the words, "I'll just get some water." She scooted into the kitchen and started pumping the pump for water.

Soon each found a place at the table, and Papa pronounced a blessing. "Dear Lord, we thank You for so many wonderful friends and the good families that are here to celebrate the coming of Your Son into the world. We thank You for great food. We ask a special blessing on Anna and the baby she carries. Amen."

Flavor and laughter burst forth from the dinner gathering. Everyone talked and ate to the full.

CHAPTER NINE

LAINEY AND ROSE PLACED THE last of the plates in the cupboard. Catherine stood on a chair to help wipe the table. Lainey sighed. "Dinner was so wonderful, but I'm a little tired."

"Me, too. But we should serve the pie now. Your mom didn't have very much to eat. Maybe she's ready for pie."

Lainey nodded. "I'll take some to her now. I know she's tired with the baby getting so close. I wonder if it's a boy or girl. I think I'd like a girl." She cut a slice of pie and placed it on one of the freshly cleaned plates.

Rose and Lainey walked into the living room with little Catherine. The sound of voices drifted down the stairs. The boys were playing a board game in the upstairs living area. Rose's mother was laughing and visiting with Marla, while the men discussed the news of the area. The women had attempted to clean up, but the girls insisted they relax after helping so much with dinner.

"Where's Mama? I brought her some pie."

Rose's mom stood. "She seemed so tired, we told her to lie down for a while. Let's check on her." The four walked into the master bedroom. Mama lay on her bed, moaning in a puddle of liquid.

"Mama!" Lainey set the pie down on the dresser. "Mama, are you okay?"

Mrs. Hanson took charge. "Her water broke. The baby is coming. Anna, Anna, look at me. How far apart are the contractions?"

"What can we do?" Lainey looked to Rose's mom. "What do we do?"

Rose's mother grabbed Lainey's hand. "Lainey, we're going to have a baby today. Go heat some water. Show Rose where the towels are. Marla, you can help by keeping cool cloths on her forehead. Tell Reinhardt to come in."

Lainey glanced at the clock. Only two hours had passed, but a whole day's weariness climbed on her. Surely, Mama felt it more. No wonder they called it labor. This was work. She kept bringing warm towels in from the water heated in the great pot on the stove. The boys earned the jobs of keeping wood in the stove and the fire stoked. The wind howled outside, wanting to know whether a boy or a girl was coming into the world.

Rose remained calm, helping Lainey to warm the towels and showing her how to lay them gently over Anna's heaving belly. They kept a few cloths cool that Marla placed over her brow. Modesty and decorum stood strong in Lainey's spirit, but she discovered that child-birth allowed for little modesty. This great shock settled on Lainey as Papa stayed by Mama's side, holding her hand. Here she was, a young woman, with an almost-naked woman, while a man stayed in the room; albeit, they were her parents. And they wanted and appreciated her presence. Mama smiled at Lainey through the sweat that streamed down her face and despite the groans from contractions that convulsed her body at ever-increasing increments.

Lainey poured a glass half-full of water and brought it to her mother's lips. She took a sip and grasped Lainey's hand. "Thank you." It was only a whisper, but it rang in Lainey's ears and heart. A bond that she didn't understand passed between them. Lainey truly belonged to this couple, and this baby was her sibling as strong as any relationship could be.

Then she saw a picture in her mind. It was a flash. She stood, an adult, full with child, and this child, now within her mama, was next to her, ready to offer assistance when Lainey gave birth. The child next to her in the vision was a girl! How could she know that? She saw it. What more could she answer? The knowledge stabilized her. Certainty of the gender rose within her, and she paused and smiled.

Rose's eyes questioned Lainey. Lainey nodded and proceeded to the kitchen to warm another cloth. Rose followed her lead and arrived next to her to help. "What? What was that? You've been so nervous, and now you look like you have a secret."

Lainey grabbed Rose's hand. "Oh, Rose, I do. I do. The baby is a girl."

Rose's eyes grew big. "But, how—how would you know that?"

"I . . . I'm not sure. But I saw myself big with child, and a young girl stood next to me. I knew it was her. It was my sister. And she is totally my sister, Rose. I can't explain it."

The outside door opened, and Clifford came through with Carter. Both carried wood for the stove. "Is the baby here, yet?"

"She'll be here soon."

Clifford tilted his head. "She? You know it's a girl?"

Rose dipped her chin at Clifford. "She knows."

Mama let out a yell, and the girls ran back to the room, careful to shut the door quietly behind them.

Rose's mom gestured for the girls and Marla to come close. "The baby's head has crowned. It'll be here soon."

"She'll be here soon, Mama. Lainey somehow knows it's a girl."

"Well, then, she'll be a special gift in the life of Lainey—that's the result of specialized information."

Mama was breathing hard, and Marla laid another cool cloth over her forehead. Mama did not seem to notice. Papa was now kneeling next to his wife, half-praying and half-talking to her. "It'll be all right. We'll have another wonderful child. Dear Lord, help my wife; make it easy, Lord. Make the child ready. We know she's early." He looked at Lainey and nodded. "Help us, Lord." Lainey knelt next to the bed as well and held Mama's other hand.

Rose's mom laid her hand on her friend's girth and pressed gently. "Anna, push. It's time to push. Yes, that's it. Push again. Reinhardt, come and catch your little one."

Papa moved into position and received the struggling little form into his arms. With tears in his eyes, he proclaimed, "It's a girl, a tiny little girl." Mrs. Hanson cut the umbilical cord as Papa drank in the child's eyes. They placed a blanket around her; and when she started to wail, Papa laid her on his wife's bosom. She quickly took nourishment from her mother, but then she began to shiver.

Rose's mom pressed her hand against her chin. "Anna, we need to provide a greater warmth than a blanket or your arms can provide. Her earliness has not allowed her to develop enough fleshiness to keep herself as warm as she ought."

Papa stood. "Should we just wrap her in an extra blanket and sit close to the fire? The boys have kept it going well."

Mrs. Hanson rubbed her face. "I don't know, but I think that's our only option. We'll have to keep Anna out there for nursing. She's suckling well, which is good. Let me clean up both of them, but we need to keep her warm."

"Mama, Mrs. Hanson. The warming oven. At the top of the stove. We can put her in there. It's just the right size for her. The stove has a good fire going, and I bet the warming oven will be just right."

Rose's mom bent over with her hands on her knees. She giggled. "Why, Lainey, I think that just might work. Anna?"

Mama nodded. "My Lainey is used of God. A gift of wisdom. She will be like a second mama to this tiny, little girl. We'll call her Christina, for Christmas—and Tina for short, since she's a tiny one. Her middle name will be that of Lainey's mother, Emma. Please place Tina in the oven and watch over her there. I must sleep a little. Bring her to me when she is ready to nurse again."

Mrs. Hanson shooed everyone out of the bedroom while she cleaned mother and baby. She then called Papa back in, gently swaddled the tiny girl already known as Tina, and handed her to Papa. Mrs. Hanson followed Papa out of the bedroom. Everyone stood.

Mr. Hanson looked at his wife. "She okay? She's a tiny thing." Tina let out a wail. "Well, that's a good sign." Mr. Hanson laughed. He held Catherine, so she could see the baby's face.

Julius peered at her. "Oh, my, what a precious little thing." He looked at Marla. "Someday." Marla ducked under his arm and leaned into his embrace.

Carter stood on his tiptoes. "Can I hold her, see her?"

"We have to put her in the oven first, Carter." Lainey patted his shoulder.

All the men's jaws dropped.

"The oven?" Carter's voice shook.

Sam coughed. "You're kidding, right?"

Mrs. Hanson laughed. "Just the warming section. We need to keep her warm until her next feeding, and her mama needs to rest. Carter, you can help watch."

Carter glanced back at Clifford. "Let's watch her."

Clifford raised his eyebrows. "She's a beautiful baby, Carter, but I'll let you and your sister have this time. Sam and I can go get more wood and do anything else you need."

Mrs. Hanson, Lainey, and Rose stood for a moment before the stove. Lainey opened the upper door. "This seems a little strange."

"It is, Lainey, but wise."

Papa placed his hand in the warming pocket of the stove. "It's not hot, just nicely warm. Okay, I'll place her in." He held her out and gazed at her face. Tina cooed. The smile on Papa's face seemed to spread a mile. "You will be just fine, little one. Christina is a perfect name with you coming at Christmastime and being such a tiny girl." Her little fist worked its way out of the swaddling cloth and grabbed her papa's finger. "You are precious, my child, and strong. This will keep you warm on this very cold day. Soon, you won't need this." He placed her on her side in the oven, not any wider than she was long. Her eyes looked from her papa to Lainey.

Mrs. Hanson put her arm around Lainey. "She knows you're her sister."

"And that I'm her brother." Carter ducked under Lainey's arm and stood on his toes again. Tina's eyes drifted to him, and her mouth puckered into a smile. "See, she knows." He reached up and touched her. "I'm Carter, your big brother." Her hand found his finger. Her eyes slowly drifted shut, and her little grip relaxed.

Mrs. Hanson put her hands on her hips. "Okay, this is the quiet room now. We can take turns watching her. Boys, you'll keep the fire in the bottom oven going, but at a steady flow, not a big fire. Reinhardt, if you want to sit with Anna, Rasmus and Julius can supervise the boys and the fire. The girls and I—and yes, you, Carter—will stay in the kitchen watching Tina."

"And I will see to it that everyone has something to eat, whether leftovers or dessert." Marla grabbed an apron from the hook and began to make sandwiches with the ham. "I think we're all a little hungry after all this excitement. And we forgot to have our pie."

CHAPTER TEN

THE FAMILY AND GUESTS SETTLED into a routine. They kept the fire going, watched Tina, and held her after she nursed. Quiet games took the place of the noisy conversations and laughter that dominated the lighthouse before Mama went into labor.

Food remained ever ready—thanks to Marla, Hannah, and the girls—and the chores required late and early hours for the boys. The wind continued to pick up, and blizzard conditions set in. The guests remained two extra days. Everyone insisted on staying yet another day to help the Engelsons pack up what they might need for the winter and shut down the lighthouse. Papa had planned to leave January tenth, but the blizzard and the early birth prompted everyone to encourage him to take his family now. No one wanted them to be stranded without help on the island should anything arise.

Julius knew his brothers would handle everything well at Pilot Island. They were experienced lightkeepers and would know that the weather detained Marla and him.

The women took care of cleaning, straightening, and properly storing all that would remain inside. The men and boys helped Lainey's father shut down and clean the light and get the animals ready for the short but wintry travel across the lake ice to Washington Island. With so many hands to help, they were soon ready to leave Rock Island until spring.

The morning for the crossing dawned sunny and clear. The wind was out of the south. Lainey noticed Mr. Hanson as he stared into the wind.

"Mr. Hanson, is a south wind a concern? Uncle Otis says the south winds are warmer."

Mr. Hanson smiled. "You're right, Lainey. As long as it stays clear, we're good. It's the best day, and despite the blizzard, much of the snow has blown far and wide, leaving only an inch or so to traverse with the wagon and the sleigh."

Mr. Hanson gave the instructions. "We'll take the sleigh across first with the women, baby, and Catherine. Then I'll bring the sleigh back, and Reinhardt and Julius will drive the sleigh with some supplies and the younger boys. The wagon will follow at a distance with the cow tied to the back and the chickens in the cages. Any remaining supplies will go on the wagon, which Sam, Clifford, and I will drive."

The chill in the air elated Lainey. The breeze smelled of cleanliness and hope and freedom. The baby was born; and even though the baby came early and Mama felt weary, Lainey knew they would be fine. She couldn't wait to be that little girl's big sister. She couldn't imagine the joy that Mama and Papa held within their being. Some day, she, too, would know the joy of motherhood. Perhaps that was part of the excitement. Not just the beautiful, crisp day, not just a sweet baby sister, but Clifford. He'd spent all that time at her home because of her—at least, she believed his presence rested on his interest in her. She wanted to sing. Such a beautiful day.

The crisp air turned a bit damp as they arrived at the Hanson home. Mama snuggled Tina close and hurried into the house, while the girls grabbed the items they carried with them on the sleigh.

Hannah kissed her husband on the cheek. "Rasmus, we can get the fire going. You need to return for the second trip. Don't worry about us."

Lainey and Rose found extra blankets to place around Anna and the baby. The wood pile stood only a few feet from the door; and as they each carried in an armful, Mrs. Hanson placed thin strips of birch bark and kindling in the fireplace. The second match sent the bark and kindling into a crackle of hot, orange flames. She carefully placed several of the short logs delivered by the girls. Soon, the warmth penetrated the comfortable living room. Marla kindled the stove fire, so she could heat the food they'd prepared at Rock.

Lainey insisted Mama lay down after nursing Tina. She burped Tina and sat in the rocking chair, where Tina's tiny eyelids slipped over her big, round, blue eyes and her breathing came in little snores. Mama, too, had fallen asleep. Mrs. Hanson took over stirring the food, while Marla sliced the bread.

A commotion outside alerted them to the arrival of Papa, Julius, the younger boys, and a sleigh filled with lighthouse supplies. Rose hurried to the door to shush them before entering, so the baby and Mama would not wake. A rush of crystalline snow and cold howled through the door with the boys. Mama stirred and sat up. She smiled as Papa and Carter hurried to her. The baby continued her light snoring.

"Mama, another storm blew up, and we can't see the wagon."

Mrs. Hanson's wooden spoon hit the floor. "What do you mean? Reinhardt, you can't see the wagon? Wasn't Rasmus right behind you?"

The door opened. Rasmus stomped in, shaking snow off his boots and coat.

"Oh, thank goodness. We thought the wagon got lost, but here you are." Mrs. Hanson retrieved another spoon and turned back to the stew she heated on the stove.

"No, the wagon isn't here. Clifford insisted he bring it. The load from the supplies was greater than we anticipated, and we decided to just have one person on the wagon. He carries supplies for his parents' store with a wagon and is very competent. However, a squall blew up from the south, and for the last part of the trip, we could not see but five feet in front of us. We kept hollering and thought we heard him holler back. But we lost him. We're going back out. If he wanders too far north or gets turned around . . . " Rasmus looked from his wife to Lainey. "We'll find him."

Sam came in the door. "Pa, I have the rope."

Papa placed a kiss on Mama's cheek and turned to Lainey. "We'll find him. This is not the first time we've had to find someone in a storm. This is our training."

Mrs. Hanson grabbed a scarf and wrapped it around her husband's neck. "We need you. Be careful. Bring that fine young man back."

Lainey hugged the baby tighter and tried to swallow the torrent of fear that bubbled up within. She and Rose locked eyes. There were no words. Even if there were, she couldn't utter them. What if he'd wandered to thin ice? He wouldn't be the first to lose his life this way. The memories, the stark grief that engulfed her when her parents died, threatened to overtake her. Mrs. Hanson took the baby. Mama knelt in front of Lainey.

"Lainey, they'll find him. Let's pray."

Rose walked over and took Lainey's hand. Mrs. Hanson stood behind them and rocked the baby as Mama prayed.

"Lord, we ask You now for Your great help. You know exactly where Clifford is, and we ask You to please protect him. Bring all the men back here safely. Please stop the winds; stop the storm. Send Your angels to bring them safely back to us. Amen."

The younger boys stood quietly while Mama prayed. Carter tapped his mother's shoulder while she still knelt. "Mama, we're kinda hungry. Is there food ready?" He turned and looked at Mrs. Hanson.

"Yes, Carter, the food is ready." She handed Tina to her mama and returned to the stove. Rose and Lainey retrieved the dishes and placed them on the table.

Clifford ducked his head against the wind-driven sleet. The first part of the trek across the channel between Rock Island and Washington Island invigorated him with the crisp air and clear, blue sky. The sun hung a bit low in the sky, its zenith being near its lowest route of the year. As he prepared to be a ship captain, the study of the times and seasons of the sun and weather patterns fascinated him. He needed to learn to efficiently read the weather. Lainey had learned a lot from her uncle about weather and clouds and storms. He enjoyed discussing those subjects with her and knew she loved living in the lighthouse.

The white expanse of snow across the ice was quite breathtaking. It sparkled in the midday sun while the swirling patterns of thick ice echoed turquoise blues and greens. The wind picked up and worked hard to take away his breath as it swirled like the ice patterns. He pulled his hat lower and his collar higher, but the biting snow still slapped his face. He ducked his head and continued forward, peering to keep sight of the rest of the men in the sleigh. He hadn't noticed signs of a squall blowing up, but they were all focused on getting everything loaded and on the way. He was glad Anna and the baby and Lainey would be on Washington Island for the remainder of the winter. The island was large—as safe as being on the mainland. He could also visit more easily.

Clifford hollered to check in with Mr. Hanson. They did a holler check every few minutes. He heard nothing but the sound of sleet slapping his face and the wagon. He yelled again. Nothing but the howl of the wind. *Wait, it's a south wind, and it's hitting me in the face. I must have turned south. I must be headed toward Pilot.* Clifford calculated just a moment and turned the horse to his right. That was better. The wind struck him now on his left.

He strained to catch sight of the sleigh ahead of him, but the snow prevented it. A haze or a fog was settling in. He could barely see in front of the horse. The sun should be in front of him and slightly to his left if he truly traveled west. Had he noticed the sun in front of him when it dawned on him that he must be traveling south? His whole body shivered, perhaps as much from confusion as the cold. He looked around. He'd brought no blanket for extra warmth. That was a serious error. He knew to always bring extra items to maintain warmth in the winter on a wagon. Probably sent all the extras for the women and the boys. He'd be okay, but he felt the dampness from the icy wind invading his clothing. Getting wet was dangerous. Clifford prayed. He could not locate the sun anywhere. If only there was a glimpse, he'd instantly know his direction.

The chicken boxes had a layer of snow on top. The now-pelting snow penetrated openings in their cages. They were hunkered down. Clifford wished he could hunker down, but he knew he needed to get the cow and the horse back safely. They were probably shivering, too. How had he gone off course? He knew to pay better attention to the weather and the wind. Still, he hadn't been out on the ice that much with his wagon. If he became a ship captain, he'd need to know how to find his way in a storm. He never wanted to run aground or climb a rocky shoal.

He still hadn't heard any hollers. He wondered if they had turned back to find him or just kept going. Maybe they heard his hollers, and he just didn't hear theirs. Well, he would keep the wind blowing on his left, and he should arrive at Washington Island soon. He must have lost track of his direction when he started thinking about Lainey.

He chuckled at how she lost all ability to function around him. Yet her beauty and her kindness really made him want to know her more. He'd never thought much about girls before her. Oh, the girls in town and at school always acted like they liked him, but he just ignored them. He had other things to do and think about. But Lainey, well, there was something about her. He didn't know if it was impor-tant like love, or just those things that happened as you got older. His dad said those feelings were inevitable, and it just meant you were growing up. He liked Lainey, but . . .

What? The wagon stopped. The wind was still from his left, so he was moving the correct direction, even though he still couldn't locate the sun. He jiggled the reins. "Let's go, Missy. Giddy up." The horse whinnied, and Clifford saw muscles strain as she tried to step forward. "I know the wind is biting, but the sooner we go, the sooner you'll be in a warm barn. C'mon, girl!" Again, the horse strained forward, but the wagon barely moved.

Clifford groaned. Maybe the wheel was stuck in an ice rut. He got out and held close to the wagon and examined each wheel. The ice under the left wheels seemed smooth. The cow stood attached to the back by a rope with her head down and turned slightly to keep the snow out of her face. He patted her head. "Sorry, Mattie, we'll get you to the Hansons' nice, warm barn soon." As he passed under her rope, it seemed taut. He made sure there was no chance the rope would work loose. He couldn't lose any of the animals.

He moved to the right side of the wagon. It provided a bit of protection from the wind. He peered up to see if the sun was somewhere but could see only a few feet beyond him in any direction. He ducked down to check under the wheels. He detected no ruts in the ice or damage to the wheels. When he came around to the horse, she, too, stood with face down. When Clifford stood in front of her, she nuzzled him.

"I know, Missy. It got nasty. Here, I'll just walk with you." He slipped his hand in her bridle and started forward. The horse tried to go, but the wagon wouldn't move. Clifford felt his way back to again check the wheels. He decided to push the wagon—maybe a bit of freezing was holding the wheels to the ice. That was probably it. The wheels turned slightly, but then the cow let out a bellow. Clifford whirled around.

"Mattie, I know it's awful out here. We'll be okay; we just need to get moving." He started to push the wagon again, and this time saw the cow move backward. "What's gotten into you? That's the wrong way." He patted Mattie on the face, and she mooed and pulled back and even shook her head. "Wait, do you know something I don't know?"

Perhaps the wind had changed. After all, it was a squall of some sort. Perhaps he had turned the wrong way. If he was going north instead of west, he was heading to open water. Just then, there occurred the slightest lull in the wind, and he heard a slap and cracks. The shivers left, and a hot sweat engulfed him. He gulped and pushed down the panic that sought to race through his being. That slap meant open water smacking the ice. He must be only twenty feet away. The cow must have known. The cracking sound meant breaking ice. They should all be lying flat right now to keep from causing more cracks.

Every step could be their last. He didn't think the cracks were behind them. If so, they would be on an ice flow heading out into Lake Michigan. Death would follow either by drowning or freezing to death. Clifford had heard too many stories from Uncle Albert of fishermen losing their lives when the place they ice-fished broke off. In attempts to stay afloat, they often fell off. Some ran and tried to jump the gap. Some made it, and some did not. Some stayed put and froze.

Clifford gently worked his way to the horse and led her back to his left into the biting sleet and snow. Now, he didn't notice. The cold didn't matter. The numbness settling into his feet and fingers didn't matter. He needed to move in the opposite direction as fast and carefully as he could. Had he continued, he would be in the frigid waters of Lake Michigan, along with the horse, the cow, and the chickens. *God, help me find the way.*

Clifford wondered if hours had gone by. It wasn't dark, didn't seem close to dark, but the cold was numbing, and still, there was no sun. He stopped, patted the horse, felt his way back along the wagon and found the rope to Mattie. "Girl, thank you." He rested his head against her forehead. Her body warmth spread into Clifford. She nudged him. "You're right, we have to keep going. Dear Lord, help us find our way."

He found his way back to the mare, took her bridle, and patted her side. "Let's go. We'll make it with God's help." He trudged forward. Perhaps he should get back in the wagon. His feet felt like blocks of ice, but he felt he needed to stay with the horse.

Sleepiness crept into his mind. Focusing became more difficult. If only he could rest. Mattie was warm. Perhaps he could just go back and lean against her. He paused. He was so cold. Missy whinnied and pushed at him. She heaved forward, almost dragging him. He startled. It was the freezing sickness. *Wake up, Clifford. Go. Walk. Listen to Missy. Dear Lord, I don't know the direction anymore. Please let Missy be led the right way.*

He stumbled forward. One step. Just one more step. He said it out loud. "One more step. Take one more step." It helped, but then it became a monotone. Clifford hollered. "One more step! Take another step! Keep going! One more step! Clifford, keep walking! Clifford! Clifford!" He hollered at himself. Wait, was that his voice?

"Clifford! Clifford!" That didn't quite sound like his voice. But then he was almost frozen. He laughed. Why should he worry about how he sounded? He needed to keep going. He stumbled again. The horse pulled. "Thank you, Missy. I must keep going."

"Clifford! Clifford!"

There it was again. Why was he hollering his own name? Something was strange. He just needed to keep going. Wait, he knew that voice. Not his voice. It belonged to . . . to . . . Mr. Hanson. It was

Mr. Hanson. He was found! He fell to the ground and yelled. "I'm here. I'm here. Can you help?" He lay down. The horse nuzzled him and whinnied. She stomped. The cow bellowed.

And then, through the swirling snow and pelting sleet, men's faces peered down at Clifford. He felt hands grab his arms and lift him into the sleigh. Blankets covered him, and a warm liquid met his lips. Now he could sleep. Someone slapped his face. "No, Clifford. Wake up. We've found you. You need to stay awake until we know you're okay. You're going to be okay."

Clifford heard voices talking about the sleigh and the wagon; and he tried to comprehend, but thinking was so difficult. His face was slapped again. Maybe it was only patted. He worked to open his eyes. Vaguely, he saw Reinhardt. "You found me. Thank you. I went the wrong way. I thought we were stuck." His voice trailed off, and he closed his eyes.

Reinhardt gently shook him. "Open your eyes, Clifford. Tell me more. It's okay."

"Okay. I thought we were stuck in a rut. But it was Mattie—you know, the cow—she knew; she stopped. I tried to go. Then I heard the slap—the waves, the open water. I heard ice cracking. I don't know how we got turned around. I walked with the horse, with Missy. So cold but then you found us. Thank you."

"We're here. We'll get you inside, Clifford. God has spared your life."

CHAPTER ELEVEN

February, 1891

THE DELIVERY WAGON WITH LAINEY'S dress finally arrived. The heavy snow and ice prevented three earlier wagons from arriving across the ice with supplies to the local mercantile. Rasmus brought it into the house at dinner time.

"Lainey, this is for you."

Lainey squealed, and Rose pushed her chair back from the table, tipping it over. "Lainey, is that the dress? Oh, thank goodness, it came. Oh, open it, open it."

"Let me wash my hands first. And you'd better pick up your chair."

Mrs. Hanson laughed and stood. "Nobody touches the dress without washing their hands. Rasmus, go ahead and eat. Boys, you stay at the table as well."

Carter rolled his eyes. "Girls—dresses. I'd rather eat."

The Hanson boys nodded and kept eating.

Catherine climbed off her chair. "I'll wash my hands, Mama. I want to see the dress."

Lainey laid the box on the settee in the corner of the room. She and Rose carefully pulled the top open and uncovered the dress from the paper wrapped around it. "Ooohhh, it's lovely. Mama, it's even lovelier than in the catalog."

Mama had just walked out of the bedroom holding the baby. "Lift it up, Lainey; let's see it."

Rose, her mother, Catherine, and Mama stood close as Lainey unfurled the dress and held it against herself.

Rose clapped her hands. "Oh, Lainey, the belle of the ball. It's perfect. Clifford will only have eyes for you."

Lainey felt the heat of a blush. "Oh, I don't know. I haven't heard from him since he recovered after Christmas."

Mama handed the baby to Rose's mom, grasped the waist of the dress, and held it against Lainey. "We may need a few tucks here. What do you think, Hannah?"

"I think you're right. I'm wondering about the sleeve length, too, but it certainly is stunning."

Lainey knew the sweet ivory color accentuated her hair and complexion.

Rose ran her fingers along the puffed upper sleeve and down the buttons of the lower sleeve. The vertical, lacy lines of the bodice met at the waist, and the skirt fell in soft folds to the hem. "It looks a perfect length. You have to try it on."

Mrs. Hanson tsked-tsked. "Not till after dinner. Let's get the meal eaten before it gets cold. I believe it's the boys turn to do clean-up, so you can try it on then. We'll get the pins and make sure we have all adjustments marked.

The week passed rapidly. Everyone at school buzzed with excitement about the coming Valentine's dance. Even Miss Juliet Pritchard, the school's young teacher, seemed excited. She let several of the older students off early on Friday to begin decorating the nearby hall for the dance.

Tables and punch bowls and lights were placed throughout the hall. The floors were swept and chairs placed on the perimeter. A small stage was cleared, so the band had plenty of room.

Lainey and Rose left the hall in the early evening. The boys left earlier and walked so the girls could take the wagon. Rose urged the horses with a slight slap of the reins. "I heard Miss Pritchard has a beau. I wonder who it might be? I haven't heard of anyone on the island. Have you?"

Lainey pulled her coat a little closer as the wind hurried across the road. "I wondered. She seems happy, like she has a secret. But I've not heard anything either. Maybe it's someone from the mainland. Are the Claflins going to make it?"

Rose shook her head. "I just don't know. Papa asked if any wagons were coming over. He thinks another supply wagon arrives tomorrow, so maybe . . . " Rose sighed.

Lainey reached over and squeezed her hand. "I hope so, Rose; I really hope they come."

"Lainey, what about Clifford? He'll come, don't you think?

Lainey shrugged her shoulders. "Oh, I don't know. He just takes my breath away, and we talked so much at Christmas; but it's been weeks since he returned home."

"I could see it in his eyes. He really likes you. Even Sam noticed it."

Lainey jerked her head around to look at Rose. "Really, your brother noticed?"

Rose laughed. "Oh, Lainey, everyone noticed. It is not just your imagination."

The girls rode in silence for a while. A gentle snow fell, and the pines shimmered in the dusky evening with a winter beauty.

"Mama said we could spend all day tomorrow primping. I can't wait to do your hair, Lainey."

"And I, yours. I think my dress is all ready. Mama said she should have all the alterations done today."

"You'll be all ivory and lace, and I'll be all green velvet."

Lainey grinned. "Rose, your dress is gorgeous. You and your mom are amazing seamstresses."

Rose nodded. "It's my mom. She loves to sew and has trained me since I was little."

"Aunt Edith taught me to mend and stitch well, but to make dresses . . . Well, there was no time, it seemed."

"Mama can teach you to make anything. And doesn't your mother sew?"

"Oh, she does, but she's been so busy with everything and now with the baby. I've mostly done the mending. One of these days, we'll do more sewing. I'd love to make little dresses for Tina."

As the day flew by, Lainey's butterflies multiplied. She knew how much she wanted to see Clifford, but perhaps he wouldn't be there. The weather held no threat of storm nor high winds, so those arriving from the mainland would have little difficulty crossing the ice to Washington Island. Clifford walked close to death crossing on the ice from Rock Island, but thankfully, he survived. Today, the ice was thick and firm; and as long as the weather stayed clear, there was no problem. If a squall came up, every family on the island opened their doors for travelers to spend the night.

"Lainey, your mind is wandering again. Clifford?" Rose laughed. "Look at your hair. What do you think?"

Lainey caught her breath when she gazed into the mirror. The ringlets Rose had created all over her head were stunning. "Rose, how did you do this? I've never seen my hair this beautiful or hold so many ringlets."

"Your hair is easy. It holds the curl much better than anyone in our family. You are so pretty. If Clifford isn't there, every young man present will want to dance with you."

Lainey looked down and felt her face grow red. "I do hope he's there; but if he isn't, I'm just going to enjoy the evening, even if no one dances with me."

"What?" Mama and Mrs. Hanson walked through the bedroom door. "No one dance with you? Look at you. You're beautiful. Any young man would be blind not to notice your beauty and want to dance." Mama placed a light kiss on Lainey's forehead, then turned to Rose. "You're an artist with hair, Rose. You'll have to show me how you did it."

Lainey stood. "Now it's my turn to do Rose's hair. Sit down, young lady. I'm going to put it up and use those gorgeous combs your mom put out for us."

"We'll be back to help you get in your dresses. Then your dad will take you to the dance in the buggy."

"I love the buggy. Thank you, Mama." Rose clapped her hands as she sat down in front of Lainey. "Do you think the Claflins will come? I guess the only one I really want to see is Niles, but I don't even know if he knows I'm alive."

Lainey grinned. "He knows, Rose. Don't be silly. You're the prettiest, nicest, and smartest girl around. I bet all the Claflin boys will want to dance with you."

"I hope so." The girls quieted as Lainey held pins in her mouth and swirled Rose's hair and fastened combs in key positions for a practical hold and a beautiful display. When she was satisfied, she turned Rose to the mirror. "I can't wait to see you in your dress. No one will be able to breathe when you arrive."

Rose sputtered, "No, we need everyone alive. That would ruin everything if they couldn't breathe."

The girls giggled, and soon, their laughter combined with tears running down their faces. As they caught their breath, they grabbed the embroidered handkerchiefs Rose's mother gave them as gifts for the Valentine's Ball.

Mrs. Hanson and Mama helped them get their dresses on and then made sure their hair remained in place. The family lined up to see the girls when they exited the bedroom. Everyone clapped. Mr. Hanson looked at Papa. "I don't know. Maybe we should keep them home. Someone is sure to arrive tomorrow and ask for their hand in marriage. I'm not ready for that."

"Maybe you're right. We should make them stay home." Papa winked at Lainey.

Rose's eyes widened. "Papa, you promised to take us in the buggy."

Mr. Hanson kissed his daughter's cheek. "You just be careful tonight. Don't let any young men talk you into running away with them."

"Oh, Papa." Rose shook her head.

She and Lainey donned the mink wraps that Mrs. Hanson laid out for them to use. Rose's grandfather had been a trapper and often went to the mainland where minks were in abundance. He'd brought some of the little animals back to the island and bred them. The furs sold well. Her grandmother learned to create one-of-a-kind mink stoles, and they sold all over the country. She taught Rose's mom, who made shawls of mink fur for all the women in her family.

Mrs. Hanson made sure the clasps were fastened and the girls had muffs to keep their hands warm before they climbed into the buggy. Every few minutes, they held the muffs to their noses to keep the chill off. Heated rocks sat on the floor where the girls placed their feet, and hand-knit, woolen blankets adorned their laps. Mr. Hanson climbed into the driver's seat, smiled at the girls, and slapped the horse's rump with the reins. The evening had begun.

The girls held hands and giggled as heads turned and smiled when they arrived and walked through the red and white decorated hall to the punch bowl. Soon, the music drew several couples to the dance floor. Rose and Lainey huddled with girlfriends as they wondered when their new, young teacher would arrive and with whom.

One of the young men trotted up to the group. "She's here, and she has a beau with her."

Everyone turned to the door as it opened, and in came Miss Pritchard. Lainey stared. Rose took the glass cup of punch from her. She squeezed Lainey's hand. "Use your handkerchief. Don't let him see you cry."

Lainey turned away. Her voice was a whisper. "Do you think your dad is still nearby and can take me home? I'll fetch my wrap and muff and go right now."

"No. Pull yourself together. There are other young men who have eyes for you. Don't let this ruin your night."

She knew Rose was right. Turning around after dabbing her eyes dry, she looked throughout the ballroom trying to see everyone else present and ignore Clifford gazing at his lovely date. She glanced his way and saw Clifford notice her and move across the room toward her. She grabbed Rose's hand and pulled her toward a small huddle of girls on the other side of the room. One of her classmates asked her to dance. As she turned with the music, she caught Clifford watching her. Why would he watch her if he was with Miss Pritchard?

When the dance ended, she looked for Rose. She spotted her talking to Niles. Lainey smiled. She knew how much Rose liked him. As the next song began, Niles took Rose's elbow and guided her to the dance floor.

Lainey turned and almost ran smack-dab into Clifford. "Oh, hi, Clifford." She wrapped her handkerchief around her finger.

"You look lovely, Lainey. It's been a while."

"Yes, are you feeling quite well? Did you have frostbite?" Lainey could not look him in the eyes. She would reveal her interest or her hurt. She determined he not see either. He obviously held no long-lasting interest in her.

"It was rather minor. I'm sure glad Rasmus and Reinhardt found me."

"Me, too." Lainey looked at the tips of her shoes peeking out from under her dress.

"Clifford." The voice was thick with sweetness. Lainey wasn't sure if it was sincere or fabricated.

"Lainey. You look absolutely stunning." Miss Pritchard stood before her. She looped her arm through Clifford's. "Lainey, this is—"

"Clifford Ruckert. Yes, we've met. I hope you have a fine evening. I need to check with Rose about something."

She realized she might have to apologize for being rude to Miss Pritchard when she returned to school on Monday, but she could not let her know how sweet she was on Clifford. She peeked over her shoulder and saw a bit of confusion on her teacher's face; but it quickly vanished as other people approached them, and she obviously delighted in introducing her new beau. And here she'd thought he was busy training to be a sea captain and helping his parents with the store or his uncle with fishing. Somehow, he found time to court the new teacher on Washington Island. Lainey wondered how often he'd come to the Island or Miss Pritchard went to the mainland to move their relationship forward. She shook her head.

"Lainey. Are you all right? Lainey?" Rose took her hand.

Lainey sniffed. "Miss Pritchard was going to introduce me to her beau—Clifford. Rose, I just walked away. I was a bit rude, I fear."

Rose smiled. "They'll be fine. I'm worried about you." She leaned in. "How about I have Niles dance with you? Maybe it'll make Clifford jealous."

Lainey shook her head. "He'll not get jealous. He'd have to be sweet on me, and he's not. He's head over heels for our teacher."

"Let's eat." Rose nodded at Niles, and he joined them. "We're going to eat. Maybe Trygve would like to sit with us as well."

Lainey lifted her head. "I didn't see Tryg. Where is he?"

Niles gestured across the room, where several of his brothers were taking off their coats. "They just arrived. I'll get him."

"Hi, Lainey! Hey, you look great. This is a nice party."

Lainey laughed. Tryg was just what she needed. He always looked on the bright side of things. She usually did, too. Right now, it was difficult, but Tryg would help. She paused. She had a lot of good friends, and she was young. She would survive tonight without Clifford. She ignored the pang in her heart and asked Tryg what he'd been doing lately.

Lainey enjoyed Tryg's easy-going personality. She supposed that being the middle of seven sons must require great flexibility. Tryg could get along with anybody. She wondered what he would become. Surely, he'd be great at it and enjoy it.

"Well, I have been doing some lumberjacking." He raised his fist and pumped his bicep muscle. "See how strong I am." He beamed unashamedly.

Lainey laughed. "You be careful. Don't get a big bump on your head by showing off your muscles out in the woods."

"I do have a few bruises, but it wouldn't do to display them in mixed company." Tryg grinned. "So, you're on Washington Island for the winter at Rose's house?"

"I am. Our parents and all the children get along so well. We'll sure miss them when we return to Rock Island. But I love it there, too."

Lainey and Tryg walked to the food table and loaded their plates. "My brother loves Pilot Island, too. I see your aunt and uncle on occasion. They actually came down to our lighthouse to visit my parents. Your uncle's leg is healing nicely, and your aunt seems . . . well, more relaxed."

Lainey nodded. "The life for her on the island was good, but hard. I'm glad she can relax now. I do miss them, but living with the Engelsons has been wonderful for me. I know God worked it out."

"That He did," agreed Tryg. They carried their overflowing plates back to the table and visited with Rose and Niles while they ate.

Niles took Rose's hand. "Let's dance." As they moved to the dance floor, Lainey saw Niles raise his eyebrows and tilt his head at Tryg.

"Lainey, let's dance." He held out his hand.

"My pleasure." Lainey enjoyed dancing with Tryg. They continued chatting, and she realized she'd forgotten all about Clifford—until he tapped Tryg on the shoulder and stepped into position to dance with Lainey.

"Thanks, Tryg." He turned to Lainey. "Is Tryg your date tonight?"

"Well, no, but he is a good friend." Lainey peeked at Clifford's eyes. They held no jealousy or what she would consider sweetness toward her. Why was he dancing with her when he was sweet on Miss Pritchard? It didn't make sense. Probably thought he owed it to her somehow. She felt the red of anger creep up into her cheeks. She could not tolerate a sympathy dance.

Clifford seemed not to notice the color rising in her face. "I'm pleased to see you here, Lainey. You look very nice."

Pleased? Does he think I wouldn't come if I couldn't be with him? The nerve! And to say I look nice—why wouldn't I look nice? Did he expect me to be in a lighthouse uniform? It was all she could do to not lash out with her words. Clifford just kept dancing and smiling at her.

"Juliet mentioned a few times how stunning your dress is. She thinks it's the latest style that she saw in a magazine."

"Yes, I'm sure Miss Pritchard keeps up on all the latest fashions."

"She says you're a smart girl, too. But I knew that."

Lainey cleared her throat. She knew if she opened her mouth, unkind words would exit.

"Lainey, you know that Juliet is my—"

"Certainly. Oh, the music stopped. Thank you for the dance. I must return to my friends." With that, Lainey turned and sauntered over to Rose, Niles, and Tryg.

Rose was wide-eyed. She leaned over to Lainey and whispered. "What did you say? He looks like you slapped him."

Lainey peered over her shoulder. Clifford walked back to Miss Pritchard's table with his head down. "I wanted to slap him."

"Well, I think he felt it."

Moroseness set in on the way home. The evening had truly been beautiful and fun. Everyone loved her dress, and she danced with three of Tryg's brothers and a few of her classmates. They laughed and told jokes and ate way too much food. Rose's dad came to pick them up just as it was time to clean up. He pitched in and helped the young men take down tables. All the girls, including Miss Pritchard, cleaned up the food and sent it home with whoever wanted it. They took the decorations down and laughed the whole time.

But she was disappointed in herself. She'd acted proud and rude with Clifford, and he probably didn't deserve it. She hurt in her heart that he was with Miss Pritchard but acquiesced to the fact that he owed her nothing. Even if he danced with her just as a friend, she could have been so much more cordial. She'd tried to bury those feelings; but on the chilly ride home, as the snow sat like a gentle blanket on the pine trees and glistened where the light from houses shone on it, she found herself all too aware of her failings and her loss of Clifford. Even if Miss Pritchard was a passing fancy, she'd done nothing to invite Clifford into her life again.

Rose grasped her hand. "It'll be okay, Lainey. I know you were hurt by Clifford tonight, but there are other young men out there." She chuckled. "You were a big hit with all the Claflin boys."

Lainey managed a smile. "They are a fun lot, now aren't they?" Still she'd envisioned herself with a sea captain named Clifford. Not a lumberjack, even though Tryg would probably always be a friend. She sighed. At least she had a family and good friends. She should be thankful. She would work at being more thankful. Aunt Edith would tell her that. She chuckled.

"What?" Rose tilted her head.

"Oh, I just remembered Aunt Edith getting after me when I'd get all upset. 'Girl,' she'd say, 'is this your drama? Pull yourself together.'" Lainey started to laugh. "I think I need to hear that."

Rose turned in her seat, threw her shoulders back, and in a deep voice said, "Lainey, is this your drama, girl? I think we've had just about enough of this." Then she snorted, and both girls wrapped their arms around each other and guffawed all the way home. Mr. Rasmus glanced over his shoulder and smiled.

CHAPTER TWELVE

THE PARTY LINGERED IN LAINEY'S mind, even though more than a month had flown by since Clifford broke her heart. Her attempts to hide her hurt were anything but successful with the Hansons. And Lainey maintained a steady politeness with her teacher, Juliet Pritchard.

Rose sauntered into the room she shared with Lainey. "Papa is taking us to the mainland Saturday to pick up and deliver supplies. We can stay with your aunt and uncle."

Lainey pursed her lips and shrugged.

"Young lady! You are no longer moping. Forget Clifford. Papa might let us visit the Claflins—you know Trygve would like to see you."

Lainey turned and smiled. "You know he's just a good friend. He's like a brother. If he was sweet on a girl, I bet I'd be the first one he'd tell. It would be fun to see him, though." She winked. "And you'd like to see Niles."

Rose twirled. "I would. So quit moping, and let's enjoy this."

Lainey and Rose arrived at school the next day discussing the clothes they would wear and eager to tell Miss Pritchard they might miss a day or two of school.

"You know the weather could turn bad." Rose smiled and raised her eyebrows after they presented their trip to their teacher.

Miss Pritchard stepped back and crossed her arms. Lainey glanced at Rose and looked down. Then she heard the chuckle. It was Miss Pritchard.

"Now, girls, you have fun. Take your good dresses in case there's a party. You know, I'm only a few years older than you. You are both wonderful students, and as long as you take your studies seriously . . . " She paused and raised her eyebrows.

Rose nodded. "Oh, yes, we are very serious, and we challenge each other, so we know we'll be ready for the big tests."

"Lainey, how long will you be with us? Do you return to Rock Island soon?"

"My parents will return mid-April. Mama is a wonderful teacher, but she and Papa think it might be best if I stay till the end of the school year, since the tests are this year. Plus, it might be too much for her to assist my studies with the baby. We haven't completely decided."

Miss Pritchard touched her shoulder. Her big, blue eyes held Lainey's. "Well, I'm sure you'll make the right choice. You have my blessing to visit the mainland. I know you'll get caught up quickly if your return is delayed. Now, will you help me set up for the younger students?"

The two girls chatted and laughed all the way to the mainland. Mr. Hanson carefully dodged ice chunks that still populated Death's Door channel. The winter had been heavy, but the thawing was ahead of schedule, due to warmer temperatures in early March. As hope for spring rode high among the residents, they were always cognizant of the possibility that storms and cold often returned to make the waters impassable.

For now, spring greeted them with damp air and glistening waves that barely crested. Lainey noticed the ice shoves had removed a few trees at the north end of Pilot Island. On occasion, strong winds pushed the ice flows onto land with such great force they cleared the area of trees and, sometimes, buildings. She wondered if her favorite tree was still there and felt the pang of the loss of her parents.

Lainey hoped the earliness of the spring melt spoke of good things to come. The longing to see her aunt and uncle rose within her. She hugged herself. She didn't realize how much she missed them.

Upon arriving at the dock in Newport Town, Lainey fell into their hugs, and warmth enveloped her. She didn't want to let go. Her uncle's big arms wrapped around her with such strength that she sensed an inner peace she'd forgotten. As happy as she was with her new family, Uncle Otis knew her like no other. They had shared so much together on Pilot Island. Even Aunt Edith emanated a relaxed demeanor and held her longer than ever before. Happiness welled within Lainey.

The Seversons invited Mr. Hanson to join them for the duration of his business on the mainland. Dinner was delicious, and Aunt Edith's pie topped off the evening as they sat by the fireplace and chatted.

"There's a gathering tomorrow night in honor of Clifford." Uncle Otis paused when neither girl responded. "You do remember him? Lainey? Rose?" Lainey felt him study her. Thankfully, Rose didn't look her way. "He's leaving next week for a time to train as captain. The *Horowitz* has taken him on as a first mate. He's been working some time for this. We hope you'll go with us. Rasmus, is that acceptable?"

"Indeed, it is. I must make some deliveries while here. Do you have an extra wagon I could use, or should I hire one in Newport Town?"

"You most certainly must use ours. We have the little surrey to attend the event."

Aunt Edith picked up her tea cup. "Girls, did you, by chance, bring your party dresses?"

"We did," both girls chimed together.

"Oh, and the Claflin boys' band will be providing music." Uncle Otis beamed when he saw the girls smile.

Mr. Hanson chuckled. "Oh, these girls will enjoy that. They were hoping to visit their lighthouse."

Uncle Otis smiled. "We have a standing invitation to visit."

Later, the girls climbed into the large four-poster bed with the rose-bud quilt. The girls whispered about their times on Pilot Island years earlier with that quilt. Soon, their conversation turned to the party for Clifford.

"Do you think Miss Pritchard knew? She told us to bring party dresses." Rose pulled the quilt closer to her chin.

Lainey shook her head. "It makes no sense. She's sweet on him and he on her. Maybe she's coming, too."

The girls walked into the cavernous room of Clayton Hall. It overflowed with smiling people. Tables sat along one side covered with a variety of colorful tablecloths and a plethora of prepared food. A hodgepodge of chairs was scattered along two walls. The fourth wall sported a small stage, most likely for the band. Women of all ages bustled about in lace, velvet, and chiffon dresses. Laughter and chatter filled the air. Winter had been long, and everyone seemed delighted for an excuse to gather for a party.

Rose linked her arm in Uncle Otis'. "This is quite exciting. I'm so glad we're here. This hall is so big."

Uncle Otis nodded. "The Claytons moved here from Racine a few years ago. They were lighthouse keepers there for several years. They purchased this building with an inheritance and hope to someday make at least part of it an eating place. That would be a big attraction for Ellison Bay. For now, they host gatherings such as this and hold roller skating nights." He turned. "Well, here's the guest of honor."

Lainey caught her breath. She watched as Clifford greeted her uncle. He quickly turned to her. "Lainey, you're here." His smile captured her. "How did you know?"

Lainey struggled to find her voice and straightened her spine. She needed to be strong. "We—we didn't. We just came for a short visit, and Uncle Otis told us. And they were coming, so here we are."

"Your aunt and uncle have been marvelous to me. They helped finance some of my training." Clifford took her hands. "It's so good to see you!"

Shivers traveled up her arm and made her tongue stumble. "It's . . . well . . . it's nice to . . . I mean, you're leaving for sea . . . tomorrow?"

"Next week. I'll probably be on the Great Lakes only for now. Someday, I hope to go to sea. How long are you here?"

Lainey woke from her daze. She pulled back her hands. "Oh, just till Tuesday. Maybe Wednesday. Rose's father has deliveries to make."

"Yes, my parents said he stopped by the store, but I had no idea you'd accompanied him."

"How do they feel about you leaving?"

"They're happy for me, but my mother is a little worried . . . you know, with all the shipwre—I'm sorry, Lainey." He tried to take her hand again, but Lainey pulled it away and took a step backward.

"That's okay, Clifford. I'll pray you remain safe." She heard his voice still talking, but she walked away. She glanced back. Clifford started to follow and call after her, but well-wishers surrounded him and restricted his progress.

Rose called to her and patted a seat beside where she sat. She leaned in as Lainey joined her. "I do believe he's still smitten. You should have seen the longing in his eyes as you walked away."

Lainey's voice was steady. "Rose, he's with Miss Pritchard now, and he's leaving. Just as well. Good news, though, the Claflin boys just arrived."

Rose tilted her head toward the door. "And so has Miss Pritchard—and in a beautiful dress."

Lainey bit her lip. "I knew it. Well, it's still a party. We're here with Uncle Otis and Aunt Edith, and the Claflins are here. Let's go see them."

The boys let out a cheer when they saw Lainey and Rose. Niles and Rose took each other's hands and said not a word. Lainey chuckled. She greeted Trygve, who set down his guitar on the stage. "They're truly sweet on each other, don't you think?"

Trygve laughed. "Niles always talks about Rose. Mom just smiles and reminds him to mind his manners when he sees her. We didn't know you were coming. This is great. How's school?"

"It's good. We didn't know we were coming either. Mr. Hanson had deliveries and asked us to come along, and Uncle Otis invited us to the party."

The brothers scurried to set up and start the music. Rose and Lainey decided to get some food. Rose nudged Lainey. She turned. Miss Pritchard was seated between Clifford's parents and holding his mother's hand.

Lainey sighed. "They look very fond of each other. Do you think he's spoken for her?"

Rose shook her head. "No. It must be something different."

Uncle Otis joined the girls. "You know I need a cane; but when this music starts, I want to dance with my girl." He chuckled and kissed Lainey on the cheek.

"Uncle Otis, you can have every dance."

"Well, now, I would get too worn out, but I'm sure those Claflin boys are good dancers. And, Lainey, I know one young man named Clifford would probably like every dance with you if you'll let him. He seems to think you're no longer interested."

"Uncle, it's the other way around. He has a new flame, and by her closeness to his parents, I think it looks quite settled."

Uncle Otis turned. "You mean Juliet Pritchard? Isn't she your teacher?"

"Yes, and Clifford is her beau."

Rose nodded. "She was on his arm most of the evening at the Valentine's Ball."

Uncle Otis took Lainey's hand and walked toward Clifford's parents and Miss Pritchard. Rose hung back. "Come with us, Rose." Uncle Otis paused until Rose joined them.

Mrs. Ruckert stood up. "Otis, we must thank you for all you've done for Clifford."

Uncle Otis smiled. "He'll be a fine sea captain."

Mrs. Ruckert hugged Lainey, then held her at arm's length. "Oh, Lainey, you are lovely. We're so happy you're here. Clifford speaks of you often."

She turned to Miss Pritchard. "Juliet, you must know Lainey and Rose. Lainey is Otis and Edith's niece."

Miss Pritchard stood. "They're two of my finest students, and I'm so glad they're here tonight."

Lainey felt her face warm, and all responses left her. None of this made sense. Perhaps, she shouldn't have come. But it was too late now. She must face the truth and just move on. Truth was better than speculation. That sounded like Aunt Edith's voice inside her. She felt a slight smile arise within her, unsure if it reached her face.

Mrs. Ruckert took Miss Pritchard's hand. "We are so delighted Juliet obtained the teaching position on Washington Island. Even though we don't see her as often as we like, having our niece here is so wonderful to us. And with Clifford leaving, we hope to see her more often, especially when school lets out for the summer."

"I'm going to help out in the store." Miss Pritchard smiled.

Rose coughed. "So, Clifford is your cousin?"

"Why, yes. Didn't he tell you at the Valentine's Ball? It was so sweet of him to come and escort me. And it was a very wonderful party." She turned to her aunt. "Lainey and Rose did most of the decorations."

Lainey stared at Miss Pritchard, trying with great difficulty to unpurse her lips. She shook her head and looked down.

Clifford's voice startled her. "I tried, Juliet, to inform Miss Lainey that I was your cousin, but she turned and walked away. I've wondered since what I did to offend her."

Rose clapped her hands. "Oh, only that you were most obviously Miss Pritchard's new beau."

"What?" Miss Pritchard took only a moment to comprehend. "Oh, Lainey. I thought . . . oh, my. I'm so sorry. You and . . . I'm so sorry. I do think I'll get some punch. Aunt Shirley, would you like to join me?"

"Most definitely." Mrs. Ruckert and Miss Pritchard hurried off, their heads together and whispering all the way.

Rose looked at Lainey and Clifford and then turned to Uncle Otis. "Perhaps, I can dance with you first."

"Excellent idea." He held out his arm, and he and Rose walked to the dance floor.

Clifford grinned, then hung his head. "So, you thought Juliet and I . . ."

"I did. It did seem obvious."

"True, but I did try to tell you."

"And I wouldn't let you."

"You hurried off to dance with Tryg."

"I did. He's a good friend."

"But not your beau."

"No."

"I know I'm leaving, Lainey, and so you might change your mind; but at least for a while, may I have the privilege of being your beau?"

"Truly? After my rude behavior?"

"Yes, Lainey. Now can we dance?"

CHAPTER THIRTEEN

EARLY THE NEXT MORNING, UNCLE Otis hitched the horse to the surrey, while Aunt Edith and the girls fixed breakfast and packed some snacks. Today was the day they would visit the Eagle Bluff Lighthouse, where the five remaining Claflin boys lived. Julius was on Pilot with Marla, and Daniel managed a resort on the west side of Washington Island with his wife. All along the way, the girls pointed and commented at the homes, the towns, and the water views. Their excitement of being together without any responsibilities delighted them. Uncle Otis and Aunt Edith smiled and shook their heads at the girls' obvious joy while they carried on their own conversation.

Aunt Edith turned in her seat. "It brings me pleasure to hear your laughter. We've all held some grief over the years." Her face softened, and she tipped her chin. "Lainey, you've brought such joy to our lives. It truly hurt to let you go, but our hearts told us it was best. And now, here you are with such grace and stability." A tear ran down her cheek. "We are blessed. You are cared for and loved and still with us. And, Rose, what a Godsend. We thank God all the time for how He's provided."

Uncle Otis slapped the reins on Fresnel's rump. "That's so. That's so."

Rose looked at Lainey, then reached forward to take Aunt Edith's hand. "I've always felt that you're my aunt and uncle, too. So, thank you for letting me come."

Lainey smiled. "I don't regret one minute with you. I'm happy on Rock Island, but I would never be who I am without you."

Uncle Otis cleared his throat. "I think we've covered that. Let's get back to giggling and watching the scenery. We're coming to Ephraim right along the water up ahead. A great port and also a destination for those looking to flee city life for a while. The Moravians founded it. Moved the church here across the ice from Marinette town on the other side of the bay. Quite a feat. We'll be to the Claflins' within the hour."

Eagle Bluff Lighthouse stood high above the waters of the bay of Green Bay. As they approached, Lainey hugged herself and willed her mind to notice the beauty of the water and the islands beyond, rather than picturing the rough waters not far from here where her parents' ship went down. She'd never been this close to the spot, and it made her stomach hurt. Aunt Edith turned and caught Lainey's eye and nodded her head. Lainey knew her aunt relived the memory as well. Uncle Otis patted his wife's hand, and Rose did the same for Lainey.

Then, the holler greeted them. "Ma, Pa, they're here!"

The boys tumbled out the door like marbles out of a bag. The surrey contingent burst out laughing. Mrs. Claflin stepped out and brushed flour from her hands, wiping them on her apron as she walked to the wagon. "Otis and Edith, Lainey and Rose, we're so glad you've arrived." Mrs. Claflin's eyes lingered a moment on Rose.

Lainey noticed a sweet smile cross her face. When Mrs. Claflin turned to the Seversons, Lainey whispered to Rose, "She likes you already. Did you see that sweet smile when she looked at you?"

Rose's face reddened. "I did."

"Rose!" Niles voice lifted over all the others. "Come see the view and the steps to the water."

She hurried to join Niles at the top of the stone steps. He grasped her hand and pulled her after him. Lainey grinned as she watched them. Tryg strolled over. "They'll be gone a while. It's seventy-five steps down to the water."

"Really? I thought our fifty steps held the record. How in the world do you get your buckets up without spilling water? I don't think I could go that far." Lainey walked to the stone fence next to the steps and peered down.

"Our dad made us yokes to carry the water—like the yokes for oxen. Come on inside, and I'll show you. It makes it so much easier to do the water every day."

As they stepped into the lighthouse parlor, the sound of a piano greeted them. Tryg smiled. "That's Ambrose, the youngest. We have a baby grand piano, and Ma loves to play. She's the one who trained all of us to love music and play instruments."

"It's lovely. He plays so well." Lainey turned full circle, taking in the crown molding and the light gray flooring. The wall held paintings and instruments—a violin, a cello, and a guitar. Next to them hung what must be the yokes.

"You should have seen what we went through to get the piano here. Ma first purchased a grand piano. It came by boat, and we had to get it from the water level up the steps with pulleys and so many people. But it wouldn't fit in any of the doors. She had to send it back and get a baby grand. It was still so much work getting it in the house, but it sure has been nice."

Lainey shook her head. "Sounds like Mama getting her stove. I thought that was a big job, but not like the piano. I'll have to tell her your story. So, are those the yokes for getting water on the wall over there?"

Trygve picked up one of the wooden pieces and slipped it over his head. The extensions rested on his shoulders, and a cord hung from each end. Lainey picked up another one. Each measured a different length of wood and was smoothed and rounded to rest comfortably on each child.

"They're beautiful and so practical. Maybe Papa could make one of these for Carter."

"We've all outgrown the smallest three. Maybe Pa would give one to Carter." Trygve picked up one. "Do you think this one would fit him?"

"I think it would. That would be a wonderful gift."

"Lainey, you're not that big. See if this one fits you." He slipped it over Lainey's head just as Trygve's parents came into the room with Aunt Edith and Uncle Otis.

Mr. Claflin clapped his hands. "That's perfect, Lainey. Did you want to go down the steps and fetch some water?"

Lainey felt her face redden.

"I'm just kidding, Lainey. We never make our guests fetch water."

"But, Pa. Do you think we could let these two go back with her? She and Carter go down fifty steps every day for water."

"Tryg, that's a grand idea. We certainly don't need them now." Mr. Claflin looked to his wife.

"An excellent idea. These have helped the boys so much."

Uncle Otis smiled. "If you're sure, I'll go put them in the wagon now. This is so kind."

Lainey removed the yoke from her shoulders, and Mr. Claflin handed the other yoke to Uncle Otis. "Happy to have them in service."

"Tryg and Lainey, would you gather the rest of the boys and Rose? It's time for lunch."

Following lunch, Rose and Niles, along with Trygve and Lainey, went for a walk in the woods near the lighthouse.

"I'll show you where I've been doing some lumberjacking. It's just a short walk. We'll let the love birds go off by themselves." Tryg pointed at the couple holding hands walking down a side trail.

Lainey laughed. "So, Tryg, have you met a girl you like?"

"Oh, not like Niles and Rose." He turned and smiled. "Or like you and Clifford. It looked like you and he worked out some misunderstandings last night, and Niles filled in some of the story. Do you think you love him?"

Lainey stopped. "You know, I'm not sure. He makes me tongue-tied and so I can't think, but is that what love is? I don't see Niles and Rose all silly like that. I guess I don't really know."

"It's okay. We've got lots of time. There is a girl that came to visit with her family. It was last month. Her name is Kate. Her parents are lightkeepers on Cana Island. I do hope I see her again."

Lainey clapped her hands. "I knew you'd tell me if you found a girl you liked. I just knew you would."

"Here it is, Lainey. See these tall pines. They are mature enough to make the best furniture. Your uncle knows the company that might buy our wood. Pa has invited some lumberjacks to come and harvest a portion of this. He doesn't want to destroy the area but wants to take enough to help pay for our college. And he's asked them to train Phineas and me so we can be good lumberjacks if we want."

"What do you think? Do you love it?"

"I really like it. I love the outdoors. I'm not sure I want to go to college, and I'm not sure I want to be a lighthouse keeper. I've talked with Clifford a couple times about being a sea captain, but I'm not sure. Right now, this feels really good."

"I'm happy for you, Tryg, and I bet Kate will like all those muscles you're building. And you can always play your music." Lainey paused again to look up at the tops of the pines. "Wait, what is that chirping? Is that from squirrels or birds?"

"Not sure. Let's go see."

Lainey and Trygve followed the sound. It was a chirping, but almost a cheeping, and quite loud. Soon, they came to a small clearing, and two huge birds stood on the side of a tree just a foot or two off the ground.

"Such big birds with such a little chirp. I would expect them to have a caw or a more commanding sound than this sweet little chirp." Lainey chuckled and moved closer.

"They're pileated woodpeckers, but I was unaware of their sound. I usually hear them tearing a tree apart with their beaks. Their cheep is pretty dainty."

One bird hopped to the ground and hopped toward another tree. Lainey laughed. "It hops, like a rabbit. It hops! It doesn't walk like a seagull or a robin."

Lainey leaned forward. "Mr. Bird, you are so big, but you hop and chirp like a little thing. You make me laugh."

"Don't get too close, Lainey. They may have babies near."

Just then, the bird that remained on the tree flew with its three-foot wing span right at Lainey. She jumped and screamed as the bird missed her by about a foot. Almost immediately, she heard its caw, caw, caw. The bird repeated its caw several times.

Trygve doubled over in laughter. "I guess he is laughing at you now. That's hilarious. I think he tired of you making fun and got right back at you."

"Oh, he did! Let's leave them be." Lainey and Tryg ran all the way back to the lighthouse and fell on the ground still laughing.

The next day, Lainey, Rose, and Aunt Edith met with Clifford and his parents for lunch in their stylish little home atop Ruckert's Supply Store. Rose and Edith stayed to visit with Mrs. Ruckert while Lainey and Clifford walked to the shore and sat on a rock near the water. The gentleness of the lapping water relaxed Lainey, yet all her senses were on alert. When Clifford took her hand in his, she gasped.

"Is this all right? Are you okay?"

Clifford's smile lit up his whole face, and she found, once again, that she could only stare. She managed a nod and allowed herself to take in the smooth roughness of his hand. It felt so strong. She'd held his hand when dancing, but this was different. This was holding hands, just the two of them.

"I'm really glad to have this time alone with you." Clifford squeezed her hand. "I know I'll be leaving soon. Our first voyage should last about three weeks. Perhaps, you can come to visit your aunt and uncle again when I get back. Or maybe I can get out to Rock Island."

Lainey nodded. "I would like that. But I might still be on Washington Island with Rose to finish the school year. Mama thinks it would be better to have Miss Pritchard teach me rather than her trying to with the baby." She grinned. "I mean, Juliet—your love."

Clifford smiled. "I'm no longer her beau. I'm interested in someone else now."

"Oh, so fickle. I'm not sure I should see you." Lainey winked.

Clifford pulled her hand to his lips and kissed it lightly. "I know, but I hope you will."

They sat in silence for a few minutes. Lainey glanced over at Clifford. "You know I'll miss you. Promise me you'll be careful and pay attention to the weather." She looked down.

Clifford lifted her chin with his other hand. "I promise, Lainey. I'll be careful, and I will come back."

CHAPTER FOURTEEN

THE GALE BLEW HARD. THE seas ran high. Clifford turned into the wind to stop the danger of waves hitting the vessel broadside. At least, he didn't have following seas, but the track could take them severely off course. He peered through the dark and rain for any range lights. The sky had been so clear just an hour earlier. The wind and waves rose suddenly, accompanied by the pelting rain. Great Lakes squalls rang with danger. He recalled talking weather with Lainey. She filled his thoughts so much lately, but now he needed to focus on the course.

"It's a nor'easter, Cliff. Worse kind." Captain Hank joined him in the steering house. "I was going to bring you a meal, but it'll have to wait with this gale."

"I know. Are you able to perform depth checks?"

"It's rocking and rolling, but I can make sure we still have a good draw. As long as we have a few feet below us, we can manage." Hank heaved himself against the driving wind and torrent of rain as he exited the steering house.

It had been a good trip thus far. Captain Hank mentioned often how pleased he was with Clifford's abilities on a boat. Each day, he had Clifford pilot the boat, utilizing and giving him practice at every time of day and night and in various conditions. This weather threatened their safety the most.

They'd traveled from Newport Town through the straits of Mackinac dropping off a load of lumber at Mackinac Island. They then traversed the length of Lake Huron to Detroit to deliver the rest of the lumber. In Detroit, they took on furniture to be delivered to Mackinac Island and to Sturgeon Bay. Every lighthouse they passed, they marked on the chart, and Clifford pictured Lainey standing on the galleries waving to him. Somehow, that girl had stolen his heart without him even realizing it until she had shunned him at the Valentine's party. That was so confusing and exasperating. But then it got straightened out just before he left. Thankfulness filled his being. But he tightened his grip on the ship's wheel. The winds were increasing, making maintaining his course a difficult feat.

Captain Hank returned. "So far, so good, but we're drifting into an area rife with shoals. Don't see range lights, only some fog rolling in."

"Hear any fog horns?"

"Not yet, but the last lighthouse we passed was the Sturgeon Point Lighthouse, just north of Harrisville. The charts reveal a large reef that extends out a mile and a half from that point. I feared these blasted winds might take us into it. I'm sure we were closer than we should be. I believe we've moved north of there; but there are more reefs all along this shoreline, and the winds are pushing us hard toward shore. The retreating waves can create a battering ram to push us back out. Hold her as steady as you can while I try to calculate how hard the seas are running in both directions. Then I'll take the wheel. We can spell each other."

The crunch surprised them both. The ship lurched, and both men stumbled. Hank recovered and ran out of the pilot house to assess any damage. Due to the shallowness of the shoal and the fierceness of the wind, a huge wave swept over the bow and then retreated.

Clifford gathered himself after the initial strike on the shoal and peered through the window to determine the direction to steer. His pulse quickened, and sweat rolled down his face. His training prepared him for this. Captain Hank would holler locations and depths to him, and hopefully, they and the ship would be saved. He heard Hank's yell and turned his head. Expecting to see Hank indicate a direction, he instead saw Hank flailing to grab the rail. Hank's head disappeared over the side. Grabbing the life ring, Clifford ran out ready to rescue Hank but slipped. His head struck the deck, and the subsequent fall into the waves did not enter his consciousness. He stirred awake enough to realize the waves had carried him away. He fought to stay conscious and above the waves but knew he was losing the battle.

A few weeks had passed since Lainey had said her goodbyes to Clifford. The girls returned from their school day and set themselves to assisting Lainey's parents, Carter, and Tina for the return to Rock Island. The May flowers would soon poke their fronds up from the soil, and warmer winds already blew across the lake. The ice was gone, so Mr. Hanson would transport them on the grocery boat. He would then begin his regular routes delivering necessities to the various islands and ports around Washington Island. He often stopped in Newport Town to get more supplies and returned with news.

Lainey, Rose, and Samuel went with the family for the weekend to help them settle in. They had planned to go in early April, but both Tina and Carter had taken bad colds. They were now returned to health and ready to go. Lainey knew she'd miss them; but she only had a few weeks left of school, and this choice worked best.

Sunday afternoon, the Engelsons were once again settled and the lighthouse fully operational. Lainey held Tina and allowed a few tears to roll down her cheek as she said goodbye. "I know it's only a short time, but I miss you already."

Mama took Tina. "Be sure to let us know when Clifford returns. We're as eager as you to hear all about his first venture on the lakes." She winked. "Well, almost as eager as you."

Papa and Carter gave the girls each a hug and shook hands with Samuel. "We'll see you all soon."

Lainey and Rose were quiet on the return trip. Lainey wondered what kind of adventure Clifford was having and prayed for his safety. Questions about how serious their relationship might be flew around her mind like the gulls flying in the clear skies above her. The blues and hues of the water filtered through her heart like flour through a sieve. The torments of life and fears for those she loved swept away, and joy filled her heart for the future. Pastor Gunnlerson had given a verse the week before that stuck with her. Jeremiah 29:11 says, "'For I know the plans I have for you,' declares the LORD, 'plans to prosper you and not to harm you, plans to give you hope and a future.'" It was like an anchor to her wonderings. Was Clifford in that future?

"If you girls aren't asleep, I have quite a tale for you." Rose's dad turned from his stance of steering the boat.

Samuel laughed. "Sleeping or daydreaming about Clifford and Niles. I've never heard them this quiet."

Rose reached out and playfully slapped Samuel's arm. "Just you wait, Sam. I've seen some girls looking at you. You'll be doing some daydreaming soon. But do tell us your tale, Papa."

"Well, this report came from Sturgeon Bay. They purchased a barge from the Michigan Car Ferry Barge Company that had been used to carry rail cars from Pestigo, Wisconsin, to Chicago. Sturgeon Bay uses it to carry pulpwood and bulk freights. They were recently traveling north in Lake Huron delivering hundreds of crates of live chickens to Mackinac Island. A storm blew up near Alpena, and they ran onto a reef near Thunder Bay's southern point. The barge began breaking up, so the crew opened as many crates as they could before they had to get away so the chickens wouldn't drown. Apparently, they've received reports that a great many live chickens, even a few of the crates, arrived on Thunder Bay Island and have made for great meals for all the islanders."

"No one was hurt?" Lainey wrung her hands.

"No, dear one, even most of the chickens survived." Mr. Hanson reached over and patted Lainey's hands.

Samuel rolled his eyes. "Sounds like the chickens didn't survive for long."

Rose giggled. "What a surprise for the islanders. Must have been like manna from Heaven. Or an invasion. Papa, where is Thunder Bay?"

"Near Alpena in Lake Huron, about as far north as we are here in Lake Michigan."

"I think Niles said his mother grew up in Alpena. She probably knows many of those that have been having Sunday dinner every day for a while. I can't wait to ask Niles if he's heard this story."

"He probably has. I guess everyone from Sturgeon Bay on north is telling the story—enjoying the humor, even though Sturgeon Bay lost a barge. Well, we're here. I'll drop you off and run a few routes. Tell your ma I'll be just a little late for dinner. Wish we had some of those chickens."

Lainey thanked Mr. Hanson for the ride. The three young people hurried to the Hanson home to relay the chicken story. Mrs. Hanson made tea for all, and Lainey offered to serve. She had just set down the teapot and picked up her cup when a knock came at the door.

Rose set her cup down and stood. "I'll get it."

The door opened, and Rose turned back. "Lainey."

Lainey looked up, and in the doorway stood Uncle Otis. His face was somber. Lainey's cup tumbled to the floor and shattered, but no one moved.

Uncle Otis stepped through the doorway without taking his eyes off Lainey.

"What is it, Uncle Otis? Who is it? Aunt Edith? Is she okay?" She felt as if she was choking.

"She's fine." Uncle Otis cleared his throat. "It's Clifford."

Lainey sank to the chair. She could utter no words. She had thought her future was bright.

"Please, sit down, Otis. Tell us what has happened." Mrs. Hanson reached over and took Lainey's hand.

Rose sat on the arm of Lainey's chair and put her arm around her.

"The *Horowitz* sank in a fierce gale in Lake Huron. They recovered most of the crew, but Clifford is missing."

Lainey rose and walked to the window. "It can't be. We hardly had time to . . . to . . . " She felt a hand on her shoulder. It must be Uncle

Otis, though she didn't hear his footsteps. She glanced back, and no one was there; yet the sensation of a hand resting on her shoulder remained. *I'll get you through this, just like everything else, but Clifford will survive. Don't be afraid. Your future is bright.*

Lainey staggered to the table. Had God spoken to her? She'd heard His voice before whenever times were tough. What was it Pastor Gunnlerson had said? "If you hear God's voice, know you'll need it to get through, so hang on to it."

The chair seemed to reach up and catch her. Rose's voice penetrated the cloud. "Girl, you're as white as a sheet. I'm sure Clifford will be found. He's a survivor. Remember the squall at Christmas. Let's go into the bedroom. Perhaps you should lie down for a few minutes."

"Yes, do that. Otis, let me get you a bowl of soup." Mrs. Hanson went to the stove.

Lainey sat on the bed next to her friend. "Rose, he will survive. I think God just told me." Lainey related word for word what she had heard within and what Pastor Gunnlerson had said.

"Then, let's write it down. We need to remember and keep praying for him. But with . . . " Rose paused, and a quirky smile played on her lips as she took a piece of paper from the night stand. "With confidence. I don't think I've ever thought of it that way. I mean, I'm confident that God is over all and loves us, but . . . "

"I know. We need to pray with confidence and tenacity." Lainey took the piece of paper and wrote the words.

She stood, and Rose gathered her in her arms. "I think you and Clifford are meant to be together, so we'll pray he's found soon."

Lainey stepped back and wiped the tear straying down her cheek. "I'm beginning to think so, too, but do you think he feels that way?"

"Lainey, I've watched him look at you. It's almost as bad as the first time you saw him. That was indeed the funniest thing I've ever seen. You stared and couldn't talk or move."

"I embraced being smitten." Lainey chuckled.

"Oh, you did. You were love-struck." Rose covered her mouth with her hand and closed her eyes. After composing herself, she locked eyes with Lainey, and they both doubled over with laughter. "And when he came for Christmas, you were so dumbfounded. And then the look on his face when you turned from him at the Valentine's Ball. That was so confusing."

"It was, but now, after finding that he truly wants to spend time with me . . . and he's lost at sea—well, the lakes. Either way, it's bad. Oh, Rose, whatever will I do?" Lainey sat down and stared at her hands.

Rose knelt in front of her. "Lainey, we're going to trust that you heard from God." She tapped the paper. "We're going to expect that Clifford will return safely."

"Oh, Rose." Lainey grabbed her friend and hugged her.

With renewed confidence and composure, the girls rejoined the grownups.

Mrs. Hanson stood. "Lainey, as soon as Rasmus returns, he can return you and Otis to the mainland. You should be with your aunt and uncle and be near Clifford's parents. Otis, does Miss Pritchard know yet?"

Uncle Otis shook his head. "I had a friend bring me here directly. Lainey and I can return with him, but I should go now and tell Miss Pritchard. Perhaps, Rasmus could let the Engelsons on Rock know."

Lainey felt her resolve begin to waver, but she shook off the melancholy that threatened to overwhelm her. "Please, give me a few minutes, Uncle. I'll get my things together and go with you to tell Miss Pritchard."

Mrs. Hanson dished up another bowl of soup. "Otis, get your friend in the boat. He can eat while you go tell Miss Pritchard."

"I'll drive you in the wagon." Rose left to hitch the horse to the wagon while Lainey quickly threw her belongings into a small chest.

Thinking came hard, but she forced herself to move. She knew this feeling too well, and she also knew she must put one step in front of the other and live.

The ride to Miss Pritchard's small cottage nestled in the woods a mile from the school was quiet. Uncle Otis sat with his arm around Lainey. She rested her head on his shoulder and fought the grief that attempted to take control of her being. Rose glanced at her every minute or two and offered a sad smile but said nothing.

Miss Pritchard stepped out her door with a big smile. "Oh, my, what a surprise. What brings you all . . . " Her words trailed off. "What happened?" Her hands flew to her face. "Lainey . . . Rose . . . Mr. Severson, please tell me."

Rose found her voice first. "It's Clifford. His ship went down, and he's missing. They found the rest of the crew, but not him."

Miss Pritchard flew to Lainey's side. "Oh, Lainey. Oh, Lainey." The tears rolled down her face. "You know, we are going to pray. Right now, we're going to pray." She grabbed Lainey and Uncle Otis' hands and nodded to Rose. "Dear Lord, we call on Your name and ask You to rescue Clifford. Wherever he is, please keep him safe and bring him home. Thank You, Lord."

Lainey climbed out of the wagon, almost falling on the ground. Her chest heaved as she and Miss Pritchard embraced for a long minute.

Uncle Otis cleared his throat. "Juliet, would you like to accompany Lainey and me to the mainland so you can be with your family? I'm sure the students will survive for a few days."

Rose stepped down from the wagon. "I can handle the students for a couple days. You know my goal is to be a teacher. I think it would be good if you went to be with your aunt and uncle."

Miss Pritchard nodded. "Yes, I should go. I just completed the plans for this week. Rose, are you sure?"

"I am. Can I help you get your things together? Lainey and Uncle Otis are leaving as soon as we get back to our place."

The day had turned to dark by the time Lainey, Miss Pritchard, and Uncle Otis arrived in Newport Town. Lainey felt a sad darkness descend upon her as they climbed from the boat and walked to the Severson home. Two dockhands offered to carry the chests belonging to the young women.

Aunt Edith rose from her seat on the porch. She said not a word but simply embraced Lainey and reached out a hand to Miss Pritchard. "I have stew ready. Juliet, you can stay here tonight. We'll go to your aunt and uncle's store early tomorrow. Lainey?" She lifted her niece's chin with her finger. "I believe they'll find him. Let's stay strong on the side of hope."

Lainey smiled. "Yes, we must. Thank you."

CHAPTER FIFTEEN

LAINEY AWOKE AT DAWN AND struggled to recall where she lay in bed. Her fingers rolled over the rose-bud pattern on her quilt. For a moment, she was back on Pilot Island, realizing her parents would never return. Present day pressed into her mind, and she sat up. Clifford was missing.

She dressed and walked to the dock in Newport Town. It buzzed already with shipment deliveries and arrivals. Men secured lines, and wagons loaded with lumber were maneuvered with great care and speed. Horses snorted and strained as they pulled the heavy cargo to and fro. Lainey dodged yelling and focused men and watched her steps as stray logs and horse droppings, though not abundant, were present. She picked her way to the end of the dock, where for the moment, no ship was tied awaiting its cargo.

She wrapped her arms around a piling and sighed. The air filled with scents of hard work. Sweat. Fishing boats readied for the day near her, still strong with fish smell from the previous day's haul. The fragrance of oak and pine wood combined with the stench of fuel. And through it all, the peaceful, sweet smell of fresh water wafted over her. She gazed at the rocks several feet below her through the shimmering liquid of Lake Michigan. How she loved it. She breathed it in. It was part of her. She was part of it. She never wanted to be far from the water.

Where could Clifford be? Would he return? Could she survive without him? She'd survived so much loss, but . . . Clifford? "Clifford, where are you? Come back to me. I think . . . I think I love you."

The tears tracked down her face and blurred her eyes. She pondered her statement. Love? Did she love him? Her mind floated back to the first time she saw him walking toward her in the cherry orchard. He captured her heart then and there without even knowing it. As he sauntered carefree with his blond hair drifting into his eyes, his image was emblazoned in her thoughts. But love?

Tryg was a good friend. She was comfortable with him, but that was it. She wondered if Tryg knew Clifford was missing. The news had probably reached him. He would worry about her, and his family would pray for Clifford. She struggled to recall the words she felt God speak to her. They jumbled inside her. Thankfulness rose within her that she'd written it down. "God, what can I do? I think I love him. Please bring him back."

A ship came into her gaze, and she realized it would dock where she stood. Lainey turned and made her way back through workers, horses, and wagons. This time, men stopped and tipped their hats. Perhaps they heard her prayer. Perhaps they knew Clifford.

Lainey returned in time for breakfast. Uncle Otis had already hitched Fresnel to the surrey, and Miss Pritchard chatted with Aunt Edith. Aunt Edith shook her head when Uncle Otis asked her to accompany them. Too much grief. Lainey hugged her aunt and climbed into the surrey.

Uncle Otis squeezed her hand tightly as they arrived at the Ruckerts' store. Lainey sighed deeply and nodded to Miss Pritchard before climbing down. The young women followed Uncle Otis into the store. Mr. Ruckert swept the floor. He glanced up and smiled sadly at Uncle Otis. Then his eyes found Lainey and Miss Pritchard. Lainey watched surprise, pleasure, and then sadness play across his face.

Uncle Otis laid a hand on his shoulder. "Any word about Clifford?"

Mr. Ruckert looked down. "Well, my friend, they found Hank, his captain, floating in the water. He was dead."

Lainey gasped. She felt her knees start to give way but steadied herself by placing her hand on the counter. She'd just met Captain Hank at Clifford's going-away party.

Otis frowned. "I'd heard the rest of the crew were found."

"Yes, the cook, the engine man, and one other were found alive. Just the one body—Hank." Mr. Ruckert shook his head. "Hank was a good man, a good friend." He looked up. "But we need to change the subject. His mama is beside herself, and I hear her coming down the stairs."

"Shirley." Uncle Otis walked over to Mrs. Ruckert. "You know, there's always hope. Edith would love to visit if you're up for it."

"Thank you, Otis." Her smile was strained. "You've been such a help to our family. We're praying for good news. I don't know what we'd do if . . . without . . . " She almost sank to the floor, but Uncle Otis caught her.

"Now, now, Shirley, just sit a minute." He guided her to a chair. "We are praying for the best. You have a strong, capable son, who will use his wits and call upon the Lord. And we brought you the next best news. Juliet and Lainey are here."

"Oh, girls . . . " Mrs. Ruckert stood and gathered both girls into her arms. With teary eyes, she stood back. "Are you each . . . okay?" She pursed her lips and wiped her eyes. "Not knowing—it's the worst."

"Aunt Shirley, we're praying, and I'm . . . well . . . I'm sure they'll find him." Miss Pritchard paused and gulped. "Alive, Aunt Shirley. They'll find him alive."

"Thank you, dear girl; your encouragement blesses me. Lainey, are you . . . okay?" A tear slid down Mrs. Ruckert's face.

Lainey twisted her fingers and looked down. "I haven't told anyone this, except Rose." She glanced at her uncle. "But when Uncle Otis came to the Hansons' home to tell me, I felt like . . . well, inside, it seemed God spoke to me that Clifford would survive this."

Mrs. Ruckert sat down and sighed. "That's good news, Lainey. I needed to hear that, and I need to believe it. I've prayed so much and probably worried more. Thank you for sharing with us. May it be soon that he returns home to us."

Lainey strolled along the shore of Lake Michigan, shoes in hand. She pulled up her skirts and dipped her feet in the lapping water. The breeze flowing across the water lifted the stray hairs not pinned up on her head. The sand welcomed her feet, but held on too long, making the walk slow.

That was all right. Her heavy heart prevented a speedy walk. She sat on a bank of sand and gazed across the lake she loved. The waves slightly crested with just a bit of white cap. The blues varied in a panorama of color that spoke peace to her troubled soul.

Where is he, Lord? Lainey gazed toward the horizon. One cloud stood far in the distance above the lake. *Is he under that cloud? Are You giving him shade? Is he hurt? Did he obtain a life preserver? Is he conscious? Or is he trapped in the wreckage? Whatever would I do if he doesn't . . . what if?* Lainey lowered her head to her hands and wept.

She'd been orphaned, and yet, besides her aunt and uncle, she'd been given parents and a family. Perhaps life could truly go on if Clifford was lost. She choked just thinking of it. She stared out at the water. It soothed her.

What did I tell you? I will return him to you. He will survive.

That must be the Lord's voice. Can it be true? The breeze swirled around her, and the rippling waves gurgled. Pastor Gunnlerson had said the Holy Spirit is like a wind. He said that when the Holy Spirit came, it was like tongues of fire. Right now, she felt on fire inside. Is that what the Holy Spirit and the Lord's voice did? Blew like a wind and set her insides aflame? Her despair seemed to leave like the retreating waves that touched the shoreline then scurried backward and disappeared.

Two weeks had passed since hearing of Clifford's disappearance. The rescue station housing the U.S. LifeSaving Service at Sturgeon Point on Michigan's Lake Huron shore had searched every day for over a week but had ceased their rescue mission. They were the ones who had retrieved the crew of Clifford's ship and found Captain Hank's body.

Lainey remained with Uncle Otis and Aunt Edith. She'd visited with Clifford's parents several times. Often, she and Mrs. Ruckert sat holding hands and praying for his safe return. It was so hard hearing that the search for Clifford had been suspended, but still they clung to the words of the Lord that Lainey had heard. Miss Pritchard had returned to school after three days with Clifford's parents but had returned each weekend, bringing work for Lainey to stay current with her studies and to spend time with family.

Tryg and two of his brothers came to visit one day. He gave her a hug and told her his family prayed daily for the rescue and survival of Clifford. Tryg was such a good friend. Phineas and Walter made her laugh and forget the ever-present grief that attempted to overtake her. They took her in their wagon to Michelson's General Store in Sister Bay to get ice cream.

The boys ordered second helpings of ice cream, but Lainey walked the little path to the docks extending into the bay of Green Bay. The water mesmerized her. How she loved gazing into the clear, shallow depths. Through the lens of ever-moving seas, she viewed the moss-covered rocks, the scattered stones on the bottom, the accordion-pleated sandy floor of the lake. The reeds that blew gently in the wind seemed to dance to the music of the breeze. *A bruised reed, I will not break.* She pondered the thought. She knew it was from the Bible. She had broken reeds herself and tossed them back in the water. She had picked up dried reeds on the beach and banks and played with them, breaking them more. Yet Jesus, Who could calm the seas with His voice, said He would not break a bruised reed. Such amazing care. She still wondered where His voice and His care were when the seas took her parents boat. Still, He had kept Lainey safe. Lainey sighed. So much she didn't understand, but strong within her dwelt the intense belief that life was good, and people should live happy and with purpose. She would do that.

Lainey turned as she heard Tryg's voice calling her. The boys needed to return her and then get back to their lighthouse. Though her heart still held a heaviness, Lainey laughed with the boys all the way back to Uncle Otis and Aunt Edith's home. She would see the good in life, no matter the circumstances.

Aunt Edith had chicken pot pie and applesauce cake waiting for them and sent several pot pies and another whole cake home with the boys.

The next morning, Lainey awoke to the realization that she should return to Washington Island and school. She needed to finish the school year and return to Rock Island. Her insides jumbled at the thought that many probably thought Clifford was lost. Too much time had gone by. How could he survive? She must go on. But first, she needed to walk along the beach again.

What would she do without Clifford? Perhaps marry Tryg. She shook her head. Tryg was like a brother and had his eyes on Kate at the Cana Lighthouse. Lainey smiled. She hoped it worked out for the two of them. But what would she do? She loved being a lighthouse keeper, but would she want to live somewhere else in order to do that? Was Aunt Edith right—that she had too much of the wanderlust of her mother to stay put? Perhaps. Could she leave the Door Islands? These were now her roots. Her branches and the fruit of her life arose from these islands and the people. Wherever life took her, she would have to come back. Still, the thought of travel to cities and lands near and far drew her. Perhaps she could stay and become a teacher. That was what Rose wanted to do. Rose. Would she marry Niles? Lainey laughed out loud. She'd be surprised if they didn't marry. And they might leave to become lighthouse keepers. Or did Niles want to be a lumberjack? Oh, it was too much to consider. Rose leaving here? What a constant friend she'd been. Still was. The conflict within of dreams and worries and realities swirled.

Place all your cares in My hands.

Yes, Lord, that was the verse Mama had on the wall on Rock Island: "Casting all your care on Him, for He cares for you."

Lainey fell to her knees. "God, You know my thoughts, my cares, my worries, my fears. I don't know the future. I feel pulled in so many directions and yet tethered to these islands. I want to roam, and I want to stay. Will You help me? Show me the way? And most of all, bring Clifford back safely." She tasted the salt of her tears. Her view became blurry. A soft breeze wafted over her. The slightly fishy and fresh scent of the water surrounded her. Lifting her eyes, she saw the lake had settled to the slightest ripple, and the sparkles of sunlight danced everywhere on the surface.

Be not afraid. Launch into the deep. I will walk with you and guide you.

The voice within was strong yet peaceful. Lainey smiled. All would be well. She could almost feel Uncle Otis' arms around her. She still didn't know her future but somehow knew the Voice was true. All would be well.

Perhaps she should be a writer and tell stories of life in the Door Islands. She did love making up little stories for Carter and Tina and the Hanson children. She should write them down. The thought pleased her.

She stood and brushed the sand from her skirts. She wiped her eyes with her handkerchief and walked back to the home of her uncle and aunt. It was time to prepare to return to Washington Island and school.

"Elaina, Elaina, please wake up."

The fog in her mind lifted. Her aunt's voice penetrated the haze. Morning. She needed to return to the island today. She shouldn't have stayed up so late getting everything ready to go and thinking about and praying for Clifford.

"They found him, Elaina. Clifford is found!"

Lainey's eyes popped open. Was she dreaming? Did Aunt Edith say they found him? She sat up. "He's alive! Or . . . found, but they found him—how?" She braced herself for the news.

"He's okay. At least, he'll be okay."

Fully awake, Lainey threw her legs out of the bed and stood. She hugged Aunt Edith and cried.

"Listen, Elaina, listen. He washed up on Thunder Bay Island in Lake Huron, the place where all the chickens were." A sly smile crossed Aunt Edith's face. "Residents were combing the beach to gather all the chickens and found Clifford unconscious. He was taken to a home where they cared for him. He finally came to, so they could send word."

Lainey sat down and wept. As she pondered Aunt Edith's words, she looked up and giggled. "The chickens that were like manna to those people caused them to find Clifford?"

Aunt Edith sat next to Lainey on the bed and took her hand. "Yes, chickens." Her shoulders started to shake, and Lainey leaned against her arm and covered her mouth. Soon, they both shook with laughter, while tears ran down their faces.

Uncle Otis walked in. "Okay, I'll join you in this. I knew I couldn't come in at first because I laughed as soon as I heard it. I should've rejoiced, but I laughed. Forgive me, Lainey."

Lainey reached out a hand to grasp his and continued laughing.

After a few minutes, they settled and wiped the tears coursing down their faces.

"Let's pray." The three held hands while Uncle Otis led them in a prayer of thanksgiving. "Dear Lord, we rejoice that Clifford has been found alive. Give him safe travel home and provide a good recovery for him. And we love that those chickens helped him be found."

"Unpack your things, Lainey. They think he'll be here the day after tomorrow. A ship passed by the day he awoke, so they sent the message he was found and that he would follow in two or three days. They wanted to make sure he ate and gained some strength before allowing him to leave. He had no memory loss but was weak."

He was coming home. Clifford was coming home. Lainey could hardly believe it.

CHAPTER SIXTEEN

LAINEY STEPPED INTO THE ROOM. The air was flavored with the antiseptic and oils used to sooth his wounds. It slightly stung her eyes, but the tears were already present. Her heart pounded, and her breath came in short gasps. He was beautiful and fragile at the same time. His blond locks covered his forehead and splayed out across the pillow. *He'll need a haircut.* His breathing was deep and steady, but even near death, he took her breath away. She stared and dreamed. Had God said Clifford was for her? Or just that he'd survive? Could she bear just being friends? She recalled the feelings of despair when it appeared he was Miss Pritchard's beau, the utter devastation upon hearing of his shipwreck and subsequent disappearance. Could it be love or just over-reaction?

A raspy voice. "Are you just going to stare? Do I look that bad?"

"Clifford, you're alive! I mean, you're awake. I missed you. I mean, I worried about you. Well, I prayed for you . . . "

"Lainey, sit down. It's so good to see you. I wondered if . . . I prayed . . . I'd see you again. I'm glad to see you." He coughed as he tried to sit up.

"Oh, don't try to move. You need to heal." She put her hand on his shoulder.

Clifford reached and grasped her hand. "Lainey."

"I'm here." She sat. The tears burst out and streamed down her face.

"Don't cry, Lainey. I'll be okay. They expect full recovery in a few weeks."

Lainey sniffed. "I'm so glad. But even if you weren't going to get well, I would lo—I mean, I would . . . I would always be here for you."

Clifford grinned and squeezed her hand. "I know God kept me alive, and I'm so sad about Hank. I saw him go overboard and tried to go after him, but I couldn't get to him. It was bad." Clifford coughed. "The waves poured over me, and soon, I couldn't even see the ship. I kept swallowing water and thought I might drown. But I heard your voice, Lainey. I heard you say, 'Clifford, come home to me.' I knew God brought your voice to me, and I fought to stay above the waves. It was hard. But I wanted to live, to come home to you. To you, Lainey."

Neither said a word for a few minutes. They simply gazed at one another and let the tears flow.

"I think I must have passed out, but then something bumped me. I couldn't quite open my eyes—I think they were swollen shut or something. I think I bumped my head trying to go after Hank. But then I determined I must be dreaming as I heard a chicken cluck. I tried to wake up and felt so confused. I felt another bump and heard the cluck again. I got my eyes open enough, and there was a wooden crate bumping me—and it had two chickens in it. Then I was sure I must be dreaming. Slowly, it all came back. The ship, the storm running us aground, Hank falling, and me trying to get him. I didn't have a lot of strength, but I grabbed onto the crate. The chickens pecked at me at first, but I tried to talk to them, and eventually, they settled down. The lake was calmer; but there were still big waves, and it took all my energy to hold on. I must have passed out again. The next thing I knew, someone was shaking me. I was on a tiny beach tucked into a cove of Thunder Bay Island.

And there next to me was the chicken crate, and those silly chickens were still alive. I think they may have been eaten by now, but they wouldn't give a lot of meat—maybe just good soup broth."

Lainey nodded. "We heard about the barge from Sturgeon Bay that broke apart near Thunder Bay Island. It carried dozens of crates of chickens bound for Mackinac Island from Detroit. They freed as many chickens as they could. Thunder Bay Island had manna from Heaven."

"Yes, they told me. And they fixed me a lot of chicken soup, and I was in and out of consciousness and couldn't tell them who I was for days. I guess several on the island knew I was missing, but this was a remote spot where only one family lived and kept to themselves. They nursed me back to health, and once I was awake enough to explain who I was and what had happened, they walked to town to tell someone. It took a couple days after that to get my strength back again so I could travel. But once I was fully awake, I insisted on coming home. To you, Lainey. I knew I needed to come home *for* my parents, but I came home *to* you."

Lainey smiled, but no words came.

"I dreamed of you, of us, Lainey. I kept seeing your face. I kept hearing you telling me to come home, asking God to keep me alive. Thank you, Lainey."

Lainey squeezed her eyes closed and bit her lip. "Clifford, that's what I did. I've prayed and thought of you all day, every day. I'm . . . I'm so . . . thankful you returned. I came to stay with Aunt Edith and Uncle Otis, so I could be here when you returned. Your mother suffered greatly. Will you go back to being a first mate?"

"Well, right now, I have no ship. I know my mother doesn't want me to go back. I can't imagine that it would happen again, but of course, it's not the safest job. I'm sure my uncle would let me work on the fishing boats, but I don't know."

"He has time to decide. Right now, we have to get him well." Lainey turned to see Mrs. Ruckert step into the room. "We're just so happy to have him safely home."

Lainey stood and embraced Clifford's mother. "Thank God, he's okay, and he's home."

"Yes, such relief. I made chicken soup." She smiled. "I'm sorry, Clifford. You're probably tired of chicken soup, but it's just what you need. Lainey, may I bring you a bowl as well? Please stay."

"I'd love to. May I help you bring it in?"

"No, Clifford looks stronger already, just being with you." She returned with two steaming bowls of soup and homemade bread. Mrs. Ruckert placed her hand on Lainey's shoulder. "You stay as long as you can. Clifford's father told your uncle that he'll take you back to their house when you and Clifford have had enough time." She left the room.

Clifford took a sip of the soup. "Lainey, I don't think I'll ever have enough time with you."

Lainey felt the redness creep up her neck to her cheeks. "This soup is hot." She fanned her face.

Clifford laughed.

He seemed to be getting better already.

Three days passed. Clifford grew stronger, and Lainey visited every day. She also took an hour or two working in the store, so

Clifford's mother could sit with him as well. Uncle Otis brought her each day, and Mr. Ruckert returned her each evening.

On the fourth day, Clifford desired to go for a walk. Going down the stairs to the main floor almost sapped his strength, but he sat for a few minutes and visited with the customers, who were delighted to see him getting stronger.

He and Lainey held hands as they walked the dirt path to the waters of the bay behind the store. They located the same big rock along the shoreline they sat on during an earlier visit and sat together. Lainey unwrapped the sandwiches she'd made, along with the apple slices. They ate in silence. The breeze from the bay wafted lightly over them, and the sweet, fishy fragrance of the water and boats hung in the air.

"I love the water, even though these very waters have taken so much from each of us."

Clifford nodded. "Me, too. My mother hopes to never let me go out there again, but I think perhaps I should. I can't live in fear."

"You're right. Fear's not helpful. I need to trust God to continue to take care of you and take care of me. I understand if you return to the water. Despite everything, I do love the water, and I—"

Clifford placed his arm around Lainey. "I love the water, too, Lainey, but I love you more." He leaned in and lightly kissed her lips.

All Lainey's strength left. Warmth encompassed her face, while chills ran up her spine. She laid her head on his shoulder, and let tears run down her face.

Clifford brought his hand to her face. When he contacted the tears, he released her. "Lainey, are you okay? Did I upset you?"

"No, no, I'm just so happy, because I'm pretty sure I love you, too."

"Just pretty sure?"

Lainey laughed. "No, no, I'm sure. I do love you, Clifford."

The two sat, Clifford's arm around her. She leaned into his shoulder and soaked in his warmth, his love. What a wondrous thing, this love. She never would have imagined it, although she saw great love between her new parents and had wondered if she would ever share such love with someone. Their love stood steady and firm and fun. She remembered sweet love between her first parents. They always expressed such happiness to be together, no matter what they did, always hugging and kissing. And she saw a steadfast love between Aunt Edith and Uncle Otis. They didn't outwardly show love in affectionate ways, but they were so faithful to do everything needed for each other. Lainey mused as to whether she and Clifford's love would continue into a marriage that held all the ways of love she'd seen in those closest to her.

Clifford sat straighter and pulled his arm from around her so he could look her in the eyes. "Lainey, I've thought about this a lot since I came to after the shipwreck. I'm prepared to return, since it looks like I'll have a full recovery." He lifted her hand and kissed it. "I'm also prepared to give it up if you would prefer it. I don't quite know what I'd do; but I could fish with my uncle, and I'm sure my parents would find a place for me in the store."

Lainey placed a finger on his lips. "Clifford, no. I cannot stand in the way of your calling, your training . . . I know being a sea captain is your dream. You need to do this. You're good at it."

Clifford hung his head. "I'm not so sure that I'm good at it. I let us run aground, and I couldn't save Hank. Not a very good reputation."

"No one thinks that, Clifford. Storms and gales come. You did your best and sacrificed yourself to try to help Hank. That's why you need to go back out there when you're able. You don't want to always wonder if you could have done it."

"I'm not sure anyone will want to hire me."

Lainey smiled. "You're a survivor. You'll have a ship."

Clifford took Lainey's hand again. "I'd like that, but more than anything, I want you in my life."

Lainey sighed. "I want nothing more, Clifford."

The two stood and returned to the store holding hands. Mrs. Ruckert glanced up as they entered the store and smiled. "You both look better. In fact, Lainey, you're glowing." She tipped her head and studied the couple.

Lainey felt the blush creep up her face and looked down. Then she looked up at Clifford, and the two burst out laughing.

"We're good, Mother. I'm feeling stronger. Shall I bring in some supplies?"

"Not yet, but, Lainey, could you assist me in the kitchen while Mr. Ruckert closes up the store? Clifford, you could help your dad."

Lainey followed her up the stairs and into the kitchen. She handed Lainey a spoon. "Could you stir the gravy while I mash the potatoes?"

Lainey lightly whisked the gravy that had been simmering on the stove. "Mrs. Ruckert, I know you don't want Clifford to return to the lakes."

Mrs. Ruckert paused and turned to Lainey. "I'm so scared for him. I didn't want him to go in the first place. Tell me you want him to stay on land."

Lainey pursed her lips before speaking. "Mrs. Ruckert, I think he needs to return."

Mrs. Ruckert sighed as her shoulders sagged.

Lainey placed a hand on her arm. "I remember the fear that en-gulfed me when my parents died and when Uncle Otis broke his leg. And, of course, when I heard that Clifford was missing. But in all that, I can't live in fear. God didn't make us for that. Clifford needs to fulfill his calling. If he finds out that it isn't meant to be long term, he'll know it's the right thing to stay here; but he can't stay here out of fear."

A tear tracked down Mrs. Ruckert's face, and she gathered Lainey into her arms. "You have wonderful wisdom for a young woman. Thank you. I don't want him to go, but I'll try not to stand in his way."

A few days later, Lainey returned to Washington Island to take her tests. She'd been able to do much of her work while at her aunt and uncle's. A friend of Uncle Otis gave Lainey an early morning boat ride to the Hansons' home. Lainey delighted to see the Hansons again and found herself longing to see her parents on Rock island.

Shortly thereafter, she and Rose took the wagon to the schoolhouse.

"Rose, are you still happy with your plan to be a teacher?" The morning haze lifted from the greening trees. New leaves unfolded in a canopy of light green across the island. The clip-clop of the horse's hooves was the only sound in the sweet-smelling late spring air.

"I do. I've thought and prayed about it. When I filled in for Miss Pritchard, working with the children was so rewarding. I think it's what I'll love."

Lainey smiled. "Speaking of love, how are things with Niles?"

Rose blushed. "We don't see each other too often, but I think it might be love." She looked over to Lainey. "How's Clifford—and what about you two?"

Lainey took a deep breath. "He's almost recovered. He'll probably be back out on the lakes this summer. But . . . Rose, he told me he loved me."

Rose pulled up the reins. She stood and almost picked Lainey up from the seat. She held her at arm's length and yelled, "Oh, Lainey! That is the most exciting news I've ever heard!" She hugged her so tightly, they almost tipped out of the wagon.

Laughing and holding their sides, they sat down. Rose took the reins, and the wagon moved forward. "I'm so happy for you, girl. This is so incredible. But what does that mean? Do you think you'll marry?"

"Oh, I don't know. Uncle Otis told me just a year ago that I'd feel this way about many boys. But I just don't know. I hope we do. But I realize things may change." She grabbed Rose's hand. "I just have to trust God. But it's such a wonderful feeling. I can't explain it. We promised to write each other every day; and whenever your dad makes visits to Rock Island, I'll send them."

"Do you want anyone to know at school?"

"No, just you, at least for a while. Right now, we'll just be happy that Clifford was found and make sure we're ready for our tests. I know you'll do well and make a wonderful teacher."

CHAPTER SEVENTEEN

WITH THE TESTS BEHIND HER, Lainey couldn't wait to return to Rock Island. It was the fifth birthday of Catherine, Rose's youngest sibling. She begged to go with Lainey to Rock Island and play with Tina and Carter.

Mrs. Hanson took Lainey aside. "Is this okay with you?"

"Absolutely. Carter will love it, and Catherine will love being with Tina. We'll take good care of her."

Catherine peppered Lainey with questions all the way to the island on her papa's grocery boat.

Mr. Hanson shook his head. "Hope you realize this will continue the whole visit. It's a phase every one of our kids went through at age five."

Lainey threw her head back and laughed. "We'll manage."

Carter waited at the dock as Mr. Hanson's grocery boat approached the landing. Lainey jumped off the boat before it was fully tied off and wrapped her arms around Carter. "Oh my goodness, look how tall you are. I've missed you so much."

"Mama isn't here because she's making a great big lunch, and Tina was taking her nap; but Papa is waiting in the wagon. The horse was acting skittish, so he stayed with the wagon, and I came to meet you. I thought you might need help with your bags. Besides I am your favorite brother." Carter paused and caught his breath.

Lainey laughed. "You are absolutely right, Carter. You are my first brother, my favorite brother, and my only brother. Catherine came to celebrate her birthday. Let's hurry to see Papa." Lainey turned. "Thank you, Mr. Hanson. Your family has been such a blessing to me."

"Especially me, right?" Catherine's feet moved in the air as Mr. Hanson handed her over to Lainey.

Lainey set her on the dock and tapped her head before the young girl rushed to Carter. "Especially you."

"Anytime, Lainey." Mr. Hanson quickly untied the lines he'd just secured and headed back to Washington Island.

Lainey, Carter, and Catherine ran the length of the dock holding hands and laughing. Papa hopped off the wagon and wrapped his arms around Lainey. "We have missed you so. Tell us. How is Clifford?"

"He's well, Papa. Praying about going back to sea, but still in need of more recovery time."

"And your school tests?"

"I had the second highest score. Rose was first, and that's good, as she wants to be a teacher. And I'm happy with my score, considering I was worrying about Clifford so much of my studying time."

After lifting Catherine into the wagon, Lainey's papa turned to take her elbow to assist her climbing into the wagon. Lainey stepped back. "Wait, Carter said the horse was skittish today."

"We've had some snakes around. Just this morning, I saw one near the barn. It's the movement near the horse that scares them so. We've cleared any long grass around the barn and put mothballs and vinegar around the barn and the lighthouse."

Carter pinched his nose. "They smell awful."

Lainey smiled and walked over to the horse and stood in front of the mare. "You're a good girl." She ran her hand over the forelock, and then placed her forehead between Missy's eyes. The horse let out a visible sigh.

"I think she's missed you, Lainey, as much as we have. Let's get home. There are a couple gals who can't wait to see you." Papa held out his hand. Lainey grasped it and climbed into the front seat.

Lainey felt tears on her cheeks as she gazed around her. The breeze from the lake delivered a sweet fragrance, and the new, light green leaves on the trees created an ethereal canopy as they entered the woods. "It's good to be home, Papa."

Papa reached over and squeezed her hand. "We're so glad you're here." Carter leaned against his sister and sighed. Catherine chattered about the trees, the boat ride, her birthday, and how excited she was to be there.

As the wagon approached the lighthouse, the door flung open, and Mama flew out with Tina in her arms. Lainey jumped off the wagon as soon as Papa pulled to a stop and ran to her mother and sister. Lainey wrapped her arms around them for a full minute.

"Lainey, we've missed you. I'm so glad you're here. How is Clifford?"

"He's getting better and expected to make a full recovery." Lainey took Tina from her mother. "My, how you've grown, little sister."

Tina giggled and kicked her legs.

Lainey laughed. She bent down so Catherine could see the baby. "Look who's here to play with you, Tina."

Mama took Catherine's hand. "Catherine, we're delighted you're here. I have food ready. Let's eat. Lainey, we want to hear everything you've done, and Carter has so much to tell you."

The next day, Lainey and Carter carried the water from the lake using the yoke carriers that Trygve's father made. Carter immediately started the times table as they went down and started the story as they returned the long trek up the fifty steps. "Lainey, I've been telling Tina the stories I make up on the steps."

"That makes me happy, Carter. You're so smart, and I bet she'll be telling stories as soon as she can talk."

As soon as lunch was over, Lainey asked Catherine to join her and Carter as they set out on a hike around the island. Catherine had never gone that far, but eagerly agreed that she was ready. Rocks and roots dotted the narrow path that wound through towering trees and descended to rippling waters along the north shore of the island. Catherine picked fanning ferns along the way, determined to present Mama with a bouquet of native plants and flowers. The gorgeous white trilliums that dotted the landscape had now turned purple, indicating the end of their time until the following May. The trio sat a few minutes on a horizontal trunk that extended out over a small bluff that dropped about ten feet to a slab of flat rock.

Carter pointed. "Can I climb down to that? I think I can."

Lainey shook her head. "It looks slippery with the water lapping on it, and climbing back up would be difficult."

Carter sighed.

Lainey patted his shoulder. "We'll find another place to get down to the water. Let's keep going."

The ferns stood taller and encroached the path, making it a bigger adventure to remain on the trail. The three of them laughed and pretended they were hiding from pirates on a deserted island. As they turned south on the east side of the island, their path tracked closer to the water's edge, and they found several spots to stand on the beach and gaze out into the lake.

"What's that way, Lainey?" Catherine slipped her hand into Lainey's. "Does the water go on forever?"

"The state of Michigan is over there past the horizon, Catherine. The lake is called Lake Michigan."

"Is there a Lake Wisconsin?"

Lainey squeezed Catherine's hand. "No, there isn't, but maybe one day, we'll discover a lake and name it Lake Wisconsin."

Carter turned back to the path. "Let's pretend we're explorers looking for the great Lake Wisconsin."

Catherine squealed and ran to catch Carter. They raced along the wider path, dodging roots and rocks that still dotted their route around the island.

They soon arrived at a very flat, grassy area. The waters of the nearby cove lapped lightly on the small, crescent-shaped, sandy beach. Ripples of aqua blue waves sported sprits of white at their crests. Lainey stopped and gazed and pictured Clifford on a ship far out in the lake. She tried to imagine the storms and gales that sunk his ship and her parents' ship. *These beautiful waters seem incapable of such devastation. How can I love the lake so much when it turns angry and destroys lives and livelihoods?*

Voices interrupted her thoughts. "Lainey, look. We discovered something." Catherine grabbed Lainey's hand and pulled her toward the spot where Carter stood. "Was it a building?"

"Yes, Catherine. What a great explorer you are." She winked at Carter. "There was once an Ottawa Indian village here." The trio walked around and found a small cemetery and read the names of those who'd lived there just forty years before. "I think many got sick and died. Many were fishermen, and they moved to other areas. Now, all that's left are their memories and gravestones."

"Let's keep going. This is a little sad. I want to keep looking for Lake Wisconsin." The five-year-old set out on the trail again. As they rounded to the south end of the island, they were greeted by mounds of soft sand and wide beaches. The south wind stirred up larger waves that crashed on the beach. Peaks of white caps rose and fell and traveled to the beach before disappearing and making room for the next series of waves.

"Ooh, the sand is warm." Catherine kicked off her boots and plopped into the sand and dug her toes into the warmth. "Can we eat our snack now?"

"Certainly." Lainey took the small pack tied about her waist and sat next to the little girl.

Carter ventured down to the water and dipped his toes into the lake between crashing waves. "It's a little chilly." He sat next to the girls and dug his toes into the warm sand like Catherine. "What do we have to eat?"

Lainey handed them each a piece of cheese and a cookie. They shared a canning jar filled with water. As they continued their exploration, they found the thimble berries abundant on the island. "Let's pick some, so we can make jam. We can use my scarf to hold them."

After filling the scarf, Catherine puckered her lips. "Ooh, they taste awful." She spit and wiped her mouth on her sleeve.

Lainey doubled over with laughter. "Oh, Catherine—that's why we make jam and tea with them. They're too bitter alone. Here, drink the rest of the water."

Catherine gulped the water. "Okay, I'm better. Let's keep going."

Carter hollered. "Hurry up, you two. The cave walls are just ahead."

Catherine's eyes opened wide. "Caves? Can we go in them?"

"Not really caves, but sheer rock walls with some indentations that seem like caves. We can certainly pretend."

Catherine grinned. "I like playing with you, Lainey." She ran ahead to catch up with Carter.

The water lapped close to the wall faces, and trees grew out of the sides of the rock. Carter lifted Catherine, so she could see the Indian drawings that were etched in the slabs. She clapped her hands then ran her fingers over the carvings. "This is the best discovery yet."

Soon, they found themselves on the familiar west side of the island with grassy hills and tall woods. They gazed across at Washington Island, tiny Pilot Island, and the mainland beyond.

"Will Rose come to visit, soon?" Carter shielded his eyes against the sun to look across the channel. "I hope Sam and David come along. I miss them."

"I do, too, Carter. I think they'll come."

Catherine grinned. "They wanted to come, but there was too much work to do. Mama said another time." She turned to Lainey. "Will Clifford come here again? We prayed for him a lot."

"Thank you, Catherine. I hope he comes sometime. Are you getting tired of walking?"

"A little—do we have much more to go?"

"Not too far. Let's get going."

As they walked through the door, Catherine walked up to Lainey's mother, hugged her, and announced, "Mrs. Engelson, we were great explorers, and I have so much to tell you; and I want to play with Tina, but I have to rest first." At that, she scurried up the stairs, plopped down on the bed assigned to her, and fell fast asleep.

Lainey showed her mama the berries and then placed them in a glass jar in the cellar room to keep them cool until jam or tea could be made.

When she returned, Mama took her hand and led her into the sitting room. Carter lay on the divan sound asleep. "Tina's asleep. I made tea. Let's sit down and catch up. How are you, and how is Clifford?"

Lainey sipped her tea and told her mama all that had transpired with Clifford, stopping short of telling her that they expressed their love to one another.

Mama squeezed Lainey's hand. "I see love in your eyes, Lainey. Does Clifford feel the same?"

Lainey looked down; then with a big sigh, she nodded her head. "Mama, he told me . . . he said . . . he loved me." She felt the heat rising in her face.

"And did you tell him the same?"

Lainey's voice was a whisper. "I did, Mama. I did." She looked up into Mama's smiling face. Was that a tear she saw?

Mama stood and pulled Lainey to her feet. She embraced her. "I'm so happy for you, Lainey. I believe you've found a lasting love."

"Really, do you think so? Uncle Otis said I'd feel this way about many boys, and that was only a year ago."

"Often, it happens that way, but not always. I liked a couple boys before I met Reinhardt, but when I met him, it was different. I was about your age, and I think I knew we were meant for each other."

Lainey sat down and took another sip of tea. "Do you think . . . I mean, could it be that we might . . . umm . . ."

"Marry?"

"Yes." Lainey knew her face must be red. It sure was hot. Maybe it was the tea. She placed her hand on her face. "That tea is really warm."

Mama chuckled. "Yes, Lainey, I think that's a possibility. But it's something only you two can decide. Are you okay with him going back to being a sea captain? He'd be gone a lot and could face danger again."

"I know, but neither of us are willing to live in fear. Mama, he actually told me he would give it up if I didn't want him to go back out there when he's well. But I know he loves it, and it's his calling. He needs to go."

"That would make you an excellent wife for him. One that would promote him and pray for him and trust God to lead him. And what a wonderful husband he would be for you, ready to lay down his life dream for you. Not many will do that, Lainey."

Lainey found she could say nothing more. Could this thought of marriage to Clifford become a reality? It was too much to take in all at once.

Mama stood. "Well, let's get dinner on the table. Perhaps, you can wake the children. I will pray that both you and Clifford will make wise decisions."

CHAPTER EIGHTEEN

TWO WEEKS LATER, PAPA RETURNED from meeting the grocery boat with a wagonload of supplies. "Lainey, I have a note Rasmus brought you from Rose."

Lainey hurried into the sitting room and tore open the envelope. As she read, she heard footsteps and looked up. There, in the doorway, were her parents and Carter.

Carter crossed his arms. "Well?"

Lainey laughed. "Rose heard from Miss Pritchard, who was on the mainland helping at the Ruckerts' store. Niles and Clifford are coming to Washington Island next week, and they want to come visit us next Saturday if it's okay."

Papa spoke up. "Rasmus told me, and I already told him to tell Rose and all to come. We're delighted to have them."

Carter turned to his father. "What about Sam? Can he come, too?"

Papa smiled. "Yes, Sam, too. We confirmed that when we talked."

Mama winked at Lainey. "Well, this is wonderful. Lainey, let's go plan the food. Carter, help your dad with the supplies and make sure the animals have water."

Mama sat next to Lainey on the divan, while Tina sat on the floor and played with her toys. "I'm so excited for you. You know, we aren't far removed from the time when all our friends, along with us, were falling in love. So, I feel a little giddy now. It's been so long since I've

208

seen Clifford—since Tina was born—so I'm excited to see you two together."

Once again, Lainey found that this wonderful mother was also a friend and wondered at her excitement for this visit.

Lainey and Clifford held hands on the walk toward the rocky overhang on Rock Island's north side. Rose and Niles had wandered south from the lighthouse. Sam and Carter watched the two couples leave and shook their heads.

Sam slapped Carter on the back. "We need to follow them and scare them to death by jumping out from behind a tree—or go split some logs for firewood."

Carter laughed. "I think Papa would like the firewood. We might get set on fire if we disturb any of the lovebirds."

"I'm going to fish with my uncle this summer. He needs help, and I can get back in the swing of managing a boat."

Lainey smiled and sat down on the rock slab that extended out from a root face on the bluff. The water slapped the shore with a musical lapping sound below them. "Are you okay with that, Clifford? I know how much you want to get back out there like before. You seem a lot stronger than a few weeks ago."

Clifford scooted across the smooth piece of rock, warmed by the bit of sun filtering through the leafy trees that hung out over the cliff.

"I am stronger. It seemed so long at first just to get my balance; and then, when all the dizziness left, I felt stronger and stronger. I'm not at full strength yet, but I'm getting there. And, yeah, this summer with my uncle is good." He paused and cleared his throat. "I do have a couple job possibilities later this summer. One is one of the barges out of Sturgeon Bay. You know, the one that had all the chickens that saved my life."

"Clifford, that's the funniest story. I mean, of course, it was serious, but chickens everywhere." Lainey's giggle turned to a snort. "I'm sorry, but . . . well . . . "

"I know. My uncle calls me chicken man."

"Nooo!" Lainey put her face almost in her lap. Clifford grabbed her arm, so she didn't slip off the rock. "That's so awful—and funny."

"I know. It's funny, but I sure am glad that crate of chickens was there. In the Bible, Jonah got a whale. Me? I get chickens. But I'm here."

Lainey threw her arms around his neck, still laughing.

They stood to continue their walk. Lainey slipped her hand into his. "What's the other possibility?"

"I'll tell you later. Let's just enjoy our time together now."

The young couple wandered the paths of Rock Island for two hours, holding hands and laughing and hinting at future plans.

"We'd better get back. Mama will need help with dinner. And who knows if Niles and Rose will find their way back anytime soon."

Clifford looked up at the treetops. "Do you think they'll get lost? I don't think Niles has ever been here. Does Rose know her way around?"

"It's been a long time since Rose and I explored; but they went toward the boat landing, so hopefully, they'll come right back from there."

To Lainey's surprise, everyone was back in the house; the dinner table was set; and the food was ready to be served. Carter and Sam kept jabbing each other in the side and laughing. Mama and Papa just seemed calm and happy. They always did; but something was different, and Lainey couldn't quite discern what it might be.

Rose pulled Lainey into her little bedroom. "Lainey, Niles kissed me down by the water. I think we might be in love."

Lainey clapped her hands. "Rose, that's the best news. I'm so happy."

Rose raised her eyebrows. "Oh, I think there might be better news."

Lainey grabbed Rose's hands. "What haven't you told me? Is someone else getting married or going to have a baby?"

Rose winked. "It's time for dinner, I think."

Dinner was delightful. Mama served a roast with mashed potatoes and carrots. Everyone seemed so happy. Lainey noticed their joy or peace just seemed up a notch from usual. Must be because Mama and Papa were so happy for company. Lainey was happy for the present company as well. These people were her very favorites. Only Uncle Otis and Aunt Edith were missing from this wonderful gathering.

Someone knocked at the door. Carter jumped up. "I'll get it!"

Uncle Otis and Aunt Edith walked in, followed by Clifford's parents and Rose's parents with Catherine and David. Uncle Otis beamed. "Hope it's okay to drop by like this. It was such a beautiful day on the water. The Ruckerts came for a late lunch, and then Rasmus dropped by with a delivery; and we just decided to come join the party."

Lainey ran into her uncle's arms. "I can hardly believe this, but I'm so glad to see you." After embracing Aunt Edith and Clifford's parents, she returned to her seat and squeezed Clifford's hand. "What a surprise."

Carter and Papa brought extra chairs to the table, so all could sit.

Mama set three pies on the table. "This is just perfect timing for dessert. Rose, could you help me cut the pies? And, Clifford, could you pass these out?" The two young people dutifully assisted.

"I can help, Mama." Lainey started to get up.

"Oh, no, we've got it. You can sit."

Lainey looked around. Why did everyone have such silly grins on their faces? Yet they all looked everywhere but at Lainey. Could Uncle Otis have gotten a promotion? Did Clifford get a better job? Was Mama pregnant again? Was Rose's mom pregnant?

Soon, all were served, except Lainey and Clifford. Clifford set his piece of the pie in front of his place and then returned with Lainey's. A napkin lay draped across her piece, except it didn't look like pie was under the cloth. She glanced at Clifford, and he nodded. She removed the napkin and gasped. There on the plate lay a beautiful diamond ring. The simple single stone set upon a white gold ring took Lainey's breath away. Clifford picked it up, pushed his chair back, and got down on one knee. "Lainey Louis, would you do the honor of becoming my wife? I love you with my whole heart. And I asked permission of your parents and your aunt and uncle."

Lainey looked around and saw the sweetest smile ever on Aunt Edith as a tear trickled down her cheek. Uncle Otis beamed. Mama and Papa were standing with their arms around each other, nodding their approval to Lainey. For once, she didn't feel the red creeping up her face, but a tear of joy traced her cheek, matching that of Aunt Edith's.

"Lainey?" Clifford still knelt.

"Yes, yes, I absolutely will marry you, Clifford. I love you as well."

Clifford slipped the ring on Lainey's finger. "This was my grand-mother's ring, and I'm so glad it's now yours."

Everyone began clapping and cheering. They all stood to give each of them a hug, then settled down to eat their pie and ask questions about wedding dates and plans. Mama set a piece of pie in front of Lainey. "I didn't forget. Here you are."

Clifford took Lainey's hand. "We haven't talked about dates, but I think a year from now would be a good date for a wedding. Lainey?"

She nodded. "That sounds perfect, but I don't know if can even think right now. I thought this might happen in the next year, and I'm so happy. Next June is wonderful. Mama?"

"It is. Your aunt and Shirley and I have talked, and we'll make your dress for you. We have time to pull all the other details together."

Lainey held her hands out. "When did all this happen?"

Mama grinned. "Oh, when you've been occupied with other things, we managed to send notes. It's been so hard to not let it slip that we knew."

Lainey pursed her lips. "Well, Rose kind of gave it away."

They all turned to Rose and let out a collective, "Whaaat?"

Rose laughed. "She thought one of you was pregnant."

Mama coughed. "No."

"But, wait, how did you all get here? We brought the wagon when Rose and Niles and Clifford and Sam arrived."

Niles chuckled. "As soon as you were out of sight today, Rose and I came back, took the wagon to the boat landing, and then walked back. That way, it was waiting for them."

Lainey set her chin in her hand and shook her head. "You really planned this all out."

Otis stood. "Nothing but the best for our girl. Come here; I need a hug."

Lainey pushed back her chair and scooted around the table to fall into her uncle's arms. He remained the most special person in her heart. Clifford was, of course, the biggest part now; but Uncle Otis had been her rock, and she would always love him.

Tina held her arms up, and Uncle Otis swooped her into his arms where she snuggled.

Lainey leaned in and kissed Tina's forehead. "Maybe Tina could be the flower girl. She'll be walking then. Of course, Rose will be my maid of honor."

Carter's eyes got big. "Can I be the ring person? What's it called?"

"Ringbearer. Indeed, you can."

Clifford reached across the table to shake Niles' hand. "You'll be best man?"

"Honored."

A small voice sounded. It was Catherine. "What about me?"

"Well, you can be a little bridesmaid or help Tina with the flowers."

"I want to help Tina. Is that okay?"

"It's perfect, Catherine. She'll need your guidance."

Mr. Hanson stood. "We are so glad to be included in this happy event, but we should return before dark. Thankfully, this time of year, we have lots of daylight. Maybe you should have your wedding on June twenty-first to take advantage of the most daylight of the year. I mean, it's a thought."

"It's a great idea, Uncle Rasmus." Lainey came to him and gave him a hug. "We're so glad you came and brought everyone."

Papa set down his fork. "Let's pray over this young couple."

The family and guests circled Lainey and Clifford, laying their hands on the couple's shoulders. Papa's voice boomed. "Dear Father, thank You for bringing Lainey and Clifford together and protecting their lives in so many situations. We ask now that You bless their engagement, their wedding plans, but most of all, their marriage. We pray for wisdom in every decision and that You guide them into every purpose and plan You intend for them. Amen."

A chorus of amens resounded throughout the dining room.

Mr. Hanson clapped Clifford's shoulder. "We should go. Why don't you and Lainey go with us to the boat landing, so you can bring the wagon back and have a few minutes to yourselves?"

Mrs. Ruckert held out her arms to Lainey. "We have a daughter now, and we couldn't be more pleased." She wiped the tear from under her eye. "I'm so happy."

She and Lainey embraced. Mrs. Ruckert grinned. "And to think we almost lost you when you thought Clifford was Juliet's beau."

Lainey's laughter filled the room. "I'm so glad I found out the truth. And I can't wait to tell her. Do you think she'd like to be a bridesmaid?"

"Oh, I'm sure she'd be delighted."

Soon, the four couples, along with Catherine and David, were in the wagon on the way back to Mr. Hanson's boat. They hugged and laughed at the boat landing before boarding the boat. Uncle Otis grinned. "Now, don't get lost going back to the lighthouse. Behave."

Clifford put his arm around Lainey and pulled her close. "We'll be good." They climbed on the wagon and waved to the others as they pulled away.

As they let the horse plod along, Clifford squeezed Lainey's hand. "I need to tell you about the other job possibility. My uncle meets a lot of people when he sells his fish. A man came to purchase fish, wondering if Uncle Albert could supply enough fish for his passenger ship that travels from Chicago to Sturgeon Bay and back. My uncle had me deliver a batch to him, and the man, Emil Lind, engaged me in conversation. I told him about the *Horowitz* running aground, being lost and found, Hank's death, and the chicken crates. He sounded fascinated, asking me all sorts of questions and even laughing a bit at the chickens."

Lainey leaned against Clifford. "Such a great story."

"True, very true. He asked if I wanted to get out on the lake again. I mentioned fishing with my uncle. He said that was not what he meant. He needs a first mate for the remainder of the summer on the passenger boat between Sturgeon Bay and Chicago. I guess the man he had in that position had a family emergency and couldn't finish the season."

Lainey took a deep breath and turned in the seat to face Clifford. "Does he want you? Do you want to do it?"

"He does, and I do; but I want to talk everything over with you first. It's only through the end of October with no promise beyond that. But it pays well and would help us save to get a house or start a business or something."

A tear tracked down Lainey's cheek. Clifford, eyes wide, pulled up on the reins. "What's wrong? Do you want me to tell him no? It's okay. I don't have to do this. I can work with my uncle, and we'll be just fine."

Lainey put a finger against his mouth. "No, no. You should take it. It's what you wanted—to be out on the lakes—and you'll make money to provide for us. I will miss you, but I think it's God's answer for us—not just you, but us. I'm so amazed at God's provision. It's so vast."

"But . . . " he hesitated.

"What is it? Do you not want it?"

"The cargo is people, Lainey. People. What if I run aground again? I didn't save the ship or Hank before."

"What did Mr. Lind say?"

Clifford looked down and shook his head. "He said it was time to get back out there, like getting back on the horse after you've been bucked off. He said everything is a learning opportunity. He said he liked my character and was sure I could handle anything now that I'd been through that. He's been on the water most of his life and knows the dangers. I can hardly understand it. I thought no one would really want me as a helmsman after the Horowitz, at least not this soon." He lifted his head. "So, you think I should tell him yes? Really? You're not afraid?"

"We already decided we can't live in fear. It's not God's plan to live that way. He tells us to be courageous and go forward. I will miss you always, but I love you and will once more trust God for you."

Clifford placed a finger under her chin and leaned forward to kiss her. Soon, they continued their short ride back to the lighthouse, Lainey leaning against his shoulder.

They spent the evening around the table eating more pie, laughing, and telling stories of growing up and making initial wedding plans. Clifford and Lainey thought the idea of June twenty-first, the longest day of the year, would be a perfect date. Mrs. Ruckert had brought a few magazines with her from the store that had wedding dress designs. Rose, Lainey, and Mama poured over them, gaining ideas for the making of her dress. Clifford shared his new job offer with Papa and Niles.

The next morning after eggs and biscuits, Papa and Lainey took the wagon with Clifford, Niles, and Rose back to the boat landing to meet Mr. Hanson on his morning grocery run. Rose gave Lainey a quick hug, then hurried to the boat with Niles.

Papa shook Clifford's hand. "You're my son now, Clifford, and I'm proud of you. I know you'll do a fine job in your new position. Know we're praying for you and expecting good things."

"Thank you, sir. I'll do my best."

Lainey and Clifford lingered, looking into each other's eyes. He gave her a quick kiss on the cheek.

"I love you so, Lainey. I'll send word about my new job."

"Can't wait to see you again. I love you."

Clifford embraced her and then ran down to the boat, turning to wave all the while they traveled away from Rock Island.

Lainey stood waving as long as she could, then returned to the wagon and climbed up to return once more to the lighthouse.

Papa patted her hand. "The year will go quickly, sweetheart. Anna will be glad for your assistance this summer. Otis said he and Edith are helping you and Rose look into your plans to take college classes by mail this fall."

"Yes, as you know, Rose wants to teach. The more I think about it, I'd like to write stories, perhaps for magazines or perhaps curriculum for schools. Clifford's parents said several college instructors come through their store in the summer, and Uncle Otis says some of them want to buy furniture and ship it back to their homes. Both the Ruckerts and Uncle Otis are going to ask their advice. Our test scores were quite high, so we think we'd qualify. Miss Pritchard already sent our inquiries out to a few places."

"Last night, while you talked wedding plans with all the women, Niles told me that Otis offered him an internship to learn accounting."

Lainey clapped her hands. "Did he tell Rose yet? That would be so wonderful. He'd be so much closer. She didn't say anything."

"He's probably telling her now and will discuss it with his parents. He'd make a great lighthouse keeper, but not everyone raised in a lighthouse wants to be in charge of one."

"I think Tryg wants to be a lumberjack. Rose wasn't sure what Niles wanted to do, but that would be wonderful if he became an accountant. And I think maybe they'll marry. Do you think so, Papa?"

He chuckled. "I wouldn't be a bit surprised."

CHAPTER NINETEEN

ROSE AND LAINEY SAT WITH their feet in the water by the rocky shore in northwest Washington Island. They had walked the pebble beach till they found a small dock on which to sit. The view to the north held nothing but blue skies and calm waters. The large harbor provided refuge from all winds, save the north. Today boasted no such north wind. A few breezes brought relief from the heat and high humidity.

Rose kicked her feet in the water. "This day is so hot. I'm almost ready to just jump in."

Lainey grinned and reached down to splash some water on her face. "I know. I could be tempted, but putting our feet in helps. The water is so cold."

"Papa said it's probably the hottest July ever. I'm kind of looking forward to fall."

"Me, too. Are you excited about your new studies?"

Rose turned on the dock to face Lainey. "I have to go to Chicago once in October after I start my studies to meet the professors and then again in May for tests. My lessons should arrive in early September. They'll let me do my practice under Miss Pritchard, and she'll write a report. She also offered to assist in anything with my assignments if something isn't clear. I might get to go on Clifford's passenger boat if Pa can book passage. I think Uncle Otis and Niles are looking into it for us. I'd love if you could come, too." She nudged Lainey. "Wouldn't that be fun? What are your studies going to be?"

"Well," Lainey rubbed her hands together. "Papa and I have looked into journalism, not just story writing, and that opened up more doors. Mrs. Ruckert gets magazines and newspapers and all sorts of journals in the store and asked Clifford to check into a few places in Chicago. I guess he's able to talk with many of the passengers on his boat. A newspaper man and his wife from Chicago really like him. They offered to bring some instructive manuals from the newspaper office and from some publishing houses. They also offered to pay my passage to visit a few places in Chicago. We just got the message yesterday."

Rose stood and pulled Lainey to her feet. She threw her arms around her best friend. "Oh, we have to go together. Wouldn't that be fun? Also, our parents wouldn't worry so much about us being alone in the big city."

Lainey smirked. "I can hear your brother Sam say, 'They'll worry more sending you two together.'"

"True. But, Lainey, we could look at wedding dresses and buy material to make your dress and the bridesmaid dresses. Even Tina's and Catherine's flower girl dresses. Oh, my, this is too exciting. We should see about booking our passage soon, so we can go together. But we should go. Niles' brother and his wife are waiting for us. I told her we'd be there by 1:00 p.m. for lunch."

Lainey rubbed her feet dry with her skirts and slipped her shoes on. "That's so nice of her to invite us. How long have they been working at Torgenson's Sunset Resort?"

Rose placed an arm on Lainey's to balance as she placed her shoes back on. "This is their second summer there. They love working for the Torgensons. It's such a pretty spot. It draws a lot of tourists, as long as they can find a boat ride out of Ellison Bay, Gills Rock, or Newport Town. My pa gives some rides but doesn't like having to meet the tourist's schedule at the end of their visit. He doesn't really charge as he's making the routes anyway, but they usually tip him nicely. He just doesn't like to have to be there for their return trip."

Lainey stopped just before they reached the wagon and crossed her arms. "Someone should do a boat solely for the tourists. I bet residents need some regular rides, too. Maybe a barge so they could take their horse and wagon across."

Rose climbed on and grabbed the reins. "That's a marvelous idea. Someone could also rent horses and wagons or give a ride for a fee from the boat landing to their destination." She winked. "Maybe Clifford would like to do that. His job only goes into the fall, right? Isn't the regular first mate returning in the fall sometime?"

"Yes, end of October, but I don't know how busy they are after that."

The horse trotted past Bethel church.

"You'll have your wedding there?"

Lainey nodded. "I can't imagine having it anywhere else. Pastor Gunnlerson has taught me so much. I should probably let him know our plans. He's been there for so many situations in my life."

Rose patted her hand. "Yes."

Soon, Rose steered the horse to the right, and they followed a winding path around a little cove on the western edge of the island. It curved through the trees after providing a beautiful view of the blue waters of the bay of Green Bay. The pines and oaks towered over them, crowding close to make the path seem like a tunnel.

"This is so beautiful. In all my years, I've never been here." Lainey stared up at the overhanging branches.

"I've only been here a few times. Mama liked to bring me here for lunch when I was little—kind of a mother-daughter day."

"I love that, Rose. When I have children . . . " Lainey paused and giggled. "I can't even imagine that yet. But when I have a little girl, I want to do that. I think my mama may have done that a few times, but since I was the only child, I didn't realize that's what it was."

The view to the west took in the vast expanse of the bay. In front of them stood a modest building with a few smaller buildings set nearby. The main building hosted a wrap-around porch with a large dining room set in the center. Large windows gave an invite to the dining room with its gingham tablecloths. The scent of the pine wood greeted them just before Daniel and Josephine hurried out to meet them.

"You made it. I'm so excited to see you." Josephine's hair reached her waist in a single braid. Her fair complexion revealed a bit of sunburn, and her eyes sparkled with joy.

Daniel stood a full foot above her and he ran his hand through his thick unruly hair. "We have to say congratulations, Lainey, to you and Clifford on your engagement. This is a great place for a honeymoon night if you plan to stay on the island."

Lainey knew a blush firmly planted itself on her cheeks. "Oh, my, I guess I haven't thought that far ahead yet."

Rose giggled.

Josephine pursed her lips and raised her eyebrows at Daniel. "I think it's time for lunch. It'll be in our cabin, and then we'll show you around."

Josephine had whitefish sandwiches and a small garden salad. "This whitefish was caught yesterday, and all of the salad is from our garden. I considered making soup, but it's just too hot. I make soup a lot for our guests. I do most of the cooking for the resort, and Daniel does the upkeep. We also do a lot of the cleaning. Keeps us pretty busy."

Daniel grinned. "Since I already sort of talked out of turn about honeymoons—don't kick me, Josie—I'm wondering if Niles has proposed to you, Rose."

Josephine rolled her eyes. "Daniel!"

Rose's face turned the color of her name. "Ah, no . . . no, that hasn't happened."

Lainey lifted her eyebrows. "Daniel, do you know something we don't know?"

Daniel held both hands up. "I know nothing. I should have said nothing, and if I don't stop now, I'll have bruises on my shin from Josie's kicks."

Everyone returned to their food, although a few giggles and chuckles broke the silence.

Josephine cleared the table and brought out cherry cobbler for dessert.

"Oh, my goodness, what a treat." Lainey took a mouthful and sighed. "Delicious. Rose, we should pick some cherries before we go back."

Daniel glanced at his wife. "We have one more thing to share with you. Lainey, have you set a date for your wedding?"

"We're thinking June twenty-first."

"Well, I have no idea what your plans are, but you and Clifford came to our minds first when we heard this."

Lainey looked to Rose and back to Daniel and Josephine. "Heard what?"

"The Torgensons are looking for new managers and, perhaps, new owners."

Lainey set down her lemonade. "They're selling? Aren't you two managing it now? Aren't you considering buying it? It's a lovely place."

Josephine reached out to take Daniel's hand. "No, we miss being on the mainland. It was nice here; but a resort in Fish Creek is looking for managers, and we want to be closer to family, especially Daniel's mom because, well, she'll be great help when the baby arrives."

Lainey and Rose each clapped their hands and squealed. Lainey ran around the table to give Josephine a huge hug. Rose followed right behind her.

When the joyous commotion settled, Lainey studied Daniel. "So, you think Clifford and I should be managers or try to buy it?"

Rose returned to her chair. "Lainey, it would be a great place for your writing, and there's a dock right out here for Clifford to use if he gets a boat."

"Oh, my, I just don't know. I'm not sure I could do everything by myself when Clifford is gone on the water."

Rose grinned. "I could help in the summer, since I'm not teaching then. In fact, that would be perfect for me."

Lainey twisted her fingers. "I'll certainly have to talk to Clifford. I . . . I don't know, but perhaps it might work."

Josephine cleared the dishes, then turned. "We'll talk to the Torgensons and have them get in touch with you. They just let us know, so there's still time to decide. I really think if you're interested in buying, they would let you pay a little at a time if you're the managers."

Daniel looked at Rose. "And Niles is learning all that accounting now. He could probably advise how to go about that."

Lainey shook her head. "I feel a little dazed. We'll need to discuss this and certainly pray. Thanks so much for thinking of us, and thanks for lunch."

Josephine smiled. "So glad you came. Let me show you around now."

Afterwards, they sat a few minutes on the expansive porch and sipped lemonade. Soon, Lainey turned to Rose. "I think we should probably leave, so we can pick some cherries and get them back to your place before dinner."

The girls said their goodbyes, then headed off to pick berries and talk more about all the afternoon had presented to them.

CHAPTER TWENTY

LAINEY, CARTER, AND TINA ARRIVED at the Newport Town dock amidst a busy unloading and loading process. Lainey always loved the clatter and chaos of this hustling activity. Today, however, she felt protective of Tina. Scooping the little girl in her arms, she stepped off Mr. Hanson's boat, thanking him once more for his constant assistance traveling to and from the islands. Carter ran ahead, dodging horses and their droppings, men carrying heavy loads, and wagons being maneuvered into place.

Lainey laughed watching Carter. He was an adventurer like she was. She heard her aunt's voice from years ago calling out her wanderlust. Even though Carter did not share the same parental heritage, he exhibited the same traits that Lainey knew would never leave her.

Lainey saw Carter hugging Uncle Otis at the end of the dock and made her way to join them. Tina reached out.

Uncle Otis laughed and took her in his arms, kissing the top of her head. "Aunt Edith has lunch ready for all of you. Niles will join us and then give you a ride over to the Ruckerts'. Clifford should arrive there about the same time as you."

Lainey loved the joy on Aunt Edith's face when she greeted Tina and Carter. Tina immediately snuggled when Aunt Edith sat the little one on her lap. This must be how it would have been with Mandy. Perhaps Aunt Edith could go there now in her heart. The pressures

and heartaches of life were less. Lainey's own heartaches only paralyzed her on occasion now, and those moments dissipated sooner
with each passing year. It happened when she heard a door slam,
and she remembered that day she waited for her parents' return.
Sometimes, it was the swirl of the water and the mournful call of
the gulls as she remembered the shipwrecks that almost took Uncle
Otis and Clifford as well. Life had continued. Love encompassed her.
Joy found her in little moments and big ones. Pastor Gunnlerson
often quoted the Bible verse that said, "The joy of the Lord is my
strength." Joy had been a strength, and she silently thanked God for
so many blessings.

She realized she'd been staring into the distance, and Aunt Edith
was watching her. The smile her aunt gave her spoke her understanding, acceptance, and love.

Soon, Niles, Lainey, and the children were on their way to Ellison
Bay. The skies were blue with wispy clouds, and the trees were in full
green. The pine fragrance filled the air, competing with the dust the
horse and wagon wheels kicked up. It reminded Lainey of the day
she met Clifford. She and Rose rode this very wagon to and from his
uncle's home.

Niles' voice intruded on her thoughts. "Dusty on the road. We're
hoping for some rain soon."

"Mr. Hanson said that, too. And he said to say hi. I'm sorry Rose
couldn't come today. She's going over her studies with Miss Pritchard.
I guess I can call her Juliet now."

"We actually spent some time on the island last week. She told
me about Sunset Resort needing managers. Do you think you might
take it?"

"I wrote to Clifford about it. We'll talk today. I just don't know. My parents think it might be a good idea."

Niles pulled up on the reins and directed their view toward the water as they'd taken the road that meandered through Gills Rock. "Carter, do you see the fishing boats? They're bringing in a big load of whitefish or perch."

"I want to be a fisherman. Lainey, can we stop on the way back and buy some fish for Uncle Otis and Aunt Edith?"

Lainey shifted Tina on her lap. "We should do that, Carter. That's a great idea."

Niles cleared his throat. "Uh, Lainey, Rose and I also talked about the possibility of Clifford having his own boat and being a transport from Ephraim and other places to Washington Island."

"I wonder if it would be enough boating for him. I think he likes the long routes down the Great Lakes."

Niles nodded. "Consider this. Rose and I discussed the need to transport from the boat docks to various places as more and more people want to visit the island. Of course, if Clifford had a barge, then the wagons could travel over; but some might want to have a service of transport or want to rent their own carriage. It would be a big undertaking to do it all, but Otis and I have been considering financing methods. What I'm trying to say is I would like to manage that part of it; and if your resort grows to all it might be and you become owners, I'd like to be your accountant."

Lainey took a deep breath. "You have really been thinking about this. I've been praying, but I just don't know if all this is possible."

"Forgive me, Lainey, but I took the liberty to write to Clifford as well and lay out all these ideas for him to consider."

Lainey's laugh was deep. "Niles, what an entrepreneur!"

"You're not mad that I overstepped?"

"Mad? I'm delighted that you and so many others have our best interests at heart." She paused. "And yours, of course. Does this mean that you and Rose . . . ?"

"I think we both know, but we've made no plans yet."

"Only that you're starting a horse and carriage rental on the island where Rose may be teaching in a year and offering to work at the resort that Clifford and I may run. No plans, huh?"

Niles' cheeks showed a bit of pink. "Well, when you put it that way . . . "

"Isn't life wonderful?"

Carter stood with his mouth open upon entering the Ruckerts' store. Lainey carried Tina around as she reached for everything. "Some day, little girl."

Carter wandered, studying the candy, the cheeses, the sausages, the lamps, and the brooms. He turned to Niles. "This is amazing. How do they get all this stuff?"

Mr. Ruckert stooped so he was face to face with nine-year-old Carter. "It's a lot of work. We have to order it and write down everything we have."

"Everything?" Carter's eyes were big.

"Yes, and then when we sell it, we have to keep track of the money and write it down again and then order more so we don't run out. And we must stack and arrange everything, so people can see it and decide to buy it. Do you think you'd like to work in a store?"

"I never thought about it before, but maybe. I think I want to be a fisherman, but maybe I'd like a store."

Mr. Ruckert chucked Carter under the chin. "Anytime you want, I'll hire you. Why don't you go upstairs now? Mrs. Ruckert has some cookies for you." He turned to Lainey. "Hello, dear. Clifford should arrive any time now."

Niles turned. "He's just tying up his horse at the post out front."

Lainey's heart skipped a beat. "Carter, carry Tina upstairs. We'll be up soon."

Carter crossed his arms and grinned. "After you kiss him?" He quickly took Tina from Lainey and started up the stairs.

Niles laughed. "I'll watch the kids. Go greet your man."

Lainey stepped out the door. Clifford had his back to her, gathering his belongings from the wagon. Lainey felt chills in her spine and heat in her face just like every time she saw him. He turned, and his face lit up.

"Lainey, you're here! How wonderful!" He set his items back on the wagon and opened his arms. She rushed into them and buried her face in his shoulder.

Lainey lifted her face. "I missed you so much. I didn't realize how much till now. I want to kiss you, but it's probably not proper here on the road."

"Oh, but it's my road, and you are soon to be my wife." He bent his head and kissed her lips. When they pulled themselves back, they heard clapping. Everyone in the store had stepped out on the porch to observe the reunion.

One of the regulars stepped forward. "Clifford and Lainey, congratulations on your engagement. We're all happy for you." The greetings continued as they entered the store.

After cookies and milk with Clifford's parents, the two were sent on their way to walk to the waterfront. Mr. Ruckert put Carter to work in the store helping him stack items on the shelves. Mrs. Ruckert played with Tina, and Niles visited with some friends at the small restaurant next door.

"Clifford, what do you think about these possible plans for the resort and the passenger transport to and from Washington Island?"

The two sat on their favorite rock next to the water. Clifford rubbed his chin. "It sounds almost too good to be true."

"But is it enough water time for you—just staying in one area?"

Clifford took her hand and kissed it. "Lainey, I love the passenger boat so much more than the cargo ships. And it would be wonderful to not be gone from you so much. This could really grow into a business—perhaps a really thriving business. I'm going to sit down with your uncle, Niles, and my dad. If we could work out the finances, it would be wonderful. We need to pray and see if this is God's great plan."

CHAPTER TWENTY-ONE

"IT'S LIKE WE'RE ELEVEN YEARS old again, exploring the rocky shoals on Pilot Island." Lainey squeezed Rose's hand as they boarded the *Michigan Queen*, the passenger boat where Clifford worked as helmsman.

Rose laughed. "Maybe someday we'll grow up, but right now, all this is just so much fun."

The early October air was cool, but with their shawls and the sun shining bright, the girls did not feel at all chilled. The excitement of traveling to Chicago filled them with overflowing elation.

They each wore their best shirtwaist with long skirts and high-ankle boots. Lainey's outfit shone softly in light blue, while Rose wore a creamy white. The girls had only three outfits each to choose from, plus the party dresses they wore to the infamous Valentine's Ball and Clifford's going-away event. After looking through magazines at the Ruckerts' store, they realized there would be exquisite dresses on the steamship and in Chicago far fancier than their dresses, but they determined to not allow that fact to make them feel dowdy.

Lainey leaned close to Rose and lowered her voice. "Remember, our smiles and our strong spirits will favor us, no matter what fashion is presented to us."

Rose grinned. "Not to mention that we sit at the captain's table, and you are engaged to the helmsman of this fine ship."

"Oh, so true, so true." Lainey pulled on the ivory door handles, and they entered the main lounge of the *Michigan Queen*. Both young women stood, mouths agape, and twirled, taking in the beauty of the room. The tables, chairs, and couches were of soft and rich rosewood. The plush upholstery boasted a purple close to plum.

"This is gorgeous. Look at the paneled flooring. Too pretty to walk on." Rose then lifted her gaze to the ceiling. "Lainey, look up." The sunlight caused rainbows of color to bounce around the room through the stained glass dome that graced the ceiling along with two glittering chandeliers.

"Uncle Otis explained that this propeller ship was designed to be like the palace steamers so prevalent in the mid-1800s. Even though the Panic of 1857 sunk the passenger business on the Great Lakes, this owner wanted to bring back some of that luxury. I guess the guest cabins are much smaller than the steamer's, but the ship itself is much smaller. Clifford said it was really nice but never relayed all this beauty to me."

"Well, he's busy with the steering and care of the passengers."

"Yes, let's find our cabin. Our tickets say we'll arrive tomorrow mid-morning. Tonight, we have dinner with the captain. I think Clifford is given a few minutes to say hi."

The girls spent the afternoon on the deck enjoying the brisk air and chatting with other passengers. They wandered the rest of the ship and found the little chapel called the bethel. They stood quietly, and Lainey silently thanked God for this trip, their futures, and for Clifford. As they exited, Rose pointed at the Bethel sign on the door.

"Our church was named after this place on ships—the chapel where the crew worshiped. I guess they've always called the chapel on ships the bethel."

"Perfect name. Pastor Gunnlerson said bethel means 'God's house.'"

They returned to their cabin to change into their best dresses for the formal evening dinner with the captain. To their surprise, the owner and his wife were on the voyage and sat with them.

"Lainey, I'm pleased to meet you and your lovely friend Rose. Clifford has told me much about you both. It delighted me to hear about your engagement. Congratulations." Mr. Lind had a narrow face, with the slightest touch of a beard, and thin blond hair.

Lainey smiled, then looked down, embarrassed and amazed that the ship's owner gave her so much attention. "Thank you, sir."

Mrs. Lind, seated next to Lainey, squeezed her hand. "I understand that as well as pursuing your path of studies, you'll be looking for wedding gowns." Mrs. Lind had a quiet, sweet voice. Lainey wondered if she sang. She wore glasses and delicate jewelry, which accented her small facial features. Her dress was a soft velvet with a brocade jacket.

"Yes, ma'am, but we plan to purchase fabric. My mother, aunt, and Clifford's mother want very much to make it themselves. Although, they each gave me a little extra money and told me if I find the perfect dress at a reasonable price to go ahead and get it."

"Oh, that's a good idea. Do make sure you study some of the designs and go ahead and try some on, so you know exactly what you want." She clapped her hands. "Would you allow me to take you to a few stores in Chicago that have the best designs and the best prices?"

Rose's face lit up. "That would be wonderful. Lainey, wouldn't that be fun?"

"Are you sure, Mrs. Lind? It would be wonderful, but I don't want to take up your time."

"I'd love it. And look who's here."

Lainey turned. Clifford stood across the table grinning. His uniform was a crisp blue with a dozen buttons down the front of the jacket. Gold stripes adorned his shoulders and his cuffs. She felt the familiar inability to function and almost dropped her glass of water.

Mr. Lind stood and shook his hand. "Clifford, we're sorry you don't have time to spend with your fiancée, but I have a few thoughts I need to speak with you about."

Clifford stood straighter. "Yes, sir. Is everything ship-shape?"

"Relax, Clifford. This is not an analysis. Sit down next to your girl."

Rose quickly moved to the empty chair, relinquishing her chair next to Lainey. A waiter moved immediately to transfer Rose's plate of food so it sat in front of her and poured Clifford a glass of water. Clifford sat down and took Lainey's hand in his, squeezed it, then turned his attention to his boss.

Mr. Lind cleared his throat and took his wife's hand in his. "Miss Lainey, we are very impressed with your young man. He is diligent, skilled, and a quick learner. His knowledge is impressive. I'm sure you know all this. However, we have observed him only a few months. Our former helmsman will return at the end of the month, leaving Clifford without a job."

Clifford held Lainey's hand a little tighter. "Sir, I knew that it was temporary, and I so appreciate the opportunity here. I'll be able to work at my parent's store, and—"

"Wait, Clifford." Mr. Lind took a sip of his water. "My wife and I are investors in small businesses. That's the way we started, and that's what will make this nation flourish. Clifford, you shared your ideas of establishing a passenger ship from various places—Sturgeon Bay and north to Washington Island. And about the possibility of purchasing a resort on the island, which opens the door to a rental facility of horses and carriages. All of that takes money."

Lainey nodded and chewed her upper lip. Clifford sat at attention. "Yes, sir."

"Relax, Clifford." Mr. Lind chuckled. "I'm not dismissing your dreams. I—we—want to help make them happen."

"But . . . " Clifford looked from Mr. Lind to his wife and back to Lainey.

"We are going to invest a small amount in your business venture. We want to help you get it off the ground. You'll have to work very hard to make it successful, but we believe you have what it takes."

Lainey felt the heat rise up her neck to her face and heard Rose suck in her breath.

"Sir, I don't know what to say." Clifford stood, so he could reach across the table and shake his boss' hand.

"We'll sit down and work out the details. I understand your uncle and the young man who is wooing Miss Rose here are both quite adept at finances and want to be involved."

Rose nodded. "Yes, his name is Niles Claflin."

"Next time we come north, we'll sit down with all of you. But for now, and with your permission, I'd like to start talks with the Sturgeon Bay Boat Company that owned that barge with the chickens that Clifford met."

Mrs. Lind covered her mouth but couldn't hide the laugh that tumbled out.

Lainey giggled. "Thank goodness for those chickens."

"Yes, yes." Mr. Lind grinned. "Anyway, they have more barges that they are refitting into cargo and/or passenger ships. Smaller than this, but a start. Need some decorating, but they could work, allowing day passengers, not overnight, and possibly two wagons with horses. If you're agreeable, I'll contact them for you and get the ball rolling."

Clifford gulped. "That would be amazing, sir. I'd be honored to have you take the lead. I mean . . . if you're sure."

"Young man, we are very sure. We'd also like to advise you on your purchase of the resort. I know you have a fine advisor in Lainey's uncle, but we deal in these types of purchases as well. Again, next time we come north, we'd like to visit the resort and assess it on our own—that is, if you don't feel like we're running over you. You'll have to work hard to get loans if needed, but we're ready to give you a good recommendation."

Clifford pulled up Lainey's hand, kissed it, and looked briefly at her. "I think we're okay with that. Right, Lainey?"

Lainey swiped a tear from her eye. "I'm amazed and grateful. Thank you, Mr. and Mrs. Lind. You have been very generous."

Mrs. Lind smiled. "Oh, we're not done."

Lainey felt her eyes go wide. "There's more?"

"Well, before we go shopping for fabric for your wedding dress, I know you both are needing to pursue your studies. Rose, we want to give you a ride to your college, so you can meet with the professors and instructors. I sit on the board of that college, and I have waived half of your fees after observing your magnificent scores on your school tests."

Rose almost dropped her glass of water. "But, but . . . thank you so much."

"I know you sent an initial fee and planned to pay over time. But those payments are now cut in half. I believe you'll make an impressive teacher."

Rose dabbed her eyes. "I'm thankful. This is so wonderful."

"And, Lainey, my uncle owns a publishing house. They publish magazines and books. They want to discuss having you do an internship with them. They're next door to the newspaper publisher who paid your fare for this trip. They have people who work with young writers in both journalism and writing fiction. Journalism is a tough business, but they'd like to meet you, evaluate you, and get you started in some courses that they supervise. You can do it all by mail—correspondence courses. Occasionally, you'll need to return to Chicago, as does Rose, to reevaluate. I know you are already staying at a nice hotel while in Chicago, and that will be fun. But for any future visits, we'd love to have you stay with us."

Lainey was now crying, as well as Rose, trying to stop the flow with her napkin. "I don't know what to say."

Mrs. Lind stood and pushed back her chair. Lainey stood and found herself in Mrs. Lind's arms. The woman then embraced Rose. "You two feel like daughters already."

Lainey looked into the kind eyes of Mrs. Lind. "I . . . I don't understand this. It's overwhelming."

Mr. Lind nodded to his wife. "You need to tell her, Claire."

Lainey felt her knees wobble and reached back for Clifford's hand. He stood and placed his arm around her.

Claire Lind stepped back, glanced at her husband, and took a deep breath. "Lainey, your mother was one of my closest friends."

Without Clifford's support, Lainey thought she might sink to the floor. "You knew Mama—my mama?"

"I did. I knew you as well. For about a year before we . . . before you lost them, we hadn't seen them as much. But you used to play with our children. They were a bit older, but they adored you." She paused and smiled at Lainey. "We had lunch with your parents right before they were to return to you."

Lainey shook her head and reached for her chair. Clifford helped her and offered her some water. She looked up at Mrs. Lind. "Right before the boat . . . before it . . . "

"Yes, the day before they left here. They had just returned from New York City, and she couldn't wait to get back to you. Your parents were wonderful, Lainey, but you know that. And she showed me the red dress she'd purchased for you."

Lainey brought her hand to her face, covering her mouth. She sat a moment with her eyes closed and slightly shaking her head. "I was so excited to get a red dress."

Mrs. Lind touched her shoulder. "Your mother said you wanted red, so you would be noticed, but not lots of ruffles or lace."

Lainey chuckled. "That's true. I didn't want to be frilly, but I wanted to be noticed. Mama loved that about me, but I just about drove Aunt Edith crazy with my personality."

"Well, after lunch, we went together and found you shiny black shoes and a pretty little red purse to match your dress."

Lainey looked up. "Oh, that would have been so special." She sighed. "I'm so happy you knew my mother. If you ever have anything to tell me about her or what she said, I'd love to hear it."

"You look so much like her, Lainey. When you walked in, I could hardly keep from calling you Emma." She looked to her husband, who nodded and handed her a bag. "There's one more thing. Our shopping bags got mixed up that day when we arrived back at our home. I had set mine aside and didn't look inside until after Emma left. I mistakenly had your little purse. I was getting ready to mail it when I heard about the accident. I kept it for such a time as this. Here's the little red purse she bought you."

Lainey couldn't see it through her tears but felt it in her hands. She wiped her eyes with the napkin Rose gave her. Rose whispered in her ear. "Lainey, wear it with your wedding dress."

Lainey jerked around. "Rose, that's a wonderful idea. I'll have all red accents."

Clifford leaned down. "I'll wear a red bow tie."

Lainey studied the beaded material and the gold clasp of the purse. It had a tiny gold chain, sufficient to carry over her wrist. She opened the clasp and felt the silky black fabric inside when her hand touched a paper. She drew it out. It was a card with a lilac design on the front. Her hands trembled as she opened the card. Her mother's handwriting. "Dear, sweet Lainey. We've had a wonderful time, but I so missed you. I can't wait until you travel with us. I hope you love your dress, and I think this purse is just like you, bright and shiny and full of life. I love you. Mama."

"Oh, Mama, I miss you so much." Long, forgotten memories rose to the surface, and Lainey didn't know whether to laugh or cry. "I have this purse and this note from my mother." She stood to face Mrs. Lind. "I can never thank you enough."

"Lainey, I never opened the purse, so I never knew about the note. I'm so glad I kept it." Mrs. Lind took Lainey's hand. "This is why you feel like a daughter." She reached over to take Rose's hand. "And you as well, Rose. I'm sure you have been great comfort—and fun—for Lainey." She winked at Rose. "I sense you both enjoy life to the fullest. Your mother and I were like you two. And that's why I'd love to help you find a dress; and even if the price isn't reasonable, I'll make up the difference."

Lainey shook her head. "I never dreamed . . . this is all so wonderful and overwhelming." She turned to Clifford. "Did you realize any of this?"

"I'm as stunned as you and just as grateful."

Mr. Lind stood again. "Clifford, we are happy to share all this with you, but now you need to return to your duties. The captain has covered for you and needs to return. Ladies, finish your meal and enjoy your evening. We'll talk again." At that, he and Mrs. Lind took each other's hands and went to visit the other tables.

Clifford gave Lainey a kiss on the cheek and left the main parlor to take his place at the ship's wheel. Shortly thereafter, the captain returned. He sat for a moment. "I understand you are the recipients of our generous owner's giving."

Rose nodded. "We are, and we're still stunned. I don't understand it."

The captain smiled and patted her hand. "You don't need to. Enjoy it. Now, finish your meal and enjoy your evening." He stood and began greeting other passengers, just as the Linds had done.

CHAPTER TWENTY-TWO

LATE THE NEXT MORNING, THE Linds accompanied the girls to their hotel. Clifford's duties demanded he remain with the boat as the return trip to Sturgeon Bay would begin late afternoon. He supervised all the prepping and inspection of the ship's worthiness for each trip.

After the girls had settled into their room at the hotel, Mrs. Lind took them to a luxurious lunch before shopping. The city enthralled Lainey. It was like the dock in Newport Town on a grand scale. Everything moved. Carriages, horses, children playing and selling newspapers, women shopping, men conducting business, people hailing carriages, people begging for food and for jobs. The finest clothes on beautiful women and in windows of huge stores graced Lainey's eyes. The rags on some people, whose eyes sagged like their clothes, caused Lainey to wonder what tragedy they lived with, and she wished she could give them a warm meal or a warm coat.

Rose kept a tight grip on Lainey's arm as they traveled through Chicago to the stores to look for wedding dresses and fabric. Lainey saw that she, too, gaped at all the amazing sights. Mrs. Lind said not a word but smiled as she watched the girls. Occasionally, they held the scented handkerchiefs, provided by Mrs. Lind, to their noses. Smells assaulted them on every block. Industrial smoke settled everywhere, coupled with the droppings from the horses. Mixed in wafted the bakery smells and the food vendor fragrances.

Lainey shook her head. "I've never seen so many buildings so close together. It's exciting; but if I lived here, I'd miss the trees and fields."

Mrs. Lind nodded. "That's why we love to travel to Door County. We love being on the water and near the water. You two are blessed to live there. However, the city offers so much opportunity."

Rose leaned out to speak to Mrs. Lind. "With so many opportunities, why do we see such poverty and begging?"

"So many people are here, and many jobs require extra training. The majority of jobs do not pay as they should, so the workers suffer. Mr. Lind has worked with the Civic Federation here to obtain legislation to assist workers in keeping their jobs and protect children from working in industry. But, here, we've arrived."

Marshall Field and Company looked just like the picture in the catalogs Lainey had seen at Ruckert's Supply Store, but the imposing seven-story building was bigger than anything she'd ever seen. The city boasted many imposing structures crammed together like fish in a net, but this building was beautiful. Straight and segmented by strong windows, she couldn't imagine a store like that at home. Soon, they were under the awnings that graced the exterior of the first floor. Men in colorful uniforms greeted and held the door for them, nodding to Mrs. Lind as though they knew her.

Mrs. Lind conversed with a woman at a desk and led the girls to an elevator. Rose grabbed Lainey's hand, while Lainey took in the high ceilings and ornately carved chairs where both women and men sat with purchases and sipped tea in a broad lounge draped with exquisite brocade curtains. Delicate tablecloths graced the café tables, and thick carpets covered the floor. The elevator opened, and another uniformed person greeted Mrs. Lind and nodded to the young women. Mrs. Lind named the floor. The doors closed, and the box rose. Lainey felt her stomach rise as well. A slight dizziness overtook her mind, and she closed her eyes to quell the queasiness she felt. Glancing at Rose, she saw paleness on her face and felt Rose squeeze her hand even tighter.

The uniformed man smiled. "First time on an elevator, young ladies? You'll adjust just fine after a few trips."

Everything lurched in her stomach as the elevator came to a stop and the doors opened. Lainey took a deep breath and stepped onto a floor filled with wedding gowns and party dresses. She gasped at the beauty before her.

Mrs. Lind stepped forward. "There is beautiful fabric here, if you choose that, but let's try on a few dresses to see what style best suits you."

Lainey almost walked into displays, unable to take her eyes off the mannequins adorned with the most elegant dresses she'd ever seen. She gently reached out to brush her fingers against the velvet, taffeta, satin, and chiffon. She stopped in front of a jewel-necked gown graced with lace all along its border. It held a soft A-line skirt of chiffon over a heavier material. Leg 'o' mutton sleeves adorned the arms, and the bodice sported a fitted waist but fell softly from the neckline.

Rose touched Lainey's arm. "It's perfect, Lainey."

The floor attendant arrived immediately and offered to let Lainey try it on. She looked questioningly at Mrs. Lind.

"This is my dear friend's daughter. She is the bride, and this is her maid of honor."

The woman's face lit up. "We have wonderful bridesmaid dresses as well."

Lainey spoke up. "In red."

The woman stepped back. "Red? Well, actually, we do have some."

Mrs. Lind smiled. "We'll look at those and at fabric as well."

"Very well." The woman looked over Lainey, then led them to a rack of gowns and found the one that appeared to be Lainey's size. "We'll start with this one."

The attendant went into the dressing room to assist Lainey with the dress. The fit was perfect. Lainey stared into the mirror, not knowing whether to laugh or cry.

The attendant scooped up her hair. "You'll be lovely no matter what; but with your hair up like this, you'll be the perfect bride. We can look at veils later. Show your friends."

Lainey opened the door and stepped out. Rose's hands went to her face, and tears burst from her eyes. "Oh, Lainey. Oh Lainey! You're so beautiful. That dress is perfect." Rose turned to Mrs. Lind. "Don't you agree? It's the one."

"I do." She turned to the attendant. "Would you bring some veils? Let's decide right now."

The woman hurried off. Mrs. Lind stood and took Lainey's hands in hers. "Lainey, I know you can get fabric and make a dress like this, but I would be delighted if you allow me to purchase this for you in honor of your mother, my dear friend."

Lainey sighed and hugged herself. She turned and looked in the mirror again. "It's everything I've ever dreamed in a wedding dress."

Rose reached for her hand. "You know all the mothers and aunts won't mind. There are so many other things they can help with."

Lainey smiled. "I think everyone is okay with us purchasing the dress. Mama, Aunt Edith, and Clifford's mom all took me aside before we left and said that it would be fine with them if I purchased the dress.

But, Mrs. Lind, I have no idea how much this costs, and I need to spend a certain amount on it. You have been more than generous with me."

Mrs. Lind grinned. "Then it's settled. You pay what you have decided on, and I will pick up the rest." She turned to Rose. "The same offer is for you. Will you allow me to bless you as well?"

"Mrs. Lind, you have already blessed us so much. I don't know what to say."

Mrs. Lind took Rose's hand in hers. "Well, then, it's settled. Lainey, let's get your veil and shoes and the flower girls' dresses and find the perfect bridesmaid dresses or fabric."

The attendant arrived with arms full. A very light and lacey veil won everyone's heart. Lainey selected ivory-toned, high-ankle, open-toed shoes that gave a filigreed look.

Rose tried on several red bridesmaid dresses and decided on a red satin dress boasting a jeweled neckline that matched Lainey's bridal gown. The three-quarter puff sleeves and the empire waist topped a flowing skirt similar to Lainey's dress. They described Juliet to the attendant, and she helped them select the correct size for Clifford's cousin. Rose knew her mom could do any alterations needed. They chose small, white satin dresses with bright red sashes for Tina and Catherine, the flower girls, and red bow ties for Carter and all the men.

The girls gave Mrs. Lind the money they'd allotted for their wedding purchases, as well as money Julia had sent with them; and at Mrs. Lind's orders, they went into the lounge for tea and cake while she completed the purchase.

Mrs. Lind soon joined them and sipped her tea. "You girls have no idea what joy this brings me. I certainly hope Mr. Lind and I will be invited to the wedding."

Lainey almost spit out her tea. "Oh, Mrs. Lind, you will be a most honored guest. I don't know how to ever repay you."

A tear ran down Mrs. Lind's face. "You have more than repaid me. Just meeting you after all these years blesses me. And I want to be able to do some of the things that I know your mother would have done. Thank you for letting me do this."

Lainey wiped the tears from her cheeks and found she had no words. She sniffed and shook her head.

Rose spoke up. "We have been truly blessed by this. I can't wait to show my mother and let Julia see her dress. She will be so very excited."

Mrs. Lind insisted on providing dinner for the girls with Mr. Lind before returning them to their hotel.

The next morning, the girls had an early breakfast at the hotel and then waited outside to meet the Linds. The carriage arrived at 9:00 a.m. This time, Mrs. Lind accompanied Rose to the college to get her established in the study of education, while Mr. Lind took Lainey to meet publishers at R.R. Donnelly and Sons, which specialized in textbooks, magazines, and catalogs. They happily discussed their requirements and recommendations with Lainey and provided instruction booklets with suggestions of articles and stories she could begin writing for magazines and textbooks.

They next visited the *Chicago Daily News* offices, where Lainey was surprised again that everyone knew Mr. Lind. Lainey sensed the tense atmosphere in the newspaper room. Men shouted instructions to each other; men and women typed furiously and scurried in and out of offices. Between barking orders to his employees, the editor described the tough requirements for reporters.

"This is journalism, young lady. It moves fast. You need to be sharp; and I've no doubt you are, or Mr. Lind wouldn't have brought you here. I suggest you get a couple textbooks over at the college and get your writing skills honed. You need to be concise and quick to edit your story. It's a quick turn-around on every story here. We do have some stories that are softer storylines—not exactly news, just interesting information. You might want to start there. You're a long ways away up there in Wisconsin. Perhaps you could write travel articles. I think that's where you could fit."

The editor stood up, indicating their time had ended. He shook Mr. Lind's hand and nodded to Lainey, then sat down to read one of the many articles on his desk. Mr. Lind took Lainey's elbow and guided her out the door.

They stepped onto the elevator. "Lainey, you can see it's a cutthroat workplace. It may not be what you want, but I wanted you to see it. At least, he's willing to look at some travel articles or human interest stories you might send."

"I can't imagine working there." Lainey took a deep breath. "But thank you so much for taking me to these places. I'd like to try my hand at writing magazine stories and articles and maybe even information for textbooks. I know I need instruction, though."

"That's why our last stop is the college where Rose is with my wife. We'll get you set up with a couple classes, now that you have an idea what you need."

Soon, the girls were having dinner once more with the Linds. Both girls had received instruction textbooks and were signed up for correspondence courses. Rose had been allowed to sit in on a class already in session. The college scheduled them to return in the spring after setting a few deadlines for material to be mailed back to them in the interim.

Mrs. Lind leaned forward. "Girls, we'll let you get some rest tonight. You must be exhausted. We'll fetch you late morning and take you to lunch before boarding the boat to return to Wisconsin. We have an extra trunk for you to place your wedding dresses and your textbooks in, so you'll be able to keep track of everything."

Rose reached out and took Mrs. Lind's hand. "We can't thank you enough. This trip has been so amazing."

Lainey nodded. "It's been unbelievable. I don't know how to thank you."

Mr. Lind stood. "Not necessary, girls. It's been our pleasure. I must say how much you remind us of your mother, Lainey. She and your father would be so proud of you. I do see a bit of your father in your ability to assess situations around you. You'll do well in your writing." He left to pay the bill and call the carriage.

Mrs. Lind sat back in her chair. "He's right, Lainey. Your mother wanted to always be on the go, but your dad was more settled. I see the best of both of them in you."

Lainey laughed. "Thank you. Aunt Edith said I had the wanderlust like my mother."

"Your aunt always lived in the shadow of your mom, but you should tell Edith how much Emma depended on her. She loved her steadfastness and always hoped she could emulate her big sister. Rose, you are going to be a marvelous teacher. The professors you met today saw that in you as well. You need training, but you are a natural."

CHAPTER TWENTY-THREE

BOARDING THE BOAT BROUGHT GREAT excitement to Lainey. "Oh, I'm so glad to be going home. I loved the city, but it's not where I would want to live."

Rose dragged her trunk into the main parlor. "I agree. This was so fun, and we did so much; but the city is smelly and, well, kind of scary. I mean, parts were beautiful, but it's so crowded. I've never felt afraid on Washington Island."

Lainey spotted Clifford coming across the room toward her. She ran to his arms. "Oh, Clifford. It was wonderful; but I missed you, and I'm so glad to be going home."

He kissed the top of her head. "What did you buy?"

Lainey looked up and saw a sweet smile play over his face. "I found my wedding dress."

"Fabric or the dress?"

Lainey clapped her hands. "The dress. Mrs. Lind helped to pay for it. Clifford, I can't believe how kind and generous they are. God has so blessed us. And wait till you see the dress . . . Oh, no, you can't. I almost forgot. Not till the wedding."

"It's okay. We'll talk later. I have to get back to the steering room. Love you."

Lainey sighed. "I love you, Clifford."

The girls found their cabin and deposited their trunks and stood by the railing as their passenger ship pulled out of the Chicago harbor.

A slight north breeze ruffled Lainey's hair. "Skies are clear. It looks like a pleasant sail." Soon, they settled into the main lounge and visited with a few of the other passengers, some of whom traveled south with them a few days previous.

During dinner, Lainey noticed a bit of rocking of the boat, but thought little of it as she'd felt that on the way south to Chicago.

Rose raised her eyebrows. "Did you feel that?"

Lainey smiled. "I'm sure it's nothing. It's a north breeze, maybe wind, so the ship has to plow a bit through the waves."

"True, I've felt that plenty of times with my pa." Rose chuckled. "I just haven't felt it while eating."

The girls lingered over tea and cakes in the parlor. A few passengers played board games, but most had already retired to their cabins.

The captain entered the room, his face stern, and hurried to the girls. "Ladies, you must return to your cabin at once and don your life jackets. We are entering a strong squall, a nor'easter. Do not lock your door, in case you need to leave the room quickly, or we need to rescue you. Please, go quickly." He paused and touched Lainey's shoulder. "Don't worry, Miss. Clifford can handle this weather. Just be prepared for all possibilities."

The captain visited each table, then exited the main lounge to alert each cabin. The passengers all scurried out the door, murmuring, with worried expressions.

Lainey sat paralyzed in her chair as a deep fog settled over her mind. A shaking caused her to open her eyes. Rose stood in front of her, eyes wide.

"Lainey, we have to go. We must return to our cabins and put on our life jackets. Please, Lainey."

Lainey stood. Already, the ship was pitching in the oncoming gale. "Is it my turn, Rose? To die? And join my parents?"

Rose stamped her foot. "No. We will ride this out. Clifford is at the wheel."

Lainey went limp, and Rose grabbed her.

"Lainey, Clifford will get us through this. God will get him through this. Now, we must go."

They felt more than heard the roar of the waves and wind. The up and down motion brought dinner to their throats.

"I'm queasy, Lainey. Are you?"

"Mm-hmm."

The tug of gravity as the ship slipped down the monstrous waves accompanied the tug of fear proclaiming to Lainey that this trip would be her end.

"I finally have all I've ever dreamed of, Rose, and now . . . "

"Lainey, can you sing?"

Lainey opened her eyes so she could roll them at Rose. "You know that's not my gifting. Are you trying to make me laugh?"

Rose smiled. "Let's sing 'Rock of Ages.' Please?"

The two young women sang the old hymn and then laughed at their inability to stay on key.

Lainey cleared her throat. "I do feel more hopeful. Thank you. Let's pray, too. Do you remember the first time we prayed together?"

"I do. We didn't know whether to kneel or close our eyes. And God answered."

"He did. Dear God, we need Your help. You've given us so much, and we ask now for our lives and all the lives on this ship. And for Clifford to be able to handle this terrible storm."

Rose whispered. "Keep us safe, Lord. Please stop these winds."

Just then, the trunks slid to one side of the room. Lainey tried to stand. "We can't let them block the door in case we need to get out."

Rose sobbed. "I'm so scared, Lainey. I thought praying would help. I mean, I believe God will help us, but I just see all the possibilities of what could happen. I love Niles. I know he loves me. I don't want him to always wonder."

Lainey staggered to Rose and wrapped her arms around her. "We've seen a lot of tragedy on these waters, but I remember God telling me Clifford would be found when his ship went down. I don't think we're going to sink like . . . " Lainey gulped. "I don't think that will happen, but even if it does, God will find us."

The next pitch of the boat almost landed Lainey on the floor, but Rose held her tight. They wept.

"Let's thank God for taking care of us, Rose. Dear God, we trust You. We thank You for taking care of all of us. We thank You that no one on this ship will miss Your plans for them."

Rose looked up. "Amen."

Though the room supplied two single berths, the girls lay down together on one so they could hold on to each other. With life jackets on, the bed barely held the two of them; but eventually, they fell asleep.

A pounding came on their door. Lainey roused. "Are we sinking? Oh, dear Lord, help us."

The door slid open, and there stood Clifford. "Lainey, Rose, are you all right? The squall is over. We're in calmer waters."

Lainey unwound herself from Rose and tried to stand. The trunks stood between them, and Clifford pushed them out of the way. He caught Lainey in his arms. "It's okay. We'll be home soon."

Rose sat up. "Was it awful trying to steer? Were you afraid?"

"I was. I remembered the other times. On the ice with the wagon. When my ship ran aground and pitched me off. But then I felt a calm, a peace, and I heard the phrase from 'Rock of Ages': 'Let me hide myself in Thee.' And I felt like God was holding me and guiding me. It wasn't easy, but we rode it out. Those winds were nasty, and the seas were running hard at us. The roar of the waves made it hard to think, but I knew God had me and, therefore, had all of us."

Lainey looked up at her fiancé. "Rose had us sing 'Rock of Ages.'"

"Thank goodness." Clifford kissed the top of Lainey's head. "I have to get back. The captain wants to go from room to room and tell everyone it's safe to go outside. Oh, it's almost time for sunrise. It should be beautiful. It's okay to go out to watch it."

Lainey and Rose could see just a hint of dawn as Clifford exited the cabin.

Lainey looked down at her dress. "Oh, my, I look rumpled." She felt her hair. "Oh, I think I'm a mess."

Rose shook her head. "We're alive, and we must live our lives. Smooth your dress and hair the best you can, and let's watch the sunrise."

Lainey laughed and did as Rose instructed. They removed the life jackets, grabbed their shawls, and stepped outside. Several other passengers were doing the same. The splash of purples and pinks spread out like a fan on the horizon. The scent of clean air and the watery fragrance Lainey loved washed over her. She breathed deeply as the fears and hurtful memories of the night before faded like the darkness of the morning. The brilliant, rounded strip of yellow grew on the horizon. The purples and pinks faded into the deep blue of a clear sky.

Breakfast was simple. Scrambled eggs and pancakes. Rose chuckled. "Probably most of the eggs broke in the rough ride. I like scrambled."

Lainey patted her hand. "Me, too. I'm surprised I can eat after feeling so queasy last night. But I'm famished, and this is wonderful."

Late morning, they arrived in Sturgeon Bay. The girls had pulled their trunks to the main lounge and then stood at the railing. There waiting for them was Uncle Otis with the wagon. Tears flowed down Lainey's cheeks. She was home, and life was good.

Uncle Otis scooped her in his arms before pulling back and noticing the tears. "Lainey, is everything okay? Were you able to find fabric and get your studies in order?"

Rose laid her hand on Uncle Otis's arm. "Oh, everything is wonderful. We have so many stories to tell you."

"Well, let's get on our way. I have some cheese and bread and apples for you to eat on the way. We missed you and can't wait to hear everything."

Lainey looked up. Clifford stood at the ship's railing and blew her a kiss. Lainey stood up in the wagon and blew back a kiss and waved.

Lainey sat back down and leaned against Uncle Otis as he led the horses to the road leading to Ellison Bay and Newport Town and to the waters that passed to Washington and Rock Islands. Her heart overflowed with joy.

I thought I'd lost it all—and I have lost so much—but I've been found, and I've found more than I could have ever imagined. She'd been given a family and now a future with the man she loved. In front of her spread a panorama of a marvelous wedding, possibly a resort to run, the prospect of a boating business for Clifford, a writing future to pursue, and friends and family they cherished.

"Uncle Otis?"

"Yes, my sweet girl?"

"I truly understand now that life is much more than our life-and-death moments. Instead, it's held together by so many moments alive with hope and possibility."

Uncle Otis patted her hand. "That's so, Lainey, that's so."

Dear God, don't let me ever forget that.

The End

AUTHOR'S NOTE

Many of the names used in the book are names rooted in the history of Door County and its islands. Most are changed to suit the narrative as are some of the dates of the shipwrecks. I have the two shipwrecks on Pilot Island as close to the actual account as possible for the purposes of the story. Other shipwrecks are a combination of factual events and fiction. Although Pilot Island lighthouse and Rock Island lighthouse each held a second floor (not including the lantern room), for story purposes I describe Pilot Island lighthouse as one floor. Lainey and her family are not true historical residents of this beautiful land but display the heart and hardships of lighthouse living in the late 1800s.

THANKS AND ACKNOWLEDGMENTS

I delight to say thank you to several people for all their contributions to this book. Captain Jim Robinson hosts a tour boat to Pilot Island and the local shipwreck sites on a daily basis. My ride on this boat was most informative as Pilot Island Lighthouse is no longer viable, sitting in disrepair. I learned about the shipwrecks and viewed their remains in the waters next to the island. We were unable to walk on the island, but when Captain Jim learned what I was writing he circled an extra time. He and his delightful first mate, his granddaughter, gave me even more information. Jim also read through a good part of the book to make sure I used correct facts and terms concerning the shipwrecks. I visited Rock Island Lighthouse a few times and appreciated the information from the docents. I enjoyed walking the perimeter of Rock Island. The docents at Eagle Bluff Lighthouse and Cana Island Lighthouse were also extremely helpful. In Michigan I took the boat tour from Alpena to Thunder Bay Island and learned amazing stories of shipwrecks and survival in that area of Lake Huron. I grew up in Harrisville, thirty miles south of Alpena and have lived in Northern Door County since 1984.

The owners of Jackson Harbor Soup, descendants of Rasmus Hanson, graciously gave me permission to use his name. He actually did build and operate a grocery boat with his brother.

Books that offered great background and details were: *Shipwrecks at Death's Door* by Chris Kohl and Joan Forsberg, *Keepers of the Lights* by Steven Karges, and *Journal of Light Station Cana Island Lake Michigan: Miscellaneous Notations and Excerpts from the Official Record of the Station 1871-1934*, Compiled and Edited by Rosie Janda for the Door County Maritime Museum and Preservation Society, Inc. Many on-line sites and local historical archives provided information as well.

My Word Weavers critique group was invaluable: Alynda Long, Dena Hobbs, Kirsten Panachyda, and Teresa Lasher have steadfastly provided wonderful corrections, suggestions, and encouragement. We've cried together and laughed together and become a family. You guys are the best. Thank you.

My local friends have always been amazing cheerleaders for my books. I so appreciate Kim Elkins, Karla Orgel, Michelle Kemp, and Julie House. Their prayer and encouragement for me and my writing have been a blessing. Thank you!!

Of course, my husband and son encourage and put up with my rollercoaster times while writing a novel and going through the publishing process.

And, without the help, the guidance, and anointing of the Lord, none of this would have begun nor been completed. I thank Him for the nudges, the ideas, and the stamina to write this book and others. All praise to His Name.

For more information about

Judy DuCharme
and
Lainey of the Door Islands
please visit:

www.judithducharme.com
www.facebook.com/judy.ducharme.18
@packerjudy

For more information about
AMBASSADOR INTERNATIONAL
please visit:

www.ambassador-international.com
@AmbassadorIntl
www.facebook.com/AmbassadorIntl

If you enjoyed this book, please consider leaving us a review on
Amazon, Goodreads, or our website.

BLOOD
MOON
REDEMPTION

JUDY DUCHARME

ALSO BY JUDY DUCHARME

An ancient relic, a puzzling prophecy, and a young woman tied together through the ages . . .

Throughout history, blood moons have always been surrounded by persecution and provision, great trials and triumphs. The blood moons of 1493-1494 provided a new world for the Jewish people. In 1949-1950, the blood moons gave them Israel, and the following eclipses presented the Jewish people Jerusalem in 1967-1968. Now a new set of blood moons is on the horizon, and Tassie's family is certain they will bring about great change.

Tassie, named for a lost religious relic, has her sights set on her career and love, and she doesn't have time for silly children's stories. Dismissing the blood moons as circumstance, her unbelief threatens to keep her from her destiny. When Tassie finds herself in the center of worldwide turmoil and a terrorist plot, can she accept her family history and fulfill her place in the future of Israel? Or will the country of her heritage finally fall to its many enemies?

Blood Moon Redemption is an end-times thriller that will keep you riveted until the very last moonrise.

More from Ambassador International

In 1817, a young man faces life with an alcoholic father and imminent financial and social ruin. In 2018, a gifted artist can't paint anything but the same theme over and over, until she unearths this young man's history and his noble rise from rags to riches in Antebellum America. Based on a 200-year-old letter collection, *Once Upon an Irish Summer* brings to life and weaves together a true story of romance, mystery, and hope.

Once upon an Irish Summer
by Wendy Wilson Spooner

Emma has high hopes when her family moves to the North Carolina mountains. Here Emma meets Edgar Moretz, an intelligent, passionate, and godly young man. Things are looking up for Emma, but when she is captured by a Cherokee raiding party, her problems have just begun.

Cleared for Planting
by Janice Cole Hopkins

Elderly Sarah returns to her hometown of Adare, Ireland, with her daughter-in-law, Anna. The suffering that World War II brought them was unimaginable, but they still have each other. With all their loved ones killed in the war, the two women have nothing but a hope that one distant relative will help them. Will this new beginning bring the healing that both of them have prayed for?

A Little Irish Love Story
by Amy Fleming

Made in the USA
Columbia, SC
06 June 2021